Henry Edwards Sutherland

The Polish Captivity

An account of the present position of the poles in the kingdom of Poland, and in the Polish provinces of Austria, Prussia, and Russia. In two volumes.

Vol. 2

SALZWASSER
VERLAG

Henry Edwards Sutherland

The Polish Captivity

An account of the present position of the poles in the kingdom of Poland, and in the Polish provinces of Austria, Prussia, and Russia. In two volumes. Vol. 2

Reprint of the original, first published in 1863.

1st Edition 2022 | ISBN: 978-3-37500-431-6

Verlag (Publisher): Salzwasser Verlag GmbH, Zeilweg 44, 60439 Frankfurt, Deutschland
Vertretungsberechtigt (Authorized to represent): E. Roepke, Zeilweg 44, 60439 Frankfurt, Deutschland
Druck (Print): Books on Demand GmbH, In de Tarpen 42, 22848 Norderstedt, Deutschland

THE
POLISH CAPTIVITY.

THE

POLISH CAPTIVITY:

AN ACCOUNT OF THE

PRESENT POSITION OF THE POLES

IN

THE KINGDOM OF POLAND, AND IN THE POLISH PROVINCES OF AUSTRIA, PRUSSIA, AND RUSSIA.

BY SUTHERLAND EDWARDS.

" Poles, we appreciate and admire the greatness of soul, the sensitiveness and the firmness which distinguish your national character, and which have been displayed in your efforts to recover the political existence of your country, which you love above everything."—ALEXANDER I., IN 1815.

" My grandmother and the King of Prussia, Frederick II., in partitioning Poland, committed a fault. . . The ruling Powers will never be able to enjoy these strange acquisitions in peace. The existence of Poland is something natural and indispensable. It would be superfluous to discuss the means of re-establishing it, for when a thing is natural and indispensable it arrives of itself."—THE ARCHDUKE FERDINAND OF AUSTRIA, IN 1848.

IN TWO VOLUMES.—VOL. II.

LONDON

1863.

CONTENTS.

APPENDIX II.

APPENDIX III.

APPENDIX IV.

LIST OF ILLUSTRATIONS.

VOL. II.

THE POLISH CAPTIVITY.

CHAPTER I.

THE POLES UNDER THE AUSTRIAN GOVERNMENT.—GALICIA AND THE "CZAS."

For the present, the Polish question is certainly a question without an answer. No probable solution can be found for it, but in the meanwhile, as the Poles are in greater force in the Kingdom than in Prussian or Austrian Poland, the Kingdom is naturally the scene of all the great demonstrations in favour of national independence. It would be a mistake, however, to suppose that the inhabitants of Galicia and Posen are a bit more satisfied with their position than those under the domination of Russia; and so impossible is it to introduce the "German element" into Poland with success that, until news was received of the Russians firing upon the people at Warsaw, the Galicians would gladly have changed the sovereignty of the Austrian Emperor for that of the Tsar. The secret of this inclination does not lie in any inexplicable affection on the part of the Poles for the Russians, but in the old invincible hatred of Slavonians for Germans, in the special hatred of the Galicians for the Austrian Government, and above all, in the general tendency of the Poles to reunite and to live together even under the harshest of despotisms, rather than remain divided under separate Governments, however liberal. What the Poles most desire is unity, which might be a step towards independence, and they would rather form one nation enslaved than remain the fragments of a nation with all imaginable political privileges except the only one they care for — that of governing themselves.

There does exist, at the present moment, a far greater unity of sentiment and purpose between the fragments of the partitioned country than people have any idea of in Western Europe, and, unless the railway between Warsaw and Cracow be broken up, and the formation of the railway between Warsaw and Posen suddenly discontinued, this sympathy and interchange of ideas between the dejected members of a body which still hangs together and lives, though long thought to be dead, will certainly go on increasing. The general liberty enjoyed by the inhabitants of Austrian

Poland appears to me, when I think of the position of the Poles in the Kingdom, immense: Cracow might still be a free city for any trouble that a visitor is put to about his passport. As for police, not only are they scarcely seen, but their action is nowhere felt except in connection with criminal cases. Go from Cracow where you please —to Lemberg, to Vienna, into Hungary—no questions are asked, no inspection of passports is necessary; all you have to do is to pay your money at the railway station, or drive quietly out of the town in whatever direction you please; whereas at Warsaw it is impossible to make an excursion of a few miles beyond the suburbs without getting your passport *visé*, while to a traveller from Warsaw to Cracow, it is an indispensable preliminary to visit three offices, and to obtain the signatures of a half-a-dozen different officials. In addition to this liberty of locomotion, the Austrian Poles have great freedom of discussion allowed them in their journals. Books of all kinds, for and against the Austrian Government, and, indeed, against and in favour of all possible and conceivable Governments, are publicly sold; and yet, with all this, there is one newspaper which is strictly prohibited, and cannot be sent through the post to Cracow, or any part of Galicia. This is the *Djennik Poznanski* or *Posen Journal*, the most outspoken in the cause of Polish nationality of all the newspapers published in the Polish language, and which accordingly has its edition frequently confiscated by the Prussian police. As the *Djennik Poznanski* is forbidden in Galicia, so is the *Czas* (equally, of course, with the *Djennik*) excluded from the Kingdom of Poland; but Cracow being the nearest town to the Russian frontier in which Polish news can be freely discussed, its chief newspaper has become, from that fact, of as much interest and importance to the inhabitants of Warsaw as an independent journal published in their own city would be. It must be remembered that in Russian Poland the press is not merely "fettered and gagged," in the vague sense in which these words are often applied to journalism in despotic countries, where the journalist, however, is allowed, now and then, to whisper a passing remark on some subject deeply affecting the interests of his country. I have already mentioned that the effect of the censorship in the Kingdom is to prevent newspapers from publishing one syllable of comment on anything that takes place in Russia or Poland, or in any other country in connection with Russian or Polish affairs, while newspaper correspondents who send their comments to be published elsewhere are threatened, and in some cases have actually been visited with imprisonment.

Thus the Warsaw journals published the list of the members of the new Council of State directly it was formed, but expressed neither approbation nor disapprobation of the appointments, being condemned to dead silence on all such subjects. The principal Cracow newspaper, however, without becoming at all enthusiastic about the Emperor's "reforms," admitted that faith had been fully kept with the Poles as regarded the nominations, and that, if not the best possible, at least a very good selection of names had been made. Every one regretted at first that the name of Count Andrew Zamoyski did not appear on the list, but it really would have been impossible to do him a greater injury than to appoint him to a place in a Council where, from the limited nature of his functions and from the absolute necessity of his working *with* the Russian Government, he would soon have lost the popularity he at present enjoys; and which, from the services he is constantly rendering to the country, he is sure to retain. The difficulty for a patriotic Pole who wishes to serve his country in an official capacity is to preserve a good name with the Poles and yet not run counter to all the projects of Russia; to do his duty fairly and honourably by the Government, and, at the same time, escape such reproaches as are constantly levelled at the Marquis Wielopolski, though it is, after all, to him that the re-establishment of the Warsaw University and the increase of the number of gymnasiums in the Kingdom of Poland from five to thirteen, and the introduction of publicity in law proceedings, are due.

Indeed, the Poles have always been ready to accept in good faith any political concessions made to them; but hitherto that seems only to have been made a reason for withdrawing them. On this subject, and on that of the Government of the Kingdom of Poland generally, it may be interesting to quote the remarks of the principal journal of Cracow, entitled the *Czas* (Hour). The reader will learn not only what the Poles living in Poland think of the Russian Government, but also to what extent writers under the Austrian Government are allowed to attack what was once a friendly Power. Russian writers attack Austria in a similar manner. Thus, the work of Russian journalists is done by Austrians, and that of Austrian journalists by Russians. Neither Government escapes and no one is punished.

This sort of thing would not have taken place in the time of Catherine and Joseph. "If," wrote the Empress Catherine, soon after the first partition, "the link best calculated to perpetuate thorough harmony and union between the three Courts remains imperfect, it will be attacked with more vigour by foreign interests, in proportion as it will be thought less indissoluble, as it will be less respected." But to proceed to the *Czas*:—

"If," says the writer (Sept. 20, 1862), "we were

not thoroughly informed—by the daily acts of the Russian Government since the days of the Empress Catherine, who, under the pretext of guaranteeing the liberties of the Polish Republic, violated, in the most open manner, not only the established laws of that Republic, but the laws of all nations, dragged the senators of an independent State from its capital, and banished them to Siberia, and, in the name of civilization and mercy, massacred the whole population of Praga—were we not informed, from its acts during the last one hundred and fifty years, what sense of right there is in its conduct, we certainly should hardly believe our eyes, seeing as we do, full of indignation and amazement, the deeds committed by that Government during the last eighteen months, which will remain in history an indelible evidence of its sense of right, and which will be looked upon by future generations with disgust.

"A new proof of this sense of right appears to be the late conduct of the Russian Government, with regard to Count Andrew Zamoyski, who, when he was asked what were the wants of the country, and an appeal was made to his good faith, submitted to that Government the openly-expressed wishes of the nobles. We say appears to be, for although the public opinion of the whole country knows the conduct of the Russian Government, it is yet loth to believe that the imprisonment of a noble and righteous man, and the consequences that will result therefrom, will close this subject; for this would be so treacherous an act, that it still awaits the last words of the Government regarding it! But before we consider the conduct of the Government in this matter, as yet incomplete, let us recall the deeds of a similar nature, though not, perhaps, of equal importance, committed by the Russian Government in the course of the past year, and which are a good specimen of its sense of right.

"After the bloody deeds of the 25th and 27th February of last year, the Russian Government allows a municipal delegation to be formed, confers with it, praises its acts, almost gives up to it the government of the town; and the delegation, without any armed force, without police, ukases, or bayonets, keeps exemplary order and peace, accompanied by complete liberty. Subsequently this same Government orders the members of this very delegation to be sent to prison, stigmatizes the course of action it pursued, and which the Government authorized, as illegal, and sends them to Siberia or the fortresses.

"About the same time, in March, last year, the Government authorizes the formation of a committee to erect a monument in memory of the victims of the 27th, to receive subscriptions for this monument, and for a relief fund for the families of the deceased. The Viceroy and the highest dignitaries send money to the committee, and praise its acts. Shortly after, the Government arrests the members of this committee, commissions of inquiry cross-examine them, military tribunals try them, and send them to Asiatic fortresses; the subscription fund is seized; an inquiry is instituted into this fund, and many persons are imprisoned on the pretext that they have secretly retained some of it; and the erection of the monument is not only forbidden, but the graves are levelled with the earth, and those who were found praying by them sent to Orenburg.

"The Viceroys, Prince Gortchakoff and General Lambert, publish addresses to the Poles, speaking of love for their country, of respect for the Polish nationality, of the anxiety of the monarch to develope it. Meanwhile, under the veil of this graciousness, the smallest manifestations of nationality, in dress, singing, or words, are treated as State crimes, and all the prisons and fortresses are filled with persons convicted of taking part in national manifestations.

"The Government loudly proclaims to Europe reforms for Poland. It informs the various courts of them by diplomatic circulars; it calls upon the nobles to vote for members for the municipal and provincial councils, it praises them for the quiet and order with which the elections are carried on.

Then, all of a sudden, when the elections are completed, the Government publishes, or rather aggravates, the state of siege which has long been in existence; forbids the councils to assemble; places under the surveillance of the police those whom it has ascertained by the elections to possess the confidence of their fellow-citizens; shuts up the whole population in their houses; gives up their fortunes and lives to the unlimited power of thousands of dictators; the accusing triumvirate, the commissions of inquiry, and the military tribunals decimate the population; and thinking that, by the severest of terrorisms, it has crushed the spirit of the nation, the Government opens, in the midst of this lawless state of things, the provincial and municipal councils: thus making the reforms a mere name, given to some small and insignificant institutions as a cloak for its arbitrary conduct.

"Notwithstanding the continuance of the state of siege, and the advice of a small and uninfluential party not to take part in the councils under such circumstances, the members elected, listening only to the voice of duty, and obeying the mandate which they received from their fellow-citizens at their election, have sat in the council so soon as they were allowed to do so, with the resolution to fulfil conscientiously their duties and attributes, as laid down by the law, notwithstanding the arbitrariness of the military government. The law orders the Municipal Council of Warsaw to visit the municipal prisons; a delegation for the Council does so, and gives a conscientious report of the dreadful state in which it found the prisons and prisoners; and the Government which ordered them to carry out this law, brutally dismisses the president of the town.

"Let us now consider the last act of the Russian Government, which is, perhaps, of the same nature, but of greater significance than those which preceded it.

"The Grand Duke Constantine issued an address in which he called on the Poles to trust in him and co-operate with him in promoting the prosperity of the country. Then, having called to his presence an honest Pole, possessing the confidence of his fellow-citizens, he asked him what would be necessary to secure to the Government the support of the nation, and requested his advice, and an open statement of the wants of the country. Count Andrew Zamoyski, after declaring his own convictions, added that he had no authority whatever to express the desires of the nation, but that he would ask the nobles in the various provinces and towns who possessed the confidence of their fellow-citizens, and lay their opinions before the Grand Duke. The Namiestnik of the Emperor, the highest authority in the Government of Warsaw, consented.

The nobles of the greatest influence and consideration, both in the towns and the provinces, assembled, and, in answer both to the Grand Duke's address and his questions, openly and confidently expressed the convictions and wants of the country. Count Andrew Zamoyski, in answer to the question put to him, forwarded the address of the nobles. What was the conduct of the Government on this occasion? On the 15th of September, the police suddenly surrounded the house of the Count; the chief of the police and the commandant of the town take him to the Grand Duke's palace; there it is said, he was directed at once to proceed to St. Petersburg, in order to give an account to the Tsar of his 'illegal' conduct. This candid and upright man is accordingly sent to St. Petersburg under escort, and the official journal, after calling the assemblage of the nobles with the knowledge of the Namiestnik an 'illegal' one, the expression of the wants of the country in obedience to an appeal from the Namiestnik an abuse, and the conduct of Count Andrew Zamoyski, who had been also appealed to by the Namiestnik, conduct for which he was liable to be called to account—announced that the Count was sent to St. Petersburg.

"Such is the present position of the question.

"The opinion of the majority in Warsaw is not as yet willing to believe that the matter initiated by the Grand Duke Constantine has been closed by the Russian Government with an act which would give its conduct in that matter the same character as that of the acts we have above alluded to. It is unwilling to believe that the Grand Duke has shut up the road to every decisive step; and that the Duke, looked upon in Russia as the leader of the Liberal and national party, has thus contradicted his own words and his own appeal. The opinion of the country is waiting to see whether in St. Petersburg, after recognizing what is the real state of things of Poland, another turn will be given to the whole matter, and whether the Grand Duke, who is compromised in it, will not take an initiative in bringing about this change. While waiting and suspending its final decision, the public opinion asks, Which Government really rules in Warsaw? That with whose knowledge the meeting of the nobles took place, and which almost sanctioned it, or that which called it illegal? That which called for an open expression of the national wants, or that which named such expression an abuse? That which appealed to Count Zamoyski, or that which declared that he should account for his conduct, as being contrary to order, and sent him to St. Petersburg? If both these Governments are one, what name shall we give to this double-faced conduct? If an act performed with the knowledge and authority of the Emperor's lieutenant can be stigmatized as illegal, does not this stigma also attach to the lieutenant? And where is the illegality? In the purport and the candour of the declaration? Or does the crime not rather lie in this, that the nobles who were asked for an expression of the wishes of the country did not falsely state its wants and rights? If, instead of three hundred nobles, possessing the confidence of their fellow-countrymen, and supported in their statements by the history of the past, by the tradition of ages, and the declaration of thousands of electors, thirty had dared to say that the country was satisfied with the reforms that have been announced, that they have been and may be introduced under the present system, that the whole of the population is on the side of the Government, and only a small party of 'agitators' against it—their statement, contrary as it would have been to the convictions, wants, and principles of the nation, would have been regarded by the Government as the voice of the nation, and their declarations would have had all the sanction the law could give them. That candour and confidence which had been appealed to, constitute, then, the whole of the offence in the reply; conscientiousness in expressing the convictions and wants of the country, all the crime. Falsehood would have been a recommendation in the eyes of the Government.

"Happen what may, if the Government persists

in its system, and refuses to satisfy the wants of the nation, as once more openly expressed, let it not think that by the banishment of one man, however upright and possessed of the public confidence, it will break the opposition of the country as shown against encroachments upon its rights, or that it will eradicate the recollection of its past, or the feeling of its wants and its mission. Not a few men of the same stamp have died or been banished since the time when, after the exile to Kaluga of the Polish senators, an ancestor of Count Andrew Zamoyski, the Chancellor of the same name, gave up his appointment, refusing to attach his seal to decisions enforced by foreign influence; and, notwithstanding all these punishments, the nation still defends its rights with an internal strength which is constantly increasing."

CHAPTER II.

THE FORTUNES OF CRACOW.

CRACOW during the last three-quarters of a century has led a more varied political life even than Warsaw, and has seen nearly as much suffering.

Warsaw remained the capital of Poland until 1795, when the ancient kingdom was put an end to, and Warsaw passed under the claws of the Prussians. In 1807 it became the capital of the Duchy of Warsaw, formed by Napoleon, and in 1815 of the little Kingdom of Poland formed by Alexander.

Cracow remained Polish until the third partition, when it fell beneath the Austrian yoke. Poniatowski cleared it of Austrians in 1808, and in 1809 it was annexed by treaty to the Grand Duchy of Warsaw. In 1815 it was made an independent Republic—under the protection of three despots. In 1833, and again in 1837, the three despots introduced various reforms in the constitution of their Republic, which they completed in 1839 by dissolving the Diet.

An old Polish tradition contains an account of an attack made upon Lekh in his cradle by a three-headed dragon. Miçkievicz pointed out, in 1842, that the cradle of Lekh was Cracow, the last resting-place of Polish independence. The attack did indeed come in 1846, when Cracow, while in a state of profound quiet, was bombarded by the Austrians, and afterwards given to them as a reward by the Emperor Nicholas—to whom it did not belong. As if to prove themselves grateful, the Austrians bombarded it again in 1848; but Austrian gratitude is not eternal, and in 1854, at the beginning of the Crimean war, the rulers of Cracow thought it advisable to erect forts outside the city, which could only have been intended as points of attack against the Russians themselves. The policy of the Marquis Wielopolski is more intelligible in Galicia than in the Kingdom of Poland, and (as I have already mentioned) it was after the massacres of Galicia, organized and paid for by the Austrian Government, that he first proclaimed it in his celebrated letter to Prince Metternich. (See *Appendix*.) Whether the Russians have or have not behaved better to the Poles than the Austrians, the Poles have, at least, more to expect from them; and if Russia went to war with Austria, she would only have to proclaim the re-establishment of Poland, in its ancient limits, under the Russian sovereignty, in order to secure at once the support of the Galicians. The only possible counter-project to this would be the re-establishment of Poland as an independent kingdom—a difficult scheme, to carry out which it would be necessary not merely to defeat a few Russian armies, but to destroy the Russian Empire. Russia will certainly never allow her actual possessions in Poland to be alienated from the Russian Crown; whereas there is reason to believe that Austria would willingly contribute to the formation of an independent Poland by the abandonment of Galicia, though she will never give it up to Russia until absolutely forced to do so.

The fact is, both the German Powers soon learned to fear the Poles, however much they may have affected to despise them. In December, 1771 (on Christmas Day) Frederic the Great wrote to Catherine the Great a magnanimous letter, in which the following passage occurs: "As for the Poles, we must expect that they will make a great outcry whenever possession is taken, for this vain, intriguing nation cries out about everything; but the army on the Vistula will soon make them cease their noise, and, after the conclusion of peace with the Turks, can pacify Poland." Eleven months afterwards, however, when the treaty of partition had been arranged between the three Powers, and Poland had been invaded by their armies, "the Great Frederic" wrote to Count Solms that, "although the Poles appeared to have given up their original project of dying sword in hand, rather than sign what they call the disgrace of Poland," yet, he thought, "their signature to the cession would never be obtained unless they were compelled to give it by force." In 1774, the partitioning Powers having made fresh demands, the Poles requested them to keep to their engagement of 1773, and to withdraw their troops, upon which Mr. Carlyle's hero observed, in a despatch to Count Solms, that "those signs were more than sufficient to prove that the Poles were not of so easy a nature as was, perhaps, imagined at St. Petersburg;" and that the Diet "would never come to any conclusion, with all this fuss, unless Russia showed her big teeth and declared plainly her intentions." *

If Frederic had lived some years longer, he would have found that the Poles were indeed "not of so easy a nature." The Germans quite understand now that they can do nothing with them beyond taking them for soldiers, taxing them to excess, robbing them of their salt-mines, and establishing German colonies on their territory. They know that there can never be any union or sym-

* *Frédéric II., Cathérine et le Partage de la Pologne, par Frédéric de Smitt*, part ii. p. 80. *D'Angeberg* (*Recueil de Documents, &c.*), p. 97.

pathy between Germans and Poles (except momentarily, perhaps, for some special revolutionary purpose), and therefore strive, with the most earnest folly, to transform their Polish subjects into Germans, and make them forget their ancient liberty and glory. Austria does not know what to do with Galicia. She *does* know that, on the first menace from Russia, she would have to fall back to the Carpathians; and that from the moment that Russia adopts a really liberal policy towards the Poles of the Kingdom, all Galicia will be Russian. Prussia, too, pleads that, in self-defence, she is obliged to Germanize Posen, which she justly regards as the advanced post of Slavonianism, and which she knows is ready to throw itself into the arms of Russia whenever Russia chooses to appear as the protector instead of the oppressor of the Poles.

This character Russia must, sooner or later, assume, for Poland, in its present state, is worse than useless to the Russian Empire; it is a constant source of danger to the Government, and is an obstacle in the way of those reforms which all the educated classes in Russia desire and expect. Russia, at the present moment, has all her right side paralysed, and cannot move forward either for peace or for war. As long as Russia remains in this enfeebled state, the German Powers have, of course, nothing to fear. But they are quite aware that when "the wound in the Russian arm" * is healed, Russia will have to make a blow at Germany for the sake of Posen and Galicia.

The German Powers are really, then, in a hopeless position as regards their Polish subjects. They know that they must some day lose them, and their plan has hitherto been to see whether it is not possible to turn some of them into Germans before the others take their departure.

An ambitious and warlike Emperor of Russia, professing advanced Liberal opinions, and a deep regard for the rights of Slavonian nationalities, ("Woe to Europe when the Tsar of Russia wears a beard!") might easily settle the Polish question in the most advantageous manner for his Empire. A really kind-hearted and, at the same time, resolute Emperor (only the two qualities are so seldom found together), might, without being ambitious or warlike, confer immense benefits on some fifteen millions of Poles, his own subjects, by simply

* M. Wuttke, a German, the Marquis Wielopolski, a Pole (*Lettre d'un Gentilhomme Polonais au Prince Metternich*), and M. Aksakoff, a Russian (the *Day*, a journal published in Moscow), all agree that Poland is a wound—the German says in the arm, the Pole and the Russian say in the body, of Russia. The Pole and the Russian are both of opinion that the wound ought to be healed; the German, however, hopes it may be kept open for the benefit of Germany, though he too foresees that, sooner or later, "Slavonia must be made whole."

executing the provisions of the Treaty of Vienna. By requiring Austria and Prussia to observe the Treaty as well, he could cause those benefits to be extended to nearly seven millions of Poles * now under German dominion, and Poland would speedily be restored to national life, though not to political unity. National and representative institutions, with liberty of navigation and liberty of commerce throughout the Poland of 1772, are guaranteed by the Treaty of Vienna to the subjects of all the three Powers. If Russia were to render the navigation of her portion of the Vistula free for the inhabitants of all parts of Poland she would have the best possible right to call upon Austria and Prussia to follow her example in that respect. Both England and France protested against the Constitution of the Kingdom of Poland being abolished after the insurrection of 1830–31; and Lord Palmerston, in a despatch dated March 22, 1831, directed the British Ambassador at St. Petersburg to remonstrate with the Imperial Government on the fact of its never having granted "national and representative institutions" to the inhabitants of the Polish provinces not included in the Kingdom. If the Emperor of Russia would begin by granting constitutional rights and the

* I call all the inhabitants of Poland Poles, without considering what provincial idiom they speak.

free use of the Polish language to all his Polish subjects, would he not have a perfect right to protest against German being maintained as the language of education and of the public offices in Posen? Would he not have a right to require that Austria should govern Galicia as a thoroughly Polish province? Would he not even be justified in announcing his desire to see the Treaty of 1815 observed in all respects—even as regards Cracow—and in adding his protest against its continued annexation to the protests entered by England and France when it was first annexed? If the act was contrary to the precise stipulations of a European treaty, it does not matter whether the Emperor Nicholas approved of it or not. Is Alexander II. obliged to set aside a treaty recognized by Alexander I. because this treaty was broken by the Emperor Nicholas? And could England and France complain if Russia even now were to declare that they were quite right in the matter of Cracow, and that Austria ought not to have absorbed it?

If Russia were to adopt this simple, safe, perfectly legal and honourable policy, what would the effect at once be on the Poles of Prussia and Austria? Simply that Warsaw would become their capital quite as much as it is now that of the Russian Poles.

Just after the first partition of Poland, when Austria and Prussia showed such greediness for spoil that scrupulous Russia was absolutely shocked, Catherine II. wrote a letter to Maria Theresa, in which (as I have already mentioned) she sought to impress upon her devout friend the impolicy of any one of the criminal Powers making demands which all three were not prepared to support. The link between Russia and Austria has been broken more than once since Catherine's time. Nevertheless, the Russian generals in 1809 manœuvred so as to avoid coming into collision with Austrian troops, and during the campaign of 1812 this attention was fully returned by Prince Schwartzenberg, the commander of Napoleon's Austrian contingent. Austria, however, had already learnt to regret the partition of Poland, and in 1814 a secret treaty was drawn up (signed January 3rd, 1815) by which Austria, France, and England engaged to declare war against Russia and Prussia if those two Powers persisted in carrying out their intentions with respect to the Duchy of Warsaw and the Kingdom of Saxony. (The Duchy of Warsaw was to have been made over to Russia, and Prussia to have taken the whole of Saxony. Alexander would thus have become king of all Poland, with the exception of a narrow strip retained by Prussia.)

Austria has behaved infamously to the Poles—that no one will think of denying—but she has found that it is to her interest to have an independent Poland placed between herself and Russia, and that, under present circumstances, there is a great chance of Galicia, sooner or later, falling under Russian power. Accordingly, in 1830, instead of openly assisting the Russians, like Prussia, she secretly assisted the Poles. Arms, provisions, and medical stores were conveyed across the Austrian frontier into the Kingdom of Poland; the political emissaries from the Provisional Government at Warsaw were well received at Vienna; and when the Emperor of Austria knew that Count Andrew Zamoyski was in his capital, though he could not receive him, he said, "Tell the Count that I feel I am about to appear before the Great Judge, and that the possession of Galicia weighs upon me like a crime. I would gladly give it up, but not to Russia. To an independent Poland I would give it up with joy."

"In that case," the Count is said to have replied, "I had better take it. I am here to represent the Polish Government."

Of course Galicia was not to be ceded in this summary manner. Of course, too, its cession by the Austrian Government would, in any case, be an act, not of simple virtue, but of high political necessity. The formation of an independent Poland would not enrich Austria, but it would make Russia (in a political sense) "poor indeed," and therefore, relatively, would increase the influence and security of her neighbours.

In 1848 Austria made another "demonstration" in favour of an independent Poland. All Germany—all Europe, except the free States and the orientally-despotic State of Russia—was in a revolutionary ferment. Deputies from Galicia waited upon the Emperor Ferdinand I. and gave a fresh proof of the moderation of the Poles—a moderation in which there is nothing astonishing, inasmuch as liberty is their legitimate inheritance—by asking merely for such rights as they would already have possessed had the stipulations of the Treaty of Vienna been fairly observed; together with trial by jury, and the equalization of all classes before the law. The address embodying these demands was presented by a number of Polish "aristocrats"—sons and grandsons of the men who had taken the first steps towards the emancipation of the peasantry in Eastern Europe, long before Russia, Austria, or Prussia, with their despotic systems, and their servile court nobility, had ever thought of such a measure. As to the question of language, the Polish "aristocrats" did not forget that in Eastern Galicia the ordinary language of the peasantry is Ruthenian, though every educated peasant also speaks Polish. Indeed, the Poles, in the whole course of their history, never once made an attempt to force their language upon the populations who had, of their own free will, joined their fate to that of Poland. This form of injustice is thoroughly despotic in its nature and origin, and no constitutional country ha ever practised it except Prussia, which, after all, is only a despotism adorned with a few unmeaning constitutional forms, to be put aside whenever it suits a strong centralized Government, supported by a privileged penniless aristocracy, and acting through a host of dependent administrative officers, to dispense with it.

Hungary, it is true, by a temporary error, sought, at one time, to oppose the Germanizing tendencies of the Austrian Government, by making the Magyar the official language of Hungary. It must be remembered, however, that the Magyar is the language of all the educated classes in Hungary, and it is simply untrue that the Hungarians tried to form their language upon the "annexes" of the kingdom. It was only in communications from the Hungarian Government that the Magyar language was to be used. They were to be replied to in Latin, the ordinary official language of the annexes, and of Hungary itself until 1848. No candid person will seek to establish a comparison between this arrangement and that by which

German has been made the local official language of Galicia and Posen—and this in spite of what the treaties expressed by stipulating that the Poles are everywhere to enjoy "national institutions."

In presenting their address to the Emperor, the Galician deputies did not conceal that the ultimate object of their wishes was the restoration of Poland in its ancient limits. In the meanwhile, they desired for the present to ensure the peace of Galicia as an Austrian possession; and after the Emperor had replied to Prince Lubomirski, who read the address, that he had the greatest pleasure in granting all his demands, the Archduke John added :—

"Now we can speak frankly. My grandmother and the King of Prussia, Frederic the Second, in partitioning Poland, committed a fault. This partition has been a great misfortune for all Europe. From that moment peace and loyalty disappeared, and the traffic of nations commenced, to the injury even of the rulers themselves. The partitioning Powers can never enjoy in peace these strange acquisitions. The existence of Poland is something natural and indispensable. It would be superfluous to discuss the means of establishing it, for when a thing is naturally indispensable, it takes place of itself. Accordingly, I think it would be more prudent not to discuss these means, but to employ them at once, so as to prepare this re-establishment. I know, gentlemen, as well as you, the dangers with which we are threatened by Panslavonianism. Russia can inundate Galicia with 150,000 troops; for that reason we must act with prudence. Another danger consists in the present organization of our bureaucracy. I regard it as a direct instrument of the fall of the Austrian Empire, and it must be completely reformed . . . . . I assure you, gentlemen, that in speaking to you as a German, I am something more than that—I am, above all, a man, and an advocate of whatever can procure the welfare and happiness of humanity," &c., &c.

The reforms promised and partly introduced by the Austrian Government in Galicia, had the fate which so many other Austrian reforms have met with.

Perhaps, before this book appears, the truth will be generally known as to the proposition for re-establishing Poland said to have been made by Austria during the Crimean war. The story hitherto circulated has been that France was willing to accept the Austrian proposition, and that England, "always devoted to her own private interests,"* refused to accede to it. Probably, England

* M. Charles Forster, in his interesting and, generally, most impartial account of Poland, writes, in a tone of complaint, that, at the time of the first partition of Poland, "*L'Angleterre, toujours dévouée avant tout à ces intérêts particuliers, tentait de*

did not care to make war for the aggrandizement of France, but would have been willing to assist in re-establishing Poland, for whose cause the greatest sympathy has always been felt by the English people, if her ally would have consented that that, and that alone, should be made the object of war against Russia on a large scale. Curiously enough, I could find no one in Galicia who believed in the good intentions of Austria towards Poland. The Galician explanation of the Austrian proposition was simple enough. The Austrian Government, say its Polish subjects, simply wished to know what the real intentions of the Allies were in regard to Poland. Had Austria learnt that the re-establishment of Poland formed any part of the plan of the Allies, she would at once have declared in favour of Russia.

The last step taken by Austria on behalf of Poland was the formation of the Galician Diet in connection with the new quasi-constitutional system introduced into Austria. Lelewel, in his *Analysis and Parallel of Three Polish Constitutions*, makes the ingenious remark, well worthy the attention of Austrians and Russians, that there are two kinds

faire rentrer dans le devoir Le Nord de l'Amérique." Ancient Poland cannot be accused of having attended much to her own interests, or the country would not have been at the mercy of Russia for many years before Russia formally consented to share Poland with her neighbours.

of constitutional monarchies. "Monarchies united by a constitution were," he says, "introduced as an intermediate form between these two extremes: the liberties of pure republicanism, and the hard slavery of despotism. In effect, constitutional monarchy tempers despotism, while it compresses the freedom of republicanism. The aim of this form of government is to keep a middle path, so as to annihilate despotism and slavery on the one hand, and, on the other, to arrest the development of democratic ideas. Such is evidently the principle of constitutionalism, but to realize it completely the exact middle path is not easy to find, and, among the various constitutions of which history has preserved the memory, there are some which lean too much to one or other of the two extremes, so that there are despotic constitutional monarchies, and republican constitutional monarchies." He then goes on to say that ancient Poland "was a true republican constitutional monarchy: a monarchy because it had a king; a constitutional monarchy because the authority of the king was restrained, and the sovereignty of the nation modified and limited by the law; republican, because all preponderance in the political life of the State belonged to the nation. It may even be said that ancient Poland was a pure genuine republic, clothed only with the forms of constitutional monarchy."

I think it may fairly be said that Austria, and Prussia still more so, are "despotic constitutional monarchies," because there "all preponderance in the political life of the State belongs to the monarch." Indeed, it may even be said that Austria and Prussia are pure and genuine despotisms, clothed in constitutional forms.

CHAPTER III.

THE AUSTRIANS IN POLAND.

Austria in her mode of governing her Polish provinces, seems at present to steer half-way between the Russian and Prussian systems. Prior to 1830 she was decidedly the least liberal of the three partitioning Powers as towards the victim. In the Kingdom the Poles had still their Constitution of 1815; in Posen they had their Provincial Diet, together with considerable liberty of the press; in Galicia they had no liberty of the press, while the functions of the Diet, composed exclusively of the Magnates—that is to say, of the highest and richest class of nobles—were little more than passive, and consisted for the most part in listening to an address from the Emperor, voting the prescribed amount of taxation, and thanking His Majesty for the interest he took in the affairs of the provinces. In Austrian Poland again, until 1848, the position of the peasants was not only worse than in those parts of Poland subject to Prussia and even to Russia, but worse by far than it had ever been in the ancient kingdom prior to the partition, when the peasants, though required to perform task-work, paid no taxes, and were not called upon to bear arms. In spite of recent reforms, in spite of liberty of the press as great almost as in Prussia, and perfect liberty of speech in the Galician Diet, there is still on the whole far less political liberty in Galicia than in Posen, though of course far more than in the Kingdom, where there is indeed none whatever. On the other hand, of that kind of freedom, scarcely appreciable by those who have never felt the want of it, which consists in being able to speak, learn, teach, and transact all kinds of business in the national language and without the interposition of foreigners, there is less in Austrian Poland than in that portion of Russian Poland called the "Kingdom," where everyone speaks Polish, where Polish money circulates, and accounts are kept in the old Polish currency, where such phantoms of journals as appear are all printed in Polish, where Polish is the language of the public offices, churches, and schools, and where, until quite lately (when, in consequence of the Poles refusing to attend it, it was closed), there was a national Polish theatre at which Polish pieces were played by Polish actors. This is just the kind of freedom which is denied to the Poles by the Government of Prussia, and which, in spite of copious promises, has only been partially granted by Austria. In short, a Pole is surrounded by more of what is called "Polonism" in the Kingdom than in Galicia or Posen, but he finds in Posen the greatest amount of political liberty. In Austria he has a little of both, but not very much of either.

Until 1848 the Galician serf, though not attached to the soil, was practically much in the same position as the agricultural serf of Russia, but with this remarkable difference, that he was subjected to the direct influence and authority of two masters; first the territorial proprietor for whom he had to labour, and on whom were imposed the hateful duties of collecting the taxes and directing the enlistment on his estate, and secondly the Austrian Government, whose officials, whatever their actions, never appeared before the peasant otherwise than in a benevolent light. Thus, when there was an increase in the rate of taxation (which for years past has been constantly progressing in Galicia until at present it amounts on an average to about 33 per cent. on clear income), it was for the landowner to proclaim and enforce the additional payments, while in each governmental district there were functionaries ready to listen to appeals and to adjudicate in cases of alleged overcharge. The existence of such officials may have been necessary and even indispensable, but it so happened that whenever the amount of taxes demanded by the proprietor was pronounced just, the decision had to be conveyed to the peasant by the proprietor himself, whereas, in all cases of remission, the officials communicated with the peasant in a direct manner. Not only were the old patriarchal relations between master and serf entirely abolished, but the master was made to appear as the serf's constant and irreconcileable enemy, while the Government insured its own popularity by presenting itself from time to time as his saviour. In the meanwhile the Galician nobles petitioned the Emperor repeatedly to be allowed to emancipate their peasants, but without avail. All they could obtain was permission to replace the *corvée* by a system of leases, attended by so many formalities and so much expense as to be impracticable. To the last proposition on the subject, made by the Magnates of Galicia in the Diet of 1845, a few months before the massacres of 1846 (concerning which, I may have a few words to say in another chapter), no reply was given. At last, however, in 1848, the peasants of Galicia were liberated with their land by the Government, which had carefully reserved for itself the credit of a measure sooner or later inevitable; and at the present moment they form, as in Prussia, a class of small freeholders having no necessary relations whatever with the proprietors, their former masters, except in the

Galician Diet. There they oppose them on every point, convinced as they are, that the chief object of the nobles in their endeavours to obtain a system of self-government for Galicia is to be able to re-establish the *corvée!* If the existing Government of Austria could have the folly and hypocrisy to stoop to such an unnecessary and discreditable proceeding, it could establish its claim to Galicia to-morrow upon the basis of universal suffrage. Equally certain is it that all the educated classes in Galicia, as low down as education has penetrated, which, unfortunately, is not very far, regards the Austrian rule with abhorrence.

"You have more liberty here than in France," M. de Montalembert is reported to have said when he was in Cracow a year or two ago. One may have more liberty than in France, and yet not become positively intoxicated with freedom; but it is a fact that in Cracow and Lemberg, books against the Austrian Government are openly sold, such as, if directed against the Government of France, could not possibly be offered for sale in Paris. Here the newspapers publish the *History of the Polish Legion*, the *Life of Dombrowski*, the *Last Debate in the Polish Diet on receiving the Constitution of* 1791, and if a journalist is now and then imprisoned for high treason (as lately happened to the editor of the

Glos at Lemberg), he has, at least, the satisfaction of knowing that he has, in a strictly legal sense, entitled himself to his punishment. But almost anything short of projects for the re-constitution of Poland, and direct incitements to civil war, may be published in Galicia, while all foreign newspapers, except that sworn enemy of Austria, *Le Nord,* and the determined advocate of Polish rights, *Journal of Posen,* seem to be freely admitted without being subjected to any purifying process at the hands of a censor. I have, moreover, travelled backwards and forwards in Galicia in various directions, some five or six hundred miles, without even being called upon to show my passport or coming in contact with a police official. All this to a foreigner seems very satisfactory, but to a Pole none of these liberties avail anything as long as he sees Germans sitting in the public offices, Germans in the schools teaching their language to children whose parents think only of bringing them up as Poles, German soldiers defiling the palaces of his ancient Kings, converted for their reception into barracks and architecturally ruined; Germans, in fact, everywhere, even in the mines of Wieliczka, where the names and inscriptions on the wonderful vaults, caverns, temples, magnificent ball-rooms, are all in the language detested by those to whom Wieliczka honestly belongs, and who still do all the important work there. Until within the last six months German was the language of the public offices and schools throughout Galicia, even to the University of Cracow, surrounded and apparently protected as it was by precise stipulations in favour of its "nationality," signed by all the Powers who took part in the Treaties of Vienna. What should we think in England of the finest University imaginable if all the lecturers appointed to it were Frenchmen, or (which comes to nearly the same thing) if all the lectures had to be delivered in French? Until the promulgation of the reforms which followed the presentation of the Galician address on December 31, 1860, there was only one professor at Cracow who was authorized to hold his class in the Polish language, and this exception, curiously enough, was made on behalf of a foreigner. At present Polish is the principal, but by no means the sole language of the Administration, and it is nominally that of public instruction. A Pole who finds it necessary to go to law has now the wonderful privilege of bringing his action in his own language. All communications from the Government to the Galician Diet have been made this year in Polish. An official is bound to reply in Polish or in German, according as he is addressed; but, as many of them do not understand Polish, it is evident that this rule cannot always be acted upon. So at the Universities of Cracow and

Lemberg (to give the capital of Galicia the name by which it is generally known in England, though the Poles call it Lwow—Leopol, and I believe, would call it anything rather than make use of its German appellation) Polish has been re-established as the medium of instruction, but by a decree which permits the numerous foreign professors who are ignorant of that language to retain their chairs. This is very generous, but it is marvellously like the generosity of the fox entertaining the crane. Poles may now drink their fill of learning at the Academy of Cracow, founded by their ancestors five centuries ago, and of which the existence as a national institution is guaranteed by the Treaties of Vienna, only they must contrive to take their Polish draughts out of German vessels. At the gymnasiums all the tuition is in German, and modern Polish history as at the Universities, is, of course, not taught at all. A student may learn that once upon a time there was a Polish Prince who was eaten by rats, and that once upon a time there was another Polish Prince who ordered the faithless wives of his officers to adopt and bring up puppy dogs, but the historical course terminates long before the black year of 1772. Indeed, to teach Polish history to a Pole, not as it is taught in Russia, but with some approximation towards the truth, is as impossible, and would be as absurd on the part of one of the partitioning Powers, as to teach reading and writing in the Slave States of America.

Before long it is expected by the sanguine that Polish will be made the sole language of public instruction in the gymnasiums, though the information hitherto published on the subject in the Polish journals is not very re-assuring. The Government shows itself as sensitive with regard to the susceptibilities of Germans as it is callous in respect to those of Poles: and, to avoid the possibility of any small German being "Polonized" against his will, or that of his parents or grand-parents, or great-grand-parents—now, it is to be presumed, no more—it is proposed that all juvenile Poles of German origin, counting as far back as the third generation, shall be regarded as Germans and educated accordingly. This is a test of nationality worthy of those electors of Southwark who, on the strength of his name, declared Mr. Layard to be a Frenchman. Applied in Poland, it would make Germans of the late Lelewel, one of the most enthusiastic of Polish patriots (in consequence of which he was exiled not only from all Polish territory, but even from liberal, sympathetic France); of Vincent Pol, one of the most popular of living Polish poets, and who was considered sufficiently a Pole in 1846 to be all but murdered in the massacres of that year; of Dr.

Dietl, the most eminent of Polish physicians, and one of the Polish representatives in the Reichsrath. For the last four or five centuries the best portion of the middle class in Poland has been composed almost exclusively of German settlers and their descendants. There are Poles in Cracow with German names, whose ancestors have been burgesses of the city since the fifteenth century, and to describe whom as Germans would be very nearly as absurd as to describe Englishmen of Franco-Norman origin as Frenchmen. Remove the Austrian troops, the German (and Bohemian) civil functionaries, and a certain number of Viennese shopkeepers established in Lemberg, and the "German element" in Galicia will be small indeed. The Government gives it a magnified appearance in the eyes of foreigners by Germanizing the names of Polish towns, and maintaining German as much as possible, in spite of protests and promises, as the public language of the country. It also keeps up German theatres, which no one attends, and German newspapers, which no one reads. The German theatre in Lemberg is supported by a forced contribution levied on the Polish municipality, amounting to 40,000 florins a year—a sum which, if the Austrian currency consisted of silver and gold and not of curl papers, might be worth £4000 of our money, and which at the actual rate of exchange is equivalent to £3000. When dramas and comedies are performed the audience is composed of about six Germans, who encourage one another the best way they can, and perhaps one Pole who has looked in simply to enjoy the dulness of the evening. Occasionally, too, as happened when I was in Lemberg, an Italian opera is performed in the German language—a fine language, certainly, for such a purpose, in which *tu m'ami* can only be rendered by *du liebst mich!* This attempted suppression of one of the manifestations of national life is the more intolerable inasmuch as the Poles have admirable actors of their own, and a comedy-writer who, as a creator or rather a presentor of national types, has certainly not his equal in Western Europe, where our dramatic works possess more or less literary merit, but have long ceased, and perhaps of necessity, to reflect in any broad manner national peculiarities. From the needy Polish gentleman of the ancient Republic, who, in spite of his utter want of cash, says to himself that he is in a political sense eligible for the Polish throne, to the Polish Anglo-maniac of the present day who sets up milestones on his estate and thinks it the height of pleasure to drive an English mile before breakfast, the comedies of Alexander Fredro abound in characters whose humour is eminently Polish. It is worth observing that this love of imitating foreigners is also in part the subject of the best Russian comedy ever written. Indeed, in spite of notable differences, there are many points of resemblance, social and intellectual, between the Russians and Poles—far more than either of them, and especially the Poles in their present most natural mood, would care to acknowledge.

To return for a moment to the question of "Polonism" among the German Poles, I may mention that though the Austrian Government maintains German theatres in Galicia, uselessly and unjustly, because at the expense of its Polish subjects, it at the same time tolerates representations in the Polish language. In Posen repeated applications have been made for permission to establish a Polish theatre, but always in vain. In the Kingdom of Poland, on the other hand, the theatre now closed was exclusively Polish; yet it would have been scarcely more a mockery to perform Russian comedies and operas at Warsaw than to give the same class of works in the German language at Lemberg.

One would imagine that the first aim of each of the partitioning monarchies, after enslaving the Poles, would have been to benefit their material position, and to spare their feelings in every possible manner; in short, to remind them as little as possible of their great misfortune, and render it, as far as could be, supportable. The contrary of all this is what Austria has done, to understand which, it must be remembered that the partition of

Poland partook largely of the nature of a common thieves' bargain, and that, political ambition apart, one great object of the three guilty Powers, and especially of Austria and Prussia, was to rob the victim as speedily and as extensively as possible. "The salt mines of Cracow," complains Frederic II., in a letter to Count Solms, dated the 20th of April, 1772, "produce a revenue of 1,000,000 florins, which is 130,000 crowns and more beyond what my share will ever bring me in." And again, he writes (25th of October):—

"The revenue of this port (Dantsic) is one of the most important branches of all that will come to me from my new acquisition, which, when everything is settled, will scarcely amount to 1,800,000 or 1,900,000 crowns. If this portion is pared off, what shall I have left? I hear at the same time from Vienna that the Empress-Queen will get 6,000,000 florins out of her share, which makes 4,000,000 crowns. I am not jealous. . . . But I should have a right to be surprised if the Court of Vienna were to take part against me in favour of Dantsic. I have said nothing about the salt mines which have fallen to Austria's lot."

At present the salt mines of Wieliczka, in the immediate neighbourhood of Cracow, are worked with such advantage to the native population that salt in Galicia costs more than six times as much as in London, and that at ordinary country inns, and even at tolerably good hotels in the towns, it is always coarse-grained and of a dirty greyish hue. So much importance does the Austrian Government attach to these mines that a spring of salt water which rises near Wieliczka has been turned into the Vistula, lest some unhappy pauper should take of the solution and extract the salt from it to the manifest detriment of the State revenue. At Rabka, some thirty or forty English miles from Cracow, there is another salt spring, supposed to possess wonderful medicinal properties. A coachman who was driving me to Cracow from the Carpathian Mountains told me of it, and as he assured me that the Government made great exertions to suppress this saline fountain I became anxious to see it; otherwise I should not, of course, have thought it worth a moment's consideration. There, indeed, was the insurgent competitor to Wieliczka blocked up and covered over with large flag-stones, and, moreover, guarded by a special functionary, housed and salaried at the expense of the Austrian Government. I had the stones removed, and up bubbled the water, very salt, very sulphurous, but tasting chiefly of foul-flavoured eggs. "A peasant must be very miserable to use such stuff as this with his food instead of salt," I observed. "They find it cheaper," was the reply. "Even now they try to steal it in the night; but in the cholera year they all came for it, and it was then that the Government found it necessary to close the spring."

As for taxation, Galicia is taxed as if Austria did not expect to plunder it much longer. A speaker in the Diet said, a few months ago, that owners of estates could no longer regard themselves as proprietors, but only as administrators for the Government. Some pay as much as forty per cent. out of their net income; but it is difficult to calculate the exact amount, on account of the irregular and arbitrary manner in which the taxes are levied. Thus, besides a land-tax and a tax for the indemnity granted to the landed proprietors on the emancipation of their peasants, with a considerable portion of land, there are taxes of the most varied and formidable kind to pay for establishing factories, iron-works, distilleries, even windmills, and I have known an instance of a proprietor being charged for erecting a portion of a mill which he afterwards found it would be useless to complete. "It is true there are no works there," said the collector, "but you must pay the tax, and you will then have the right to put them in and to grind corn whenever you please." If an artist takes pupils and sets them to copy pictures he is taxed as an employer; if a peasant is caught mending his own boots he runs the risk of being taxed as a cobbler. Sydney Smith, who thought our Government had exhausted all possible means of levying imposts, would have found, could he have visited Galicia in the year 1861, that in England we are only at the beginning of the art. To be sure, Austria is very nearly at the end, for she is fast ruining her taxpayers, and in Galicia there are already too many instances of estates confiscated for non-payment of dues and because the arrears are nearly equal to the mortgageable value of the land. In fact, on the immense majority of estates it is as much as the proprietor can possibly do to satisfy the exorbitant demands of the Government, and at the same time provide himself with the reputed necessaries of life, which are, in some respects, smaller in Poland than in any other civilized country. So true is it that the Poles, from being the most ostentatious and luxurious people in Europe, have now become the most simple, frugal, and sober. In the city and district of Cracow the weight of the actual taxation is felt more oppressively than elsewhere in Galicia, because when Cracow was prosperous and self-governed the inhabitants paid scarcely any taxes at all. It was then one of the cheapest cities in the world, and, in a commercial sense, one of the most flourishing. Since its absorption by Austria, its trade with Breslau, which, in the days of the free city, was very considerable, has been annihilated, prices generally have doubled, and taxation has been increased, at the smallest computation, six-fold. I could mention the case of a landed proprietor, living in his own house, and following no profession or trade, who now pays in house-tax sixteen times what he was charged in 1846; but I find that tradespeople, on the average, pay 600 fl. where, formerly, they paid 100 fl., and that shopkeepers are usually taxed to an amount equal to their rent. A house proprietor who lets a large house in flats told me that all the rent of the first floor went to the Government. The arbitrary manner in which taxpayers are assessed would be another cause of complaint, if it were of any use to complain on the subject. It is found more efficacious to bribe the collectors, and many tradesmen in Cracow have assured me that but for the fortunate venality of the officials they would be unable to carry on their business. Immense sums of money, something like four millions of florins, have been spent on the fortifications of Cracow, and for this, according to the custom of paternal governments in such cases, the unfortunate inhabitants are taxed. Every height around Cracow has been made the site of a fort, "as if," say the Cracovians, "the artillery from the Castle was not sufficient to destroy the city, while, if a liberating army once made its appearance outside, all the fortifications in the world would not prevent us from joining it." So little secure, however, does the Government feel itself, even now, that no one is allowed to build a house in Cracow unless he first signs an agreement binding himself to knock it down at his own expense in case the ground should be required for military purposes! In the admirable and ancient library of the University of Cracow there is a vigorously-painted picture of the Swedish soldiers under Charles XII. stealing the books. The Austrian Government has not plundered the library, perhaps because its printed and manuscript contents had no great value in its eyes; what, indeed, would such trifles as Kosciuszko's autograph, or a letter from John Sobieski to his wife, dated immediately after the deliverance of Vienna, fetch at an Austrian auction mart? But it has sacrificed, in the most shameful manner, the revenues of the Academy. These were derived for the most part from estates in what is now called the Kingdom of Poland, and concerning which Austria cannot well trouble Russia, after receiving at its hands such a magnificent present as the republic of Cracow. I learn from a little book published with the authorization of the censor appointed by the three Powers when Cracow was still a "free city," that at the beginning of the year 1846 "the greater part of the property belonging to the University (valued at 8¼ millions of florins) was situated in the ancient Polish provinces, now governed by Russia, Austria, and

Prussia, and that the liquidation of the various sums due is not yet terminated;" that is to say, 74 years after the first partition! I believe that the liquidation is quite terminated now.

Austria has, moreover, confiscated property belonging to the municipality of Cracow; she has confiscated Church property, and she has not scrupled to convert three of the most ancient and interesting chapels (the Italian chapel, the Goldsmith's chapel, and the chapel of the musicians in the Franciscan convent), into tobacco depôts! The Castle, the residence of the ancient Polish Kings, has, as I have already mentioned, been turned into a barrack; the staircases remodelled, the graceful characteristic architecture of the windows destroyed, the painted walls whitewashed. The Polish crowns, with all the State jewelry that could be laid hands upon, were of course stolen long ago. The State rooms are now filled with soldiers. Their trousers and stockings hang out of the Palace windows, and the courtyards swarm with troops to such an extent that a pestilential odour pervades the whole place, and renders it impossible to pass through the Castle to the Cathedral which adjoins it, and to which, fortunately, there is another entrance. In the Cathedral, together in one vault, lie the bodies of John Sobieski, Kosciuszko, and Poniatowski—the two latter placed there during Cracow's brief existence as a republic. The saviour of Vienna, the leader of the insurrection of Cracow, the hero of the battle of Leipsic, are all now in the hands of the Austrians.

Outside Cracow are three funereal mounds, such as were raised by the ancient Slavonians in memory of heroes and demi-gods. One of these commemorates Cracus, the reputed founder of Cracow, a personage whom I should be disposed to class with Prussus, the founder of Prussia; Russ, the founder of Russia; Tchekh, the founder of the empire of the Bohemians, or Tchekhs; and others of the same fabulous tribe. The second, Wenda, a Princess much revered in Poland because she drowned herself to avoid marrying a German; and the third, Kosciuszko. In 1820, on the anniversary of Kosciuszko's death, General Pazkowski laid the foundation of the Kosciuszko monument with a barrowful of earth and bones brought from the battle-field of Raclawice. He next deposited in a marble coffin the bust of the Polish chief with his biography, and placed by its side an urn containing some of the earth from the field of Maciéiovicé where Kosciuszko "fell." Then the spectators who had assembled in tens of thousands, all contributed to raise the mound, which is about 120 feet high and half a quarter of a mile round the base. This was just what the Austrians wanted. "Kosciuszko's Tomb" had been erected on the highest ground that Poles might see it from afar, and that from its summit the ancient palaces, churches, and monasteries of Cracow, to every one of which some national legend is attached, might be seen. What better site could there be for a military position? Accordingly, the Austrians proceeded to wall it in and fortify it, and the tumulus of the Polish patriot is now one of the chief strongholds of the army which occupies Cracow.

When I was in Galicia (where I spent three months in the summer of 1861), the Government paid little or no attention to "demonstrations." Soon, however, the demonstrations assumed a certain importance, and the Government then forbad the performance of .masses in connection with presumed patriotic objects, such as those for Prince Czartoryski and Lelewel. The service for Prince Czartoryski, forbidden absolutely at Leopol, was only permitted at Cracow on condition that the patriotic hymn should not be sung. It was sung, however, by the public as soon as the priests had left the altar. When, soon afterwards, an attempt was made to prevent the celebration of the union of Poland with Lithuania, the religious service was performed, in spite of the orders of the Bishop of Cracow (who it appears sides with his Roman Catholic government), by an unattached priest of the United Greek Church. On the anniversary of the Polish and Lithuanian union many of the shops in Cracow were shut. All were closed on the day of mourning appointed for "the martyrs of Wilna," and after the mass a number of persons, accused of creating disturbances in the streets were arrested. There has long been a secret press in Cracow. I do not know where the printed addresses come from which circulate all over the town, but they somehow or other find their way into every house. One, entitled *A Voice to the Inhabitants of Cracow*, which was issued the day before the celebration of the mass for the Poles who fell at Wilna, commences as follows :—

"You have proved your right-mindedness and readiness more than once. But heavier and heavier days are now approaching. The liberalism of Austria already shows its Muscovite claws. Do not allow yourselves to be intimidated by threats and bayonets, and do not let the ancient city of the Jagellons abase itself before those who formerly begged on their knees for Polish help. Of late the police has become more brutal, following in the track of the Muscovites. It forces its way into our houses during the night, to put out the lights, seizes our property, forbids us to shut up our shops when it pleases us to do so, breaks up our assemblies for prayer, threatens the personal liberty of every one of us, and arrests peaceable men in the streets."

Such, indeed, are now the general complaints

in Cracow, though, on the other hand, it must not be supposed that any amount of liberality on the part of the Austrians would ever reconcile the Poles to an Austrian Government.

In spite, however, of the general detestation in which the Austrian Government is held by the intelligent classes in Galicia, its power seems almost as firmly established there in the present day as it was in 1846, when the Polish insurrection prepared by the nobles utterly failed, and the peasantry rose to defend the Emperor, to massacre their masters, and to gain the possession of land which shortly afterwards was duly granted to them. Putting all patriotic feeling and all love of liberty out of the question, the territorial and commercial classes in Galicia cannot be well disposed towards a Government to which they are forced to pay a third part of their incomes in taxes. But the peasant class sees only in the Government the power to which it owes its emancipation, and is grateful to it *à la* Rochefoucauld, hoping at the first opportunity for fresh favours, such as the right of cutting wood in their late masters' forests, and of sending their cattle to graze on their late masters' pastures. The assembling of a Diet in which the old proprietors and the new peasant proprietors sit together has demonstrated in the plainest manner the existence of the chasm which separates them. In the eyes of the liberated peasants, the reconstitution of ancient Poland, or even the establishment of local self-government in Galicia, as petitioned for in the Galician address presented to the Emperor two years ago, signifies, as far as they are concerned, a return to the *corvée*. With regard to their conviction and attitude on this point there can be no doubt. I have conversed with deputies elected by the nobles, deputies elected by the towns, and deputies elected by the peasants themselves, and have found not the slightest difference of opinion on the subject. The peasant representatives sit apart, and form an Opposition—in a country in which to belong to the Opposition means to support the Government. On such "liberal" principles is the Diet constituted that the most ignorant class in the province—ignorant to such an extent that it does not even look upon reading and writing as necessary qualifications in its deputies—elects 72 members, while the nobles—that is to say, all the old landed proprietors, great and small, have only 42 representatives, the townspeople only 22. The Universities of Cracow and Lemberg are represented through their rectors, who sit *ex officio;* the Chambers of Commerce of Lemberg, Cracow, and Brody send one member each to the Diet, who is elected. But as the influence of the landed proprietors and citizens is negatived by that of the peasants, so is that of the educational and commercial bodies by a formidable clerical party, consisting of three archbishops (one Roman Catholic, one United Greek, and one Armenian) and four bishops (three Roman Catholic and one United Greek). With the intelligence, patriotism, and property of the country on the one side, but with the priests and peasants on the other, the Government, putting its faith in numbers calculated and carefully balanced beforehand, does not find the Galician Diet such a troublesome body as might have been expected. To give an example of the exclusiveness and spirit of caste which animate the nobles of Galicia, I may mention that in the district of Cracow they have chosen as their representatives a physician and an advocate. The citizens, on the other hand, were almost unanimous in electing a nobleman, Count Leon Skorupka, author of a work just published on *The Autonomy of Galicia*. They have also named a Jew, who is as good a Pole as any Polish Christian. The Cracovian peasants have given their votes to two noblemen, Count Potoçki and M. Wielogloski. The Deputy for the Chamber of Commerce is M. Kirschmeyer, the proprietor of the *Czas* newspaper. It would have been difficult for the ancient capital of Poland to show in a more striking manner that in politics it knows no class interests, and that there all classes are animated by the same sentiment. But it is only in these parts of Galicia, where the peasants are tolerably well educated, that their aid can be at all counted upon, and out of their 72 deputies only five sympathize with the true Polish party—that is to say, with the nobles, the citizens, and the educated classes generally. The Government knows where to look for its friends, and has taken care not to stipulate for the first elements of learning on the part of not only voters, but even of representatives; and accordingly there are Ruthenians sitting in the Galician Diet and giving their support to the champions of Ruthenian "nationality," who do not even know the difference between the Ruthenian and Polish alphabets.

For the patriotic party is opposed, not only by the mass of Galician peasants, who dread, or affect to dread, the re-establishment of the *corvée* and who are sincerely and naively eager for more land, and for fresh forests and pastures, but also in a special manner by a Ruthenian section, who have been taught by their priests and by their Government officials to weaken the movement in favour of "Galician Independence" by raising a factious cry in behalf of "Ruthenianism." Before speaking in detail of the curious and newly-invented thing called "Ruthenianism," let me state clearly that the Ruthenian peasants and the peasants of Western Galicia are thoroughly agreed as to the desirability of encroaching upon the property left to their late masters by the terms of the emancipative measure of 1848. They have been encouraged to look upon the land they now hold as a reward granted to them for "saving the monarchy" in 1846, and many of them say openly that the land might all be theirs, that the Emperor wishes them to have it, and that it is only the selfishness of their late proprietors which keeps them out of it. At present the great object of Galician politicians is to free the province as much as possible, and by perfectly legal means, from the control of Vienna, so that it may regulate its own local taxation, and appoint its own officials; and certainly, if the suffrage were intrusted to the same classes only as those which exercise that right or rather privilege in England, but one voice would be heard in favour of self-government. The peasants, however, have been persuaded that their interest consists in maintaining the existing state of things, and they present a stolid opposition to a movement which is supported by all the rest of the Polish population, from the artisan to the highest magnate, and including even the Jews, who now understand, here as in the kingdom of Poland, that the Poles are their best friends. The *Year-book of the Israelites* (for 1861) contains, by the way, some excellent advice on this latter subject; but it was scarcely needed by the Israelites of Cracow, who were for a long time under the spiritual guidance of the Rabbi Meisels, now, as every one knows, the superior rabbi in Warsaw. There is as much unity among the Hebrews of Poland as among the Poles themselves. Indeed, as a writer in the *Year-book* remarks, they *are* Poles, only of a different religion.

It would be difficult to persuade Austria that Galicia, whatever local liberties might be granted to it, would be contented to remain an Austrian province. The Poles have not undergone a century of suffering, unexampled in the history of the world, to end now by acquiescing in their subjection to any foreign Power, and least of all to a German one. But in the meanwhile it has been represented to the Austrian Government that it may lose its Polish provinces by more than one means, if the present system is persisted in, and without any great gain to the Poles themselves. The introduction of a tolerably liberal and rational system in the Kingdom would at once attract the Galicians to Russia; and Russia is already doing her utmost to undermine not only the Polish, but also the Austrian influence in Eastern Galicia, to which she has precisely the same claim as to Podolia, and a better—or rather I should say a more plausible and less preposterous one—than to the western portion of Lithuania. The eastern part of Galicia constituted formerly, with a portion of Podolia, the Duchy of Halitch, or Galitch, for a long time governed by Russo-Norman (Varangian) Princes, one of whom, named "Lev," or "Leo," founded "Lvoff," or "Leopol." Eastern Galicia, or Ruthenia, has, moreover, a Little Russian peasantry whose language closely resembles, and whose alphabet is almost identical with, that of the Great Russians. It received its religion from Kieff, and its actual Greek Archbishop, Jachimovicz, though as a Uniate he acknowledges the authority of the Pope, is shamefully calumniated if he does not regard St. Petersburg rather than Rome as his true religion's metropolis. Jachimovicz headed the Ruthenian deputation, which proceeded to Vienna in January, 1861, to protest against the exclusively Polish spirit of the address presented by the Galicians the month before. It is true this second address was followed by a third, in which a large body of Ruthenians assured the Emperor that they regarded their interests as identical with those of the Poles; but there exists, none the less, a Ruthenian party in Galicia, composed for the most part of ignorant peasants with intriguing priests at their head, which supports the Austrian Government and its bureaucracy against the demand for Galician self-government, and, turning the convenient weapon of "nationality" against Poland, claims Ruthenia for the Ruthenians. The Austrian Government is delighted at this divergence in the views of its Galician subjects, but in the meanwhile it has been warned not to rejoice too soon, and to remember that to cultivate a Ruthenian question is, sooner or later, to play into the hands of Russia, who has already presented herself as the future liberator of the Ruthenian peasantry and Church. I learn from *Le Nord*, and from a little work which describes Ruthenia, or Red Russia, as "the Russian Bosnia," that that unhappy land is oppressed by the Poles, and that if the oppression continues it will become the duty of Russia to interfere on behalf of her ill-used brethren. I certainly thought the Poles had long ceased to oppress any one, but this is not the first time that the wolf has protested against the tyranny of the lamb, and if Poland has not maltreated Ruthenia recently, she may have behaved harshly to her several hundred years ago, and in any case Russia does not mean to stand it much longer. Russia's claim to Ruthenia, or "Red Russia," has also been recently asserted by Prince Troubetskoi in a pamphlet on the subject, and all the Russians who justify their country's title to the so-called "conquered provinces" of Poland—that is to say, the provinces annexed at the various partitions—are logically bound to agree with him as regards her right to Eastern Galicia. It must be remembered that Russia claims, as legally belonging to her at the present moment, *all the territory that was ever ruled at any time by any of the descendants of Rurik.* This would give her not only the eastern provinces of Poland already in her possession, and of which she maintains that she was unjustly deprived by Lithuania during the Tartar occupation, but also the whole of the Ruthenian portion of Galicia. The learned Oustrialoff, in his amusing history, presents the third partition of Poland as marking the period at which "*nearly all* Russian territory was united into one whole," but without stating what is yet wanting to complete the unity of the empire. Say that the missing portion is Ruthenia, and the articles in *Le Nord* on "Russian Bosnia," and the attitude of the Ruthenian priests in the Galician Diet, become intelligible enough.

For the present all the Ruthenians, or rather those of the Ruthenian deputies who are elected by the peasants, simply protest against Polish being made the official and educational language of Galicia. But all the educated classes in Ruthenia speak Polish just as the educated classes in Brittany speak French; and the Poles say that a Ruthenian peasant, if left to himself, would not hesitate for a moment as to whether his child should be educated in the popular idiom or in the literary and general language of his province—which, be it observed, is the language always spoken by the present advocates of Ruthenianism among themselves. Nor do the Poles say a word against the establishment of Ruthenian primary schools, though they deny that they would ever be attended.

In the meanwhile, the true peasant deputies of Ruthenia (as distinguished from the political Greek priests, also elected by the peasant class) forget the question of their nationality so soon that they are always ready to depart from it and from every other question to join with the pure Galician peasant deputies in demanding fresh forests and pastures. Indeed, during the first meeting of the new Diet at Leopol (Lemberg), no one subject was brought forward but the debate was interrupted by the peasants asking how it affected the forest and pasture question. When a project for re-organizing the system of education in Galicia was being discussed, the peasants would rise to propose that the right of property in forests should cease. If the Austrian police system was protested against, the peasants came forward to suggest that the first thing to do was to throw open to them all the pastures of their late proprietors. In vain the President explained that there was one appointed subject before the Assembly; the forests and pastures were introduced on every occasion. If by chance they were neglected for a time, there were peasant electors present to remind the peasant deputies that they were failing in their mission, and at any inopportune moment the cry for more property, or rather for the abolition of existing property, was raised. Apart from the minor question of Ruthenian nationality (which, if left to themselves, the Ruthenian peasants would never have thought of), the peasant-orator in the Galician Diet has hitherto had only one idea—that whatever else takes place, the right to forests and pastures must be destroyed. "*Hoc censeo et delendam esse Carthaginem.*"

Sooner or later the Galician peasants will certainly understand that their interests are with the rest of the Poles, and not with the Austrians. Hitherto the Poles have left them entirely to their own devices, that they might convince themselves of the impossibility of obtaining from the Government any fresh partition of the estates of their late proprietors; and in time, if they learn nothing else, they will discover that it is only by combining with the great territorial and commercial classes that they can hope to free themselves from the weight of taxation which presses upon them as upon the rest of the Galicians. They have, if possible, even a greater antipathy to the Germans than the educated classes throughout Poland, and on this subject a good anecdote, which has the further advantage of being true, is told of a Galician peasant who accused another peasant of vilifying the Emperor. "He called him a German," said this loyal Pole; and as soon as it is generally understood that the Emperor of Austria cannot divide the estates of the old proprietors, and that, moreover, he is an Austrian, his Germanism and his anti-communism will render him equally unpopular with the peasants.

One word now as to the feeling of the proprietor towards the peasant of Galicia. The massacres of the year 1846 are so little forgotten, so little likely to be forgotten, that they form in part the subject of the second of the two religious hymns which are sung everywhere throughout Poland. "Many Cains are among us," says the fourth stanza of hymn No. 2; "but, Lord, they are not guilty, though through them our future has been thrown back. Other demons were at work there; oh, punish the hand, and not the blind weapon." Whatever we may say about these massacres having been to some extent provoked by the tyranny of the proprietors, I maintain that you will find no one living in Galicia who shares that opinion. At least, I have spoken to scores of persons of all classes on the subject, some interested, others in no way interested except as Poles in the question, and, whatever the truth, the universal belief is that the peasants murdered their masters, and plundered and burnt their habitations, because they were tempted and incited to do so by the Austrian Government. The hateful *corvée*, which the proprietors had begged repeatedly to be allowed to abolish, still existed, and the peasants were assured that if they defended the Emperor against the insurrection which was to overthrow his rule they would be rewarded with lands, which were in fact granted to them soon afterwards. The popular tradition on the subject is simply, that the Government offered a sum of money for the head of every landed proprietor; but this, like all traditions, is partly true and partly false. Persons who have studied the question thoroughly, and are familiar with all its details, explain the measures of 1846 by the peasants' detestation of the *corvée;* by the fatal influence exercised by the emissaries from the Polish democratic party, who hoped to restore the country by appealing to the communistic instincts of the most ignorant and unpatriotic class: and, finally, by the Austrian Government taking advantage of the two motives which already inclined the peasant to attack the owners of the soil, and adding a third—namely, the hope of an immediate reward in money and future landed possessions. Two movements were being prepared in Poland at the same time—one founded upon a democratic and socialist, the other upon a national basis under aristocratic leadership. The Austrian Government played off the former against the latter, called the peasants to its aid, and offered them liberation from the *corvée*, land, drink, and ready money if they would only rob and destroy those whom they had been taught to regard as their natural oppressors. Such a movement, directed as it was by Government officials, could not possibly fail, and it, in fact, succeeded only too well. None of the peasants, or of the disbanded soldiers who aided them and led them on, were brought to justice; but, what is still more noteworthy, those who organized means for resisting their attacks and preventing fresh destruction of life and property were punished for "levying war against His Majesty's subjects." To prove fully the first of these statements would clearly be impossible; of the truth of the latter, which goes far to establish that of the former, I possess positive evidence.

The feeling then produced in Galicia by the massacres, and now existing in full force, is one of hatred, not towards the ignorant peasants, corrupted and excited as they were in every possible manner, but against the Government. Those who suffered ought to know best who were their tormentors, and men do not usually excuse the murderers of their fathers and brothers; yet, from persons whose nearest relations were massacred I heard the same account and the same accusations as from those who were merely driven from their habitations in the night, and returned some weeks afterwards to find them in ruins. In most cases, the peasants on one estate were excited and directed against the proprietor and his family on another; but however this may have been, all agree in considering the peasant as the instrument employed, and the Government as the true author of the crimes, and doubtless the memory of these atrocities had no small effect in inducing the Galicians, until quite recently, to prefer even the domination of Russia to that of Austria. The Russian soldiers who passed through Galicia to Hungary in 1849 had meat and wine given them by the people of Cracow—doubtless not from any sympathy for the Tsar, and least of all for the cause he was about to support, but from a disposition to turn from the abhorred Government of the Austrians to a people of the same race as themselves; and at this very moment the most determined patriots in Galicia—believing fully as they do, in common with the Poles everywhere, that Poland must one day be re-established—will nevertheless say that if all hope vanished, and they seemed destined to remain the slaves of Austria, they would avert that fate by uniting with Russia, so as to form an immense Slavonian empire, in which they would play an important part, and stop for ever the encroachments of the Germans. The partition of Poland has been a political failure—at least as regards the German Powers—in so far that, instead of being absorbed, the separate portions tend more and more every year to reunite. Probably the only question soon will be, whether there shall be a strong, independent Poland—to produce which result it would be necessary, as a preliminary, to destroy the Russian Empire—or a united Poland under Russian protection. The great promoters of Galician self-government say that it is Austria's interest to reconstruct Poland, and that in the event of its reconstruction, Prussia might be indemnified in Germany for the Grand Duchy of Posen; but they acknowledge that no arrangement is possible with Russia, which, since the third partition, has been constantly gaining Polish territory at the expense of Austria and Prussia, and more recently in defiance of treaties signed by all the European Powers, and which, for the last 200 years has acquired province after province in Poland without once receding. The formation of the Duchy of Warsaw in 1807 and its extension in 1809, were both accompanied by fresh cessions of Polish soil to the great Polish invader. In 1831 Russia acquired absolutely the central provinces of Poland, of which the government had been intrusted to her in 1815, under conditions more or less precise, and now she is preparing to lay claim to the eastern part of Galicia—a pretension which, in Russian books and journals is already plainly put forward, and which quite explains the intense sympathy expressed by the St. Petersburg newspapers and reviews for the "rights of nationalities." If Napoleon III. were to talk of reconstituting the Empire of Charlemagne, his well-educated, and, after all, moderately-ambitious people, would laugh at the project; but the Russians will not laugh—they will enthusiastically applaud and support the first Tsar who proposes to complete the Empire of Ruric by occupying and annexing Eastern Galicia, otherwise Ruthenia, or Red Russia. The Poles waste words, politically speaking, when they discuss the historical question with the view of proving that the alleged Russo-Norman Empire never existed for any length of time, and that in any case the modern Russian Emperors are not its inheritors. The Tsar styles himself the Emperor of All the Russias, and one of the Russias is Red Russia. Ivan IV. once claimed all Poland, on the ground that he was the fourteenth descendant of Prussus, brother of Octavius Cæsar, who had conquered the country. The title was not a good one, but Ivan captured Smolensk all the same. So, whether or not the Duchy of Halitch formed part of a federated Russo-Norman Empire in the 14th century, Russia, as soon as Austria is sufficiently weakened, and Western Europe is occupied with other quarrels, will attempt to seize what the Government affects to regard, and what an immense number of Russians seem to regard in all sincerity, as one of her ancient possessions.

In addition to the nonsense talked about "Ruthenian nationality" in the Galician Diet; in addition to the Russian articles and books promising support to the Ruthenians against their Polish tyrants; in addition to the significant inexplicitness of the official historian on the subject of the territory *not* re-annexed to Russia at the third partition of Poland,—it is worth observing that the order for establishing a state of siege issued by the Minister of Justice in Lithuania in 1861 makes Russia's claim to that portion of the old Polish Republic rest upon the very title which would also give her Eastern Galicia.

CHAPTER IV.

THE POLES UNDER THE PRUSSIAN GOVERNMENT IN THE GRAND DUCHY OF POSEN.

In pursuing the Polish question from the Kingdom to Galicia, and from Galicia to the Duchy of Posen, it would appear at first sight that in this last-named section of Polish territory there must at least be an end to persecution, and that the Poles of Prussia can have nothing whatever to complain of, except that they are not citizens of a free and independent Poland—a matter which regards every Power that signed the Treaties of Vienna quite as much as Prussia herself. You cannot take ten steps in Warsaw without perceiving that you are in the midst of "a nation in mourning." Every lady is in black, every man, as nearly as possible in black, or in the national costume, which, itself under a foreign Government, is a sign of tribulation. There, moreover, are the insulting Russian monuments and the Russian soldiers at the corner of every street and under the portico of every house. Add to this the agitated groups and the excitement noticeable in the physiognomy of almost every one you meet, and without going into private society, without even entering a church in which the patriotic hymn is being sung, you cannot fail to understand that the people you see around you want not an atom of extra provocation, but only the slightest possible opportunity, to rise in insurrection. In Cracow there are no outward visible signs of oppression, such as would be evident in Warsaw to a man who might just have arrived in a balloon from another world. The place is surrounded by forts, but these might have been constructed solely as a defence against enemies from without. There are, moreover, plenty of soldiers in the town, in which also there is nothing very remarkable. What *is* remarkable, however, in Cracow is the extent to which the national costume is worn—so much that among the men it is, with very few exceptions, universal. There is as yet no national costume for the Polish ladies, but in Cracow, as in Warsaw, they all wear mourning and crucifixes, and black brooches inscribed with the fatal date of the 27th of February. In Posen none of these individual manifestations of patriotism strike the eye, and here you seem really to have arrived at the end of Poland, the true *finis Poloniæ*. The despondent exclamation falsely attributed to Kosciuszko has recently been

blasphemously misapplied by several German writers, who have made it the title of works on the hopelessness of the Polish cause; but on entering Posen one cannot help thinking for a time that they may be right, and that in Prussia at least Poland is no more. At the railway station no language but German is heard. You see German inscriptions over all the public offices, you are driven by a German to a half-German, half-Polish hotel, a ploygglot waiter brings you the bill of a German theatre, and when you ask if the Polish theatre is open, he stares and tells you that in Posen no such thing is known. If you were a Pole and had a son whom you wished to send to a Polish school, you could not at the present moment do so, even if you did not object to his learning everything in the fourth, fifth, and sixth classes in German, which is the invariable rule at all Polish schools in Posen. "This is as it should be," say the Prussians, "for you are no longer in Poland, but in Prussia. Nevertheless, Posen was the cradle of the Polish monarchy; it was Poland when the partition was plotted and perpetrated, it was Poland under the Duchy of Warsaw, and it was given to Prussia to be governed as a Polish province with "national institutions" in 1815. It is just the fact that beyond the names over the shops and the books in the shop-windows there is nothing Polish to be met with in Posen, which makes the Poles say that, as Poles, they suffer as much hardship and injustice under the liberal government of Prussia as under the Russian despotism. The Prussians shoot no one in the streets, and could not, under any circumstances, be guilty of such atrocities as were committed under the auspices of the Austrian Government in 1846; so, in the absence of any striking acts of cruelty and barbarity to be laid to its charge, we take it for granted that the Prussian rule in Posen is about as humane and equitable as, under very difficult circumstances, is possible. In Warsaw, however, though in the streets you may see bloody sights, you there behold at once, in its worst form, the most horrible part of the Russian system. Every one knows that a Pole who, with thousands of other Poles, cries out before the palace of the Lieutenant-Governor for his ancient liberty, will be shot, or, at least, shot at. On the other hand, let him sink his political aspirations, and he will find himself surrounded by other Poles, with Poles in the public offices, and Polish professors in the schools, and scarcely a sign of the governing Power anywhere but in the power itself. I do not say that this is an enviable state of things, nor am I inclined to give overdue credit to the actual

Government of Russia for its existence, such as it is; so impossible was it found under the Emperor Nicholas to introduce a thoroughly Russian system into the heart of Poland, in the manner in which Prussia has introduced her German system into the outlying province of Posen. But, nevertheless, many Poles belonging to Posen have found their life here so intolerable that they have left the place and gone to take their chance with their fellow-sufferers in the Kingdom. The proceeding may not seem wise, just as it may not appear a sagacious idea on the part of the Lithuanians to join their fate to that of their unhappy brethren in Poland generally; but it is a course to which Poles may be incited by a sincere, fervent love of their native land, and in Posen they are made to remember, in every possible way, that they are in a foreign country.

I do not think the history of our Channel Islands can be well compared with that of Poland. At least, I never heard of their Copernicus or their Sobieski, and they have not yet been called upon to produce a Kosciuszko. Yet, think of the effect that would be caused in Jersey by an Order in Council making English the language of the administration and law courts, and limiting the number of French schools, with the further stipulation that in all so-called French schools the instruction in the first three out of six classes should be given in English. There is nothing, except common decency and honour and prudence, to prevent the adoption of such a course, if the English Government determined upon it; at least, there are no pledges on the subject given to the Jerseyites. In Posen, however, the Prussian Government is bound by the treaties of 1815—bound neither more nor less than Russia, against whom they are so frequently invoked—to give "national institutions" to her Polish subjects. I will make no remarks about Prussia's inattention to the clauses regarding the free navigation of the Vistula, because they have been equally set at nought by all the three Powers, and because in this matter the Poles have been injured only in their material interests. To levy unlawful dues is bad enough, but it is as nothing compared with the suppression of national education—an iniquity which the most dexterous misinterpretation of the treaties imaginable could not excuse. Prussia may plead that the general Act of the Treaty of Vienna only requires the three Powers to give their Polish subjects "a representation and national institutions *regulated according to the mode of political existence which each of the Governments to which they belong may consider useful and suitable,*"* and that the "national institutions" most suitable

* See *La Prusse et les Traités de Vienne*, and compare with it *Finis Poloniæ*.

to the Grand Duchy of Posen are those which the Grand Duchy of Posen now enjoys. But this, it has been suggested, would be like a man engaging to supply another man with board of such a kind as he might think fit, and afterwards determining to give him no board at all. Moreover, Prussia in the special treaty between herself and Russia, promises in precise terms that the Poles shall obtain under her government "institutions which shall insure the preservation of their nationality." Frederic William III. interpreted the treaties of 1815 almost as literally as Alexander I. After a long correspondence on the subject, he decided not to form Polish regiments in Posen, at the express recommendation, it is said, of the Russian Emperor, who did not wish any counter-scheme of absorption to his own to be founded in Prussia; but he named a Pole, Prince Radziwill, Viceroy of the province, appointed another Pole the Director of Civil Administration, and allowed all the Polish officials of the "Duchy of Warsaw" to keep their places. At present there is not one Pole in the Government service of Posen, except in the tribunals, where if a few were not employed the affairs of the province could not possibly be carried on; and Prussia, with all her liberalism, violates the treaties of 1815 in as flagrant a manner as either Russia or Austria. In the Grand Duchy of Posen the village mayors appointed to Polish villages are

Germans. The district counsellors (*landrathe*), elected in the rest of Prussia, are in Posen Germans named by the Government. A knowledge of Polish is not required of any of these functionaries, though the persons with whom they are chiefly in contact are Polish peasants. In the Prefecture there are two interpreters, but not one official who understands Polish. In every department under Government control—and what is not under Government control in Prussia?—the same system exists. No Poles need apply. The clerks, conductors, even the stokers on the railway, are Germans. In all this there is a double injustice. If Polish and German were spoken indifferently throughout the province, it would still be unfair that none of the places at the disposal of the Government should be given to Poles; but the crying shame is that, by appointing Germans to every office, the Government *imposes* its language upon the Polish population, causing inconvenience to many, positive injury to a few, and natural, legitimate offence to all.

The first, then, of the "national institutions" granted by Prussia to her Polish subjects is a German administration. Now for the schools, which are divided into two classes—not Polish and German, but Catholic and Protestant. This, however, comes to much the same thing, as by far the greater number of the Catholics are Poles, while nearly all the Protestants are Germans. It appears from the Government returns, that there are in the Duchy of Posen, in round numbers, 900,000 Catholics and 400,000 Protestants and Jews. Accordingly there are four Protestant gymnasiums, in which everything is taught in German, while there are only three Catholic gymnasiums, in which Polish is the language of the three lower, and German that of the three higher classes! The Government will not consent on any terms to the establishment of a thoroughly Polish gymnasium, nor will it even allow a fourth Catholic one to be opened, on the lower-half Polish, upper-half German system, though the Poles are ready with the building, and have subscribed the greater part of the funds. A fourth Catholic gymnasium is declared to be unnecessary, and yet an advertisement appeared in the papers when I was in Posen, announcing the commencement of the autumn term, and informing parents who might wish to inscribe their sons' names on the books of the Posen gymnasium that it was useless to apply, as there were no vacancies. In the existing Catholic gymnasiums there are special classes for the German Catholics; but in the Protestant gymnasiums there are no special classes for Polish Protestants. The Polish Protestants in the Grand Duchy of Posen are, nevertheless, not yet an extinct race—only they are not recognized by the Government. The gymnasium of Lissa was founded by them at the time of the Reformation. This institution is at present exclusively German. I may add that a large amount of property left at various times by Poles for the support of national and Catholic schools has been applied to the maintenance of Protestant and German schools by the Prussian Government. This is not merely a "Jesuits'" cry. It is a complaint which has been brought forward at various times by the Poles of Posen generally, and it must be remarked that until last year the head of the Polish party here (the late M. Potvorovski) was a Protestant.

The Russian Government has often been accused —sometimes, in my opinion, unfairly—of "obscurantism;" though, from its very nature as a despotism, it is compelled to forbid, and does publicly and precisely condemn, all publications directed against its authority. In the present day, the charge of obscurantism is justly considered one of the most disgraceful that can be brought against a State, and no State prides itself so much as Prussia on being quite beyond its reach. Yet the history of Poland is a proscribed subject in the schools of Posen. No history is certainly better than false history, just as it is better to remain silent than to utter lies. But is not this attempted suppression of all the past life of a noble nation not only unjust but also scandalously immoral? If there were any descendants of the inhabitants of Gomorrah, it would doubtless be to their advantage not to familiarize them with the deeds of their progenitors. It is precisely, however, because the history of Poland abounds in instances of virtue and patriotism that the Prussians, in common with the Russians and Austrians, dare not teach it publicly, and even venture to forbid its being taught in private. It is all very well to quibble about the Treaties of Vienna, and argue, with the ingenuity of a Jew lawyer, that the words "*qu'il jugera convenables*" give either of the three Powers the right of setting at defiance the principles which are "*convenables*" to every civilized State. The evident meaning of the treaties relating to Poland was to secure to the Poles the right of existing without abandoning their nationality. At present, their life is intolerable in Prussia unless they become Germans—a kind of metamorphosis which, fortunately for the liberty of the world, is impossible. Fancy our French fellow-subjects in Canada being forbidden to study the history of France and to establish French schools; fancy Hebrew schools being denied to the Jews; and only think what an outcry would justly be raised by our philanthropists! Yet the Poles have done rather more than the Jews for Europe. I know an instance of a schoolmistress in Posen being reprimanded by the Government inspector for giving a lesson in the history of Poland to her pupils once or twice a-week, on the ground that, as this subject was not taught in public schools, so also it ought not to be taught in private ones. It is also a fact that a Polish professor in Posen, who proposed as a theme "the necessity of understanding one's native tongue," was in consequence dismissed from his place. After this, it only remains for the Prussian Government to offer a prize for the best essay in Polish on "the disadvantages" (evident enough in Poland) "of knowing the history of one's native land."

Apart from the baseness (necessary as that baseness may seem under a villanously tyrannical system) of endeavouring to destroy in a child the very idea of patriotism, the professors of Germany must moreover understand that to teach European history without the history of Poland is as impossible as to teach astronomy while omitting all mention of one of the great planets.

The Poles of Posen are allowed to publish a newspaper, and, from the frequency with which it is proceeded against under a Government not generally hostile to discussion, we may conclude that it speaks out vigorously on behalf of Polish rights. To do the Prussian Government justice, it must be mentioned that, though often seized, the *Djennik Poznanski* is seldom condemned; but, on the other hand, it might be argued that since it is never condemned it ought not to be seized at all. The accusations, however, come from the police, the acquittals from a judge. In Posen, too, an editor has at least the satisfaction of knowing that he cannot be punished for attacking the Government until his attack has been fairly issued and circulated. In Austria, a specimen number of every journal must be sent to the police an hour before its publication, when if anything objectionable is found in it, the publication is stopped, and the responsible editor clapped into prison merely for his evil intentions.

Although Polish papers are now published with comparative freedom in Posen, they are, as independent organs, of quite recent introduction, and two years ago there was as much liberty for the Polish press in Russia and Austria as under the Prussian Government. This was not the result of any law on the subject, but simply of an intimation from the President of Police to the various printers that if they produced objectionable journals they might find themselves deprived of their licences. From 1852 until 1859, no independent Polish journal was suffered to exist in the Grand Duchy of Posen. In the one newspaper printed in the Polish language which *was* tolerated, Polish affairs were so little discussed that, by express command of the police authorities, the Polish deputies in the Berlin Assembly were never even mentioned in it.

I have already said that there is no Polish theatre in Posen. The Poles have never asked the Government to found one at its own expense, or with such privileges as are accorded to the German theatre; but they have applied repeatedly to be allowed to establish a national theatre by subscription, and this permission, under one pretext or another, has always been refused. In Posen, as in Lemberg, the Poles make a point of not attending the German performances, nor, as a rule, do Poles and Germans ever associate here in private life.

One very droll argument employed by the Prussians to justify their continued possession of Posen is that they have civilized the country! They have numbered the houses, which formerly were known only by the names of the proprietors; they have introduced passports, the secret police, and a system of printing-licences which enables them to dispense with the censorship, properly so-called; and they have established German schools for Polish children. That is what German civilization amounts to in Prussian Poland.

"The Germans declare that they have civilized us," said a Polish gentleman to me one day in Posen. "Perhaps they mean that they have broken our spirit, but I am not at all sure of that; as for civilization, I cannot understand how the Prussians of the eighteenth century could civilize anyone. Even now they are only civilized, in a political sense, in so far that they have adopted some of the principles of our Constitution of 1791, which they joined the Russians in subverting, and the promulgation of which was made the pretext for destroying the existence of our country. As far as I am concerned, I can boast that they have not civilized me. I may be a Polish barbarian, but I certainly owe nothing to German civilization. No German ever sets foot in my house, and neither I, nor my father, nor my grandfather, ever had a German master, or a German steward, or a German servant, or ever had anything to do with the Germans except in the way of fighting them, and suffering from their persecution."

The Prussians will never understand that every nation ought to be allowed to civilize itself in its own way, that amity between nations is only possible on those terms, and that the best form of civilization, whatever that may be, can only prevail on condition that it is imposed upon no one. Under present circumstances, I confess I like to see the Poles of Posen and Galicia rejecting everything that is German, and that is precisely what we should do in their position. It cannot be said that the Poles have nothing to learn from the Germans; but all they have hitherto learnt from them—all that they possibly *could* learn—has been to detest them.

But, after all, it may be said Posen is now not a

Polish but a Prussian province. So some Prussian writers assert, and, putting aside the Treaties of Vienna, point triumphantly to the actual position of the Grand Duchy, in which a considerable portion of the population can speak German. I believe at present that the Poles in the Grand Duchy are to the Jews and Germans as eight to five. The Government represents the disproportion between the numbers as somewhat less, but acknowledges that there are 900,000 Catholics to 400,000 Protestants and Jews. Out of the 900,000 Catholics 100,000 may be Germans, and, as a rule, the Catholic Germans side with the Poles.

With regard to the sentiment of the province, as expressed through the number of Polish and German deputies returned to the Berlin Assembly, there were seventeen of the former and only thirteen of the latter in 1861, when I was in Posen. It is a remarkable fact that in the Assembly of 1855-8 the Polish party reckoned but five members, while the German party counted twenty-five. The explanation of the striking increase in strength of the Polish party was accounted for by the Government having ceased in a great measure to influence the elections and intimidate electors through the agency of its functionaries. This system was formerly carried to such an extent that for three years the city of Posen was represented by its President of Police, a functionary who gained some notoriety two or three years ago by inventing a conspiracy. The invention was brought home to him by M. Niegolewski, one of the Polish deputies. At present nearly half of the thirteen German members are independent, and all of them are opposed to the Poles. Of the five or six independent members, two belong to the National-Verein, where, treaties and promises apart, the absolute necessity of keeping Posen as an integral part of Prussia is maintained in the alleged interest, first of Germany, and finally of Europe.

It will be readily believed that Prussia, as a highly-civilized State, must be ashamed of her government in Posen, and that she would like to behave justly and humanely to her Polish subjects if they would only let all Polish national spirit perish within their breasts. Prussia probably thinks Europe ought to sympathize with her in the difficult position in which she is placed. But it is for all honest persons to rejoice at her dilemma, and to observe with glee her awkward endeavours to pass for an enlightened liberal Power, while she is condemned in spite of herself to practise despotism and obscurantism. It is quite certain that she cannot educate her Polish subjects as Poles, and that to retain them in subjection she must deprive them even of the memory of their historical existence. This is the natural consequence of the partition, one following the other as naturally as murder does robbery. All that can be said in favour of Prussia is, that she does her murdering as gently as possible, partly not to attract attention, and partly because she really does not like the work, and would be heartily glad not to have to do it at all. The Polish deputies are even convinced that she would give up a certain portion of her plunder to-morrow if it were possible that the remainder could be positively guaranteed to her. So, it is said, would Austria, and even Russia, provided the Poles would formally renounce all claim to Lithuania and to the Russian "Polish Provinces" on the Dnieper, which they naturally will not do. In the mean-time, while Russia declares, with brutal frankness, that she cares nothing for the Treaties of Vienna, that the Poles had better be quiet, and that, if not, she will establish order in their streets, Prussia coolly maintains, in the first place, that the stipulations in these Treaties have been scrupulously observed by her, which is impossible; secondly, that the Poles have nothing to complain of under her government, which is ridiculously false; and, finally, that they are contented, which, to adopt the language of one of Prussia's advocates, is *plus que faux*. "Russia," say the Poles, "is a bear, Austria a hyæna, and Prussia a fox—a fox with a large liberal tail, which she loves to exhibit to the eyes of Europe, but a cunning, fraudulent, destructive fox nevertheless."

CHAPTER V.

POLISH PRUSSIA AND PRUSSIAN POLAND.

"*Germania omnis . . . . a Sarmatis Dacisque mutuo metu aut montibus separatur.*"

Insuperable obstacles separate Poles and other Slavonians from all Germans.

Or, as a very ancient Polish proverb says:—

> "Never till all nature ends
> Can Poles and Germans live as friends."

The Poles detest the Germans now most decidedly, and for special reasons. Otherwise the mere fact of "Slave"* in all the Germanic languages having acquired the meaning of "captive," whereas in its original native sense it signifies (man of) "speech," (man of) "fame," (*slovo*, word, *slava*, glory); this alone would indicate the impossibility of reconciliation between two races which have always hated and misrepresented one another, which have always been fighting, and

* *Slave* in English and Danish, *sklave* in German. Hence, *schiavo* in Italian, *esclavo* in Spanish. So, among the Romans, "*servus*" meant "captured Servian."

which must have one more great struggle before long, in which the Germans are already tolerably sure that this time they will not be the victors. If the Poles of Russia form a sincere alliance with the Russian people; if the Emperor of Russia grants them the rights to which they are entitled by the Treaty of Vienna; if they even submit blindly to the Panslavonian policy of the Marquis Wielopolski—in either case Prussia must give up Posen to the Poles; or the Poles, backed by the Russians, will seize it, and afterwards take their revenge on the Prussians for the trouble they will have caused. "Poland in its integrity!" is becoming the cry of the Poles now more than ever; independent if possible (the possibility is not great), otherwise under the sceptre of the Tsar, and with the Tsar for its avenger.

Tu l'as voulu Georges Dandin! you tied yourself to Prussia without thinking how much younger, stronger, more powerful, more enterprising, and even more unscrupulous she is than you. The Poles may yet rise against you; your long thin country may again be broken in pieces as it was in 1806, and as it remained until 1813; when, finding that your French master was running from the Russians, you turned upon him and magnanimously kicked him!

But whatever happens to Prussia, it will still

have Mr. Carlyle for its historian. Only it must not lose Posen until the life of Frederic II. is quite finished, for if a nation does not prosper, it clearly does not deserve to prosper. The historian will justify the ways of Providence towards Prussia up to the moment of going to press. It must not, then, before the last volume is completed, fall back to the position it occupied fifty years ago.

"Of the partition of Poland," says the historian, "everyone has heard, but of the partition of Preussen, 307 years before, everyone has not heard."

Everyone, however, has heard of it who has read a history of Prussia or a history of Poland (which latter Mr. Carlyle appears *not* to have done). The whole story of the so-called partition of Preussen is told—not in Polish, but in Latin — by Dlugosch, or Dlugossius, otherwise Longinus, a writer of the period. Mr. Carlyle without quoting Dlugossius) gives a plain and, of course, truthful account, as far as it goes, of the transaction; but having done so it is not a little astonishing that he should afterwards speak of the so-called partition of Preussen as at all analogous to the partition of Poland.

And to justify a sovereign in going back 307 years to establish a title in opposition to the most solemn treaties and obligations! Did we not hold Calais three centuries ago? And if, after arranging with two other Powers to invade France at other points, we were to enter Calais on some futile pretext and then refuse to go out on the ground that Calais had belonged to us three centuries before—why, we should then be acting precisely as Mr. Carlyle's hero did in 1772 in the matter of Poland.

Mr. Carlyle himself tells us that St. Adalbert, a Polish bishop, was the first man who preached Christianity to the heathen Prussians; that Conrad, Duke of Mazovia (the province of which Warsaw is the capital) sent to invite the Teutonic Knights to occupy Prussia on certain conditions (which they did not fulfil); and that two centuries afterwards all Prussia called upon Poland to deliver it from the Teutonic bondage.

The cry was one of real distress. "So it had gone on," says Mr. Carlyle, "from bad to worse till 1440; when the general population, through its heads, the landed gentry, and the towns, wearied-out with fiscal and other oppressions from its domineering Ritterdom, brought now to such a pinch, began everywhere to stir themselves into vocal complaint. Complaint emphatic enough: 'Where will you find a man that has not suffered injury in his rights, perhaps in his person? Our friends they have invited as guests, and under show of hospitality have murdered them. Men, for the sake of their beautiful wives, have been thrown into the river like dogs,' and enough of the like sort. No want of complaint, nor of complainants: town of Thorn, town of Dantzig, Kulm—all manner of towns and baronages proceeded now to form a *bund*, or general covenant for complaining; to repugn, in hotter and hotter form, against a domineering Ritterdom, with back so broken; in fine to colleague with Poland, what was most ominous of all. Baronage, Burgherage, they were German mostly by blood, and by culture were wholly German; but preferred Poland to a Teutsch Ritterdom of that nature. Nothing but brabblings, scufflings, objurgations; a great outbreak ripening itself. Teutsch Ritterdom has to hire soldiers; no money to pay them! It was in these sad years that Teutsch Ritterdom, fallen moneyless, offered to pledge the Neumark to our Kurfurst, 1444; that operation was consummated. All this goes on, in a hotter and hotter form, for ten years longer.

"Period third begins early in 1454, with an important special catastrophe; and ends, in the thirteenth year after, with a still more important universal one of the same nature. Prussian Bund, or anti-oppression covenant of the towns and landed gentry, rising in temperature for fourteen years at this rate, reached at last the igniting point, and burst into fire. February 4th, 1454, the town of Thorn, darling first child of Teutsch Ritterdom—child 223 years old at this time, and grown very big, and now very angry—suddenly took its old parent by the throat, so to speak, and hurled him out to the dogs, to the extraneous Polacks first of all. Town of Thorn, namely, sent that day its letter of renunciation to the Hochmeister over at Marienburg; seized, in a day or two more, the Hochmeister's official envoys, dignitaries of the order; led them through the streets, amid universal storm of execrations, hootings, and unclean projectiles, straight to jail; and besieged the Hochmeister's Burg (Bastille of Thorn, with a few Ritters in it), all the artillery, and all the throats and hearts of the place raging deliriously upon it. So that the poor Ritters, who had no chance in resisting, were in a few days obliged to surrender, had to come out in bare jerkin, and Thorn ignominiously dismissed them into space for evermore—with actual 'kicks,' I have read in some books, though others veil that sad feature. Thorn threw out its old parent in this manner; swore fealty to the King of Poland; and invited other towns and knightages to follow the example. To which all were willing, wherever able."

And yet this country, which in its barbarous state was first explored by the Poles; into which

Christianity was first introduced by St. Adalbert, a Polish missionary and martyr; where the Teutonic Knights were invited to establish themselves on the understanding* that they were to be joint proprietors with the Dukes of Mazovia of all Prussian territory rescued by them from the pagan Prussians; where "the general population, through its heads, the landed gentry and the towns," "all manner of towns and baronages" of their own accord kicked out the Teutonic Knights, threw themselves into the arms of Poland, and entreated Poland to help them; this country three centuries afterwards,—that is to say, after three centuries of a common political life with the Poles — no more formed a natural part of the Polish State than it did of a half-imaginary Prussian State, of which the full idea was only realized at the first partition of Poland, and to cut away this country with the German sword in 1772 was the same sort of act as cutting it away with the Polish sword in 1466! That the population, high and low, were unanimously in favour of the Poles in 1466, and unanimously against

* Mentioned by Dlugossius (who also narrates, from his own knowledge, how the Polish Diet delayed, considered and examined titles before it consented to assist the Prussians and accept them as fellow-citizens); by Miçkievicz (*Lectures on the Slavonians*), Lelewel (*History of Poland*), &c., &c., but not even alluded to by Mr. Carlyle.

the Prussians in 1772, are facts not worth considering!

Perhaps, in a future volume, Mr. Carlyle will explain by what title Prussia took possession of Warsaw at the third partition of Poland. He has already told us how Frederic William I., the first Duke of Prussia, from whom Poland consented not to claim homage, fought against his sovereign at the battle of Warsaw in 1656, and how, in the thick of the fight, he treacherously, but greatly to the advantage of Poland, changed sides, and attacked his former allies, the Swedes. If a Prussian duke saved Warsaw from the Swedes* in 1656, why should not a Prussian king claim Warsaw for himself in 1795?

As for Frederic II., to do him justice, he never seriously pretended to want West Preussen for any other reason than because he felt it necessary to *arrondir* his dominions, and to join Brandenburgh and East Prussia, separated as they were by West Prussia and the Vistula.

That all Prussia, east and west, should not belong to the King of Prussia, seems, at first sight, something marvellous and unnatural; and that

* "Shortly after which, Frederic Wilhelm, who had shone much in the battle, changed sides—an inconsistent, treacherous man! Perhaps not, O reader! Perhaps a man advancing 'in circuits,' the only way he has; spirally, face now to east, now to west, with his own reasonable, private aim sun-clear to him all the while." In other words, consistently treacherous.

is why the electors of Brandenburgh and dukes of Prussia called themselves, after they had been released from the homage they owed to Poland for the East Prussian Duchy, first, Kings in, and secondly, Kings of, Prussia. The title of "King of Prussia" was not recognized by Poland till 1764, and then only on Frederic the Great making an express declaration that it involved no claim on his part to any of the possessions of the Polish Republic.

"Since the most serene Republic of Poland, following the example of all the other Powers, has consented to recognize the title of King of Prussia, in order that this recognition may in no way injure, in no way interfere with the rights and possessions of the said Republic, in the name of H.M. the King of Prussia, We, his ministers," wrote the Prussian ministers at the Court of Warsaw, "declare that the King has no intention, no desire, in making use of his title to infringe on the treaties and conventions existing between him and the most serene Republic; that, on the contrary, he engages to give the guarantee of his power for the maintenance of the rights and liberties of the Republic."

"We, after seeing this declaration, and maturely considering it, accept it and ratify it," added the Great Frederic at the foot of the copy forwarded to the Polish Diet. "We approve it and confirm it with our Royal word in our name, and in the name of our successors. We promise to respect it religiously, and not to permit anyone, for any reason whatever, to infringe it. In faith of which we sign this act of ratification with our hand, and affix our royal seal to it." *

This act was delivered to the Diet two years after the signing of the secret treaty between Frederic and Catherine, binding them mutually to allow no candidate but the one proposed by themselves to occupy the throne of Poland.

If the Prussia of the Teutonic Knights had been suddenly invaded, in time of peace, by Poland and two other States acting in combination and in pursuance of a secret plan, there would have been some resemblance between "the partition of Preussen" in 1465, and that of Poland in 1772. In speaking of this, the most criminal incident in the history of modern Europe, Mr. Carlyle, like the Hohenzollerns themselves, "does not walk in altogether speckless Sunday pumps or much clear-starched into consciousness of the moral sublime." Herr von Raumer, writing on the partition of Poland at Berlin, where he was Professor of History, is far less Prussian than Mr. Carlyle. On the other hand, he is far more impartial, and, at the same time, more generous. He can look to Polish as well as German authors for his facts; he can admire

* *D'Angeberg* (*Recueil des Traités*, p. 25).

the Poles in spite of their misfortunes, and cannot admire the partition of Poland, though Prussia may appear hitherto to have profited by it.

Nevertheless, eleven years after the third partition Prussia lost all the territory of which she had robbed Poland, and then for nine years (until 1815) had no Polish subjects to torment by endeavouring to turn them into Germans. Even now, nearly all the chestnuts which Prussia pulled out of the Polish fire during the insurrection of Kosciuszko are in the possession of Russia, and if Russia should resolve to do tardy justice to her Polish subjects, and grant them a liberal measure of self-government, it will be difficult to prevent Posen from going of its own accord the way that Warsaw was forced to go.

It is easy to understand why the Prussia that was ruled by the Teutonic Knights desired, like Lithuania, Livonia, and even Bohemia, to unite itself to Poland. It was tired of German persecution, and desired Polish liberty. We learn from Mr. Carlyle's own pages, that long after West Prussia had become Polish (or Royal) Prussia there was much sympathy for Poland and Polish ideas in East or Ducal Prussia. This was manifested in several instances, when the Duke of Prussia first became an independent sovereign, many of the German "barons and burghers," evidently thinking it would have been better had it remained a Polish fief. "He had some trouble now and then," says Mr. Carlyle, "with mutinous spirits in Preussen. Men standing on antique Prussian franchises and parchments, refusing to see that the same were now antiquated, incompatible, not to say impossible, as the new Sovereign alleged; and carrying themselves very stiffly at times. But the Hohenzollerns had been used to such things: a Hohenzollern like this one would evidently take his measures, soft but strong, and ever stronger to the needful pitch, with mutinous spirits. One Bürgermeister of Königsberg, after much stroking on the back, was at length seized in open Hall, by Electoral writ—soldiers having first gently barricaded the principal streets and brought cannon to bear upon them. This Bürgermeister, seized in such brief way, lay prisoner for life, refusing to ask his liberty, though it was thought he might have had it on asking."

Mr. Carlyle also tells us how one of the nobles of this German Prussia, (the country of which Königsberg is the capital—not to be confounded with Polish Prussia, now West Prussia, of which the chief town is Dantzig,) actually appealed to John Casimir, King of Poland, for justice; who, under the circumstances, even had he been a firm instead of a very feeble monarch, could scarcely have interfered. The affair is thus narrated by Mr. Carlyle:—

"Another gentleman, a Baron von Kalkstein, of old Teutsch-Ritter kin, of very high ways, in the Provincial Estates (Stände), and elsewhere, got into lofty, almost solitary, opposition, and at length into mutiny proper, against the new 'non-Polish' Sovereign, and flatly refused to do homage at his accession. Refused, Kalkstein did, for his share; fled to Warsaw; and very fiercely, in a loud manner, carried on his mutinies in the Diets and Court-Conclaves; his plea being, or plea for the time, 'Poland is our liege lord' (which it was not always), 'and we cannot be transferred to you, except by our consent asked and given,' which, too, had been a little neglected on the former occasion of transfer. So that the Great Elector knew not what to do with Kalkstein; and at length (as the case was pressing) had him kidnapped by his ambassador at Warsaw, had him 'rolled into a carpet' there, and carried swiftly in the ambassador's coach, in the form of luggage; over the frontier, into his native province; there to be judged, and, in the end (since nothing else would serve him), to have the sentence executed, and his head cut off. For the case was pressing! These things, especially this of Kalkstein with a boisterous Polish Diet, and parliamentary eloquence in the rear of him, gave rise to criticisms; and required management on the part of the Great Elector."

This may amuse Mr. Carlyle, but it will not amuse Prussia to find her Polish subjects turning to their brethren in the Kingdom of Poland, which they will do more and more when the Russian Emperor has granted them those liberties which (unless he means to lose Poland altogether) he cannot now any longer withhold.

CHAPTER VI.

POLAND, PRUSSIA, AND THE "NATIONALITY" THEORY.

For some years past few phrases have been so often used in political writings as that of "the rights of nationalities," though there is far from being any general understanding as to what a "nationality" is, or what the rights claimed for it are. As a rule, a man who declares himself in favour of "the rights of nationalities" passes for a person of liberal sentiments; and it is taken for granted that any one who questions those rights must be an enemy to freedom, and that their greatest opponents are the despotic Governments of Europe.

The fact, however, is that the nationality theory, owing to the vagueness of the terms employed in setting it forth, is one of the most dangerous ever broached. It is a weapon equally well suited to despots and revolutionists, and which, in the hands of either, may be turned against the best interests of civilization.

Originally, no doubt, the theory sprang from a liberal and just idea, and signified (to quote examples) that Italy and Hungary ought not to be governed by Germans, nor Poland by Russians, but that every nation should be allowed to rule itself and develope freely the kind of civilization peculiar to it. These rights, however, whether allowed or not, would have been called, fifty years ago, "national rights," and not "the rights of nationalities."

The word "nationality" was frequently used in 1814 and 1815, when the Treaty of Vienna was in preparation, but it simply meant the fact of being national. Thus, when it was desired to guarantee to the Polish subjects of Prussia their continued existence as Poles, a clause was devised binding the Prussian King to grant them "institutions calculated to ensure the preservation of their nationality." Sixteen years afterwards, when the French Chamber of Deputies adopted, for the first time, the declaration, which it so often repeated, that "Polish nationality shall not perish," every one understood this to be the expression of a determination that the Poles should not be extinguished as a nation, though Poland had long ceased to exist as an independent State. No one at that time said that Poland was "an oppressed nationality," or that the Poles under the Russian, Austrian, and Prussian Governments were "oppressed nationalities." It was stated simply and correctly that the Poles (who have never ceased to form a nation, in all but the political sense of the word) were oppressed in reference to their nationality, which the partitioning Powers had, individually and collectively, promised to see respected.

In course of time, however, as the expression *la nationalité Polonaise* became popularized, a concrete instead of abstract meaning was given to the substantive, and people began to look upon a "nationality" as signifying something less than a "nation"—either the fragment or remains of one, or the nucleus of one that had not yet existed. When the Revolution of 1848 broke out, "oppressed nationalities" were heard of everywhere, and meant, in the language of the period, not only oppressed nations, but any oppressed bodies of population, or, indeed, any bodies of population differing in race, language, and national feeling from the governing race of the State to which they belonged; such, for instance, as the Bohemians in the Austrian Empire.

The rulers soon found that the game of nationalities was one at which they also could play. Almost every "oppressed nationality" in Europe has some other "nationality" connected with it, which, if it does not oppress, it at least has not succeeded in inspiring with any solid feeling of attachment; and many of these minor "nationalities" are mean in proportion to their pettiness and historic insignificance, and willingly join with the despotic monarch to resist the just claims of their superiors, simply because they are jealous of them.

Thus, the Croats did their best to paralyze the Hungarian movement. They were tempted by the Austrian Government to attack the Hungarians, for centuries their fellow-citizens, and to raise the banner of Croatia, which never before had a banner. They were determined that Croatia should no longer be known simply as an annex of Hungary, and preferred that their political parent should perish rather than that she should continue her existence with the adopted Croatia as one of her provinces.

If the Hungarians say now, "We wish to be governed as Hungarians," the Austrian Government replies, "Yes; but a majority of the inhabitants of the ancient kingdom of Hungary, including Croatia, is not Hungarian at all, but Slavonian. We feel bound to attend to the interests of this loyal, though uncivilized, portion of the population;" and the effect of this apparently liberal move, to which no one who is a thorough supporter of the nationality theory can possibly object, is to check-mate the Hungarians.

In Italy the Germans could make no use of the "nationality theory." However they might differ ethnologically, the races of Italy had all adopted the Italian language, or dialects of it; and in Lombardy it was impossible to set the lower against the higher and middle classes of the population by appealing to national antipathies, the only national antipathies known, being those which separated Italians from Germans. The sole way to beget the good favour of the peasantry and working classes of Lombardy was by exempting them almost entirely from taxation. This plan was tried, and so successfully that there is no reason to believe the Austrians would ever, without the assistance of the French, have been expelled from the Lombardian territory, where the labourers took but little interest in the struggle one way or the other, though, on the whole, their sympathies were naturally with the Italians.

In Galicia Austria has discovered an inferior race of men called Ruthenians, and endeavoured to persuade them that they form a "nationality" quite distinct from that of the Poles. The efforts made by Austrian officials to raise up the Ruthenian or Russine * nationality have enfeebled the Polish cause to some slight extent in Austria,

* *Rossianin*, Ruthenian, or Russine, as distinguished from *Ruski*, Russian. The author has had, and may again have, occasion to explain that the Ruthenians are of the same race as the pure Russian (or Normanno-Slavonian) race in the

though, to an equal degree, they have advanced the interests of Russia in that Empire. In the Western provinces of Russia, or Eastern provinces of Poland, the Russian Government has also Ruthenians to deal with, and seeks to raise up these "peasant slaves" against the educated Poles, who represent all the civilization of the said provinces. Here, again, the cause of nationality is made to serve that of despotism, which knows that it can always find supporters among the lowest classes, and that it has only to fear opposition from persons who have inherited feelings of independence, and cultivate freedom as a sort of tradition.

In Finland, too, Russia has contrived to profit by the theory of nationality. She has raised up a Finnish peasantry against a Swedish aristocracy and merchant class; and now, if any one talks of "rights of nationality" in Finland, Russia may say, with truth, that she observes them, though by so doing she openly places herself in a better position to deny the educated men of Finland the political franchises expressly guaranteed to them.

No Power, however, in all Europe makes such a strange use of the theory of nationalities as

Russian Empire; but for four centuries (until the partition of Poland) they had a different history, and, those who were civilized among them, a different civilization.

Prussia. She ignores it altogether in Posen, where she has to deal with Poles, and proclaims it loudly in Schleswig, where Denmark has a number of German subjects whom she governs under circumstances of great difficulty with strict justice, and whom, until German propagandism compelled her to abandon her own natural system, she ruled with a liberality of which the Prussians have taken the meanest advantage.

So it has been in the provinces of West-Preussen and Posen, where the German settlers enjoyed, under the Polish Government, from time immemorial, the freest use of their language, and, in their own colonies, of their laws. So incapable have the Germans shown themselves of appreciating these privileges in a becoming spirit, that they now basely turn round upon the Poles and, quoting these very privileges against them, assert their right to rule as Germans wherever Germans and Poles are found together; that is to say, the right not only to use their own language, but to prevent the Poles from using theirs!

This treacherous argument has been employed against the Poles everywhere. Under their Government, as under that of Great Britain, no one thought of forcing any part of the population to adopt a language not its own. Uniformity was not aimed at; all the provinces composing the Republic were on a footing of perfect equality, and Prussians spoke German or Polish, Ruthenians Ruthenian or Polish, without the least restriction, and without any rule beyond the convenience of the parties concerned.

The Polish language was gradually becoming the language of politics and literature all over the Republic, and was replacing Latin in the higher spheres, and the provincial idioms in the lower; but it was never imposed upon anyone. Those Ruthenian peasants, whom the Russians, in Lithuania, and the Austrians, in Eastern Galicia, are now kind enough to regard as forming an "oppressed nationality," that they may have a pretext for raising them up against the Poles, spoke their own dialect among themselves, but were glad to have an opportunity of learning Polish; and educated Ruthenians were and are Poles in the sense in which educated Irishmen and Welshmen are Englishmen.

If the Ruthenian peasant-deputies in the Galician Diet could read they would be able to convince themselves that two Kings of Poland, Michael Wisnowicçki and John Sobieski, were Ruthenians; that they never considered themselves oppressed, and that they knew of no national distinction between Ruthenians of Poland and Poles. This distinction has been invented by the Russian and Austrian Governments, and has been made a pretext for suppressing the Polish language, on the ground that it is not the language of the majority—which is quite true, just as English certainly was not, and perhaps is not even now, the language of the majority in Ireland, Wales, and some parts of the Highlands of Scotland.

There is something very touching in this tenderness of despotism for the least noble, least civilized classes of the community. It does not, and cannot, raise them to the position of their superiors, but it can, at least, bring down their superiors to theirs.

"We will have no aristocratic tyranny here! no Polish language spoken among a Ruthenian—or Russian — population," say the Russians in Lithuania.

"We will have no aristocratic tyranny here! no Polish language spoken among a Ruthenian—*not* Russian—population," say the Austrians in Eastern Galicia.

Accordingly, in the one case Russian, in the other German, is made the official language. The Ruthenians, after all, are in no way benefited, but, at least, the Poles are injured.

The division between Poles and Ruthenians would be far greater than it actually is if the Poles could only be induced to furnish some grounds for the ridiculous charges of persecution brought against them; if, for instance, the Polish deputies in the

Galician Diet, in making their demands for provincial self-government, could be led to object to the official use of the Ruthenian language and the establishment of Ruthenian schools. But they know their own traditions too well. Accordingly, when a Ruthenian deputy, who had had his cue given to him, but did not know his part throughout, rose one day to ask by what right the proud Poles proposed to ignore his native *patois*, they simply replied that they gave it their full recognition; that their only desire was for the Poles to be allowed the use of the Polish language, and that they quite admitted the right of the Ruthenians to use whatever language suited them best.

It is not the fault of the Poles if this ready admission of the equality of Poles and Ruthenians involves no real sacrifice on their part. The Ruthenian, as a modern literary language, has yet to be invented; and some ingenious and energetic Russians are really endeavouring to invent it: though, even if they succeed, it will not be very easy to get the invention accepted for general use. The Ruthenian priests who lead on the Ruthenian deputies in the Galician Diet invariably speak Polish among themselves; and the Ruthenian can no more prevail against the language of Miçkievicz than Welsh (fine poetic language as it may be) can prevail against the language of Shakspeare and Byron.

I am told that a Ruthenian peasant will often pretend to understand Polish thoroughly (because it is the language of his superiors), when he is, in reality, but little acquainted with it; and this will be quite intelligible to anyone who knows that Highlanders sometimes affect a greater familiarity with English than really belongs to them. I read, only the other day, in a Scotch newspaper, that at a church in the Highlands, where the service was performed alternately in English and Gaelic, the English service alone was attended; upon which the minister, one day, at the end of his English sermon addressed the congregation in Gaelic, and told them he was quite aware that they had scarcely understood a word of what he had been saying to them. The Poles have no more wish to suppress the Ruthenian than the Highland proprietors have to suppress the Gaelic. They know that their language, left to itself, can take care of itself, and it is for this reason that the Russian, Austrian, and Prussian Governments look upon it with so much disfavour.

In Posen, however, where the peasants are of pure Polish race, and where Polish is the language of all the Polish population, high and low, and where German is the language of a minority consisting chiefly of shopkeepers and Government officials—there the democratic nationality theory will, of course, not work. The peasants are Polish; the clergy and the landed proprietors are nearly all Polish; the members for Posen in the Prussian Assembly are, in the Upper House, all Polish, and in the Lower House, Polish in the proportion of about four to three. In other words, the aboriginal population and the really cultivated classes are Polish. In the face of these facts the Prussians, with characteristic non-perception of the absurd, maintain that the German bootmakers, bureaucrats, and spies, represent the "civilizing" element in Posen!

Putting all treaties on one side, it cannot be maintained for an instant, either in the interest of the most civilized or of the most numerous class, that German ought to be the official and educational language of Posen. But that small body of Poles who believe in universal suffrage and the right of uneducated majorities to dictate the law to educated minorities, should be prepared to give up all claims to Galicia and to Lithuania, where, under present circumstances, the Russian and Austrian Governments can always get a multitude of peasants to oppose the wishes of the "noble" or lettered class. That is why I regard the Polish democrats as a misguided, heretical, and essentially anti-national sect, and not from any community of interest or sentiment with Polish "aristocrats;"

it never having happened to me to meet with any Pole, however highly born, or however distinguished by his own personal merit, who was an "aristocrat" in the exclusive and tyrannical sense attached to the word by the exclusive and tyrannical democrats who are so fond of using it.

CHAPTER VII.

THE POLES ON GERMANY IN GENERAL.

The Prussians are often regarded, on false ethnological grounds, and, perhaps, also because Blucher helped us to beat the French at Waterloo—as our natural allies. Our sympathies, however, were not either with the Prussians or Austrians when Prussia and Austria took part in the dismemberment of Poland; nor when they joined Napoleon's European league against England, to which they remained bound until the French reverses in Russia gave them an opportunity of rising treacherously against their enfeebled master and ally; nor when they united with Russia to destroy the independence of Cracow; nor when, from fear of Nicholas, they abstained from even expressing an opinion as to the justice of the Crimean war, undertaken solely to resist the encroachments of Russia; nor, recently, when Austria was fighting against the Italians with all Germany wishing her success.

If we are of opinion that the Italians, the

Hungarians, and the Poles have been cruelly treated, and are cruelly treated now (which all accounts from Venetia, Hungary, and Poland prove to be the case), we cannot have any high esteem for the Powers under whose auspices, or with whose connivance, these cruelties are perpetrated. Nor ought we to separate the Governments, either of Austria or of Prussia, from the people; for, as a general principle, nations are worthy of their rulers. If subjects cannot be looked upon as answerable for the acts of despotism committed by their Sovereign, they may at least be regarded as guilty of culpable negligence, indolence, or cowardice, in allowing themselves to be governed under a system which allows the ruling power to act in an irresponsible manner.

Of course, in an ethnological point of view, we are related to the Germans, though not to the Prussians, properly so-called. So, in a remoter degree, are all the European races; so, in a still more remote degree, are all the sons of Japhet related to all the sons of Ham, though hitherto they have not shown themselves very proud of the connection. On the other hand, we have grown up for centuries under a political system entirely different from any that has been known in Germany since the formation of regular Governments in that land, and which differs essentially from those of Austria and

Prussia even now, when both these monarchies are nominally of the constitutional pattern. They possess what may be called fine-weather Constitutions, which, as soon as a political storm is seen to be brewing, are taken in. In reality, the power of the Monarch is no more limited in Prussia than it is in France, while in the Austrian Empire it has not even the appearance of a counterpoise either in Hungary or in Venetia.

The recent setting aside of the decision of the Prussian Chamber of Deputies in the matter of the Budget ought not to be regarded as an exceptional act, for it is one which, from the nature of the Prussian Monarchy, the King may commit with impunity as often as he pleases. Even if he were to drive the middle and lower classes to resistance, which, from their inherited habits of submission, they are not likely to attempt, he would still have the whole of the nobility on his side, and an army in which all the officers of superior rank, and a great majority of the subalterns, are nobles.

The so-called "constitutional" struggle now going on in Prussia is not a struggle between the King and his Parliament, but between the King, supported by the Upper House of Parliament, the Government officials, the landed proprietors of the noble class, and the troops, on one side, and the Lower House of Parliament, supported by the professional and commercial classes, on the other. The King need not fear the result of such a contest as this. What he would really have cause to dread—unless he were prepared to do his duty honestly to the nation—would be a union of the upper and middle classes to obtain a Parliamentary system resembling that of England. This he knows to be out of the question as long as a class of privileged nobles is kept up in Prussia. When the nobility—that is to say, not the heads of illustrious houses, nor the members of the Upper Chamber alone, but all the descendants or representatives of the old feudal landowners—are themselves exempted from paying taxes, does it matter to them whether the taxation imposed on the rest of the population be light or heavy? Indeed, the heavier the better, for there will then be more money to spend on the army, in which the commissions are looked upon as the natural perquisites of this indigent, selfish, and inglorious order.

All classes are, it is true, represented in the Prussian Chambers; but the nation being divided into two camps, nobles and plebeians, the Parliament is divided in a similar manner; and instead of the two Houses working together harmoniously, as they do in England, they are always in opposition. They have different interests and a different policy. The nobles join with the King in demanding unlawful imposts from the people, and the King joins with them in declaring that *they* shall pay no imposts at all.

When a trial takes place, whether with or without a jury, of course that in itself is a show of legality, if nothing more. But the Prussian police possesses irresponsible despotic power to such an extent that its action often takes the place of legal proceedings, so that alleged offences (especially in Posen) are often punished, without any intervention of the law whatever.

Indeed, it is an offence in Prussia to do anything to which the Administration may object, without any reference to the legality of the act. Thus, it is an offence to sell or offer for sale any book which, either for religious, moral, or political reasons, is displeasing to the Government; and, to avoid all unpleasantness, works, chiefly of course of a political nature, are often proscribed beforehand by the police —though it is well known that in Prussia no censorship exists. If the offence, however, is committed, if the forbidden books or newspapers are offered for sale, then the bookseller or newsvendor is reprimanded, his contraband goods are seized, and he may esteem himself a fortunate man if his licence to sell is not taken away. He has no means of justifying himself, for he is brought before no tribunal. An excuse, according to the French proverb, is a species of accusation, but a man cannot even excuse himself when no accusation is brought against him.

In short, the great art of Prussian government consists in gaining and keeping up a reputation for liberalism while practising despotism. Austria has never been such a hypocrite. She also might have said, long ago, "The censorship is abolished," while constituting every policeman a censor. She also might have said, "Trial by jury is established," and then have added, "except in political cases," —the only ones in which that great safeguard is absolutely indispensable. Austria might, moreover, have proclaimed the complete liberty of the newspaper press, and yet have so managed matters that not a journal should be started in all her empire without the special sanction of the Government, and that every journal not possessing that sanction should be suppressed. This desirable end is attained in Prussia in the following easy and simple manner:—

The code proclaims the press free, but renders it incumbent on printers to obtain permission to open printing-offices from the police. Under this arrangement you are at liberty to print whatever you like if you can only get a printer to undertake the work for you, which, if the printer has received a caution on the subject from the police-office, he will take very good care not to do. Russia and Austria, with the frankness of acknowledged despotism, say that they will not tolerate opposition from the press beyond a certain point. Prussia, however, is too much of a Western Power to venture upon such a course as this. She accordingly invites writers publicly, through the law, to express themselves freely on all subjects, and takes care privately, through the Administration, that they shall do nothing of the kind.

All this is known and felt by the Poles, and if we knew the Prussian Government as well as they know it, we should admire it even less than we do now. Nevertheless, Prussia is not Germany, and there are numbers of high-minded Germans who have always shown the greatest sympathy for the Poles. The popular Polish notion of the German is, that he is a man given up to eating and drinking, and to sensual enjoyments of the lowest and most unpoetical kind. Caring so ardently as they do for their own country, the Poles despise the German workmen and shopkeepers, who, as it seems to them, will leave Germany at any time to "better their position"; the German bureaucrat, who, for the sake of a salary, will take office under any despot; and the German Protestant princes and princesses, who despise their own souls, and for the sake of a good marriage, will at any moment change their religion.

They remember, too, that in Alsace, in the Baltic provinces, wherever they are under a foreign domination, they are always contented as long as they can get enough bread, meat, and beer; and that the only instance of the Germans making a really national movement occurred when they rose at the heels of the French, under the protection of Russian bayonets, and with the aid of English money.

Nevertheless, there are plenty of Germans who do not bind their faith to the actions of Austria and Prussia, and think of other things besides *butter-brods.* Indeed, the latter accusation against the countrymen of Göthe, Schiller, Schubert, Weber, Beethoven, and Mozart, is in the last degree ridiculous.

There are some political Germans, moreover, who really admire the Polish character, and all that was good in ancient Polish institutions. Those few Poles who talk of their Slavonian "brethren" in Russia should remember how the Poles, after their unhappy insurrections, have been received, not by Prussian troops, but by the German people. "As long as the world is the world," the Pole (in proverbial language) will, perhaps, not be the brother of the German; but the officers and soldiers of the Polish army of 1830 received a truly fraternal reception in all the German towns they passed through.

Finally, the Poles should not forget that a German professor, professing history at the university of Berlin, wrote, at the special command of the Prussian Government, the best book that has ever been written on the fall of Poland. The French and the Poles themselves may have written more enthusiastic accounts of the virtues of Poland and the qualities of its sons, but no history will last very long, or, indeed, bear more than a moment's examination, in which the writer does not look at the bad as well as the good side of his subject. The Poles have no reason to fear any such impartiality, and the Berlin professor has given not only the fairest, but also (because it is so truthful) the most flattering account of the noble endeavours of the Poles to save their country after its integrity had been shamefully violated by Prussia, Russia, and Austria. Here, for instance, are Professor Raumer's remarks on the Constitution of the 3rd of May. It is difficult to understand how any Pole can read the passage and not admire the honesty and nobility of thought which certainly characterize the German, and above all the scientific and literary German, when he has not allowed himself to be corrupted by a despotic Government.

"Among all the Constitutions," says the German historian (writing in 1831),* "which have been framed within the last forty years, the Polish Constitution of the 3rd of May, 1791, is, with the exception of the North American, the most ancient. Any defects in it would be, therefore, much more excusable than if it had taken birth at a period of more mature experience, or if it had been planned under more favourable circumstances, or by nations having attained a higher degree of civilization. How praiseworthy is it not, therefore, that the Poles succeeded, under the most difficult and the most deplorable circumstances (such, indeed, as would have rendered desperate resolves excusable), to give themselves a Constitution, which, superior to almost all the subsequent attempts of the kind, conciliates in a most satisfactory manner the general claims of reason and sound theory, with the order of things established by history, and with the requirements of the age, and kept all within the limits of the practicable! Had the theoretical point of view and the subsequent means been obstinately insisted on, it

* *Untergang des Polen.*

would have led to wild dreams alone, while too great concessions to tradition would have led to the idolatry of the past; but Kollontay, Ignatius Potoçki, and the other admirable originators of this Constitution, happily steered their way between the dangers of these Scylla and Charybdis.

"For if any one would find fault with certain provisions concerning religion and the relative position of the two Chambers, let him remember that Great Britain settled the first point only forty years later, and that France is still in doubt (1831) on the subject of the latter. All the other provisions were decidedly improvements on the existing order of things. Take, for instance, the extension of religious toleration, the enfranchisement of the towns, the regulation of all the dues of the peasantry, the new organization of the Diet, the increased power of the senators, the form of elections, the abolition of the confederations and of the *liberum veto*, the establishment of an hereditary monarchy, &c. And this Constitution the Poles had given to themselves without plunder, assassination, bloodshed, or injury to the rights of property. They combined the most tender respect for all vested rights which could possibly be maintained, with the extermination of all radical evils, with wisdom, moderation, and perseverance. Such an admirable work was indeed deserving of the greatest possible success; doubly responsible, therefore, are those ruthless hands, which polluted the pure, spotless deed, the calumniators who reviled it, and the miscreants who have destroyed it. . . . The first dismemberment, had, no doubt, at least partly, been brought about by the own fault of the Poles; by their neglect of their duties to themselves, and the anarchy which prevailed in their country; since then, however, they had advanced in a laudable manner towards a better state of things, and had even, in respect to the legal forms of public life, outsped their accusing neighbours. What right had, therefore, these latter to disturb instead of assisting—to destroy instead of upholding? The tenth part of the forces which they set in motion for their unhallowed ends would have sufficed to extirpate all that was wrong in Poland, and insure victory to all that was good. In 1772, Catherine declared that she was supporting the cause of Polish liberty, while, from motives of covetousness, she was promoting anarchy. In 1791, she received the congratulations of the Confederates of Targovitza for having checked the *ultra-monarchical* innovations in Poland; and, in 1792, she designated those very innovations, as *jacobinical and democratic!* In the same manner, Frederic William, following the triumphal car in Russia, shifted about in word and deed. War was made upon France because the royal power had there been diminished, and upon Poland because it had there been increased; and this increase was ascribed to the Jacobins (the enemies of all kings). Whilst, in France, licentiousness, assuming the mask of a false philosophy and philanthropy, led ambitious innovators to the overthrow of all governments; in Poland, the infatuated kings seemed to have entered into a conspiracy with their adversaries, to surpass the latter in jacobinical practices, and to destroy amongst nations all respect for right, property, the sanctity of oaths, and the duty of subjects!

"Indeed, the Poles were more unfortunate than those nations who were conquered in an open, simple war. Their friendship was sought with a view of betraying it; it was considered a pleasure to break treaties solemnly concluded with them; they were driven into courses which were afterwards condemned, and sentiments were ascribed to them which they never had harboured. At the present day, it is only blind prejudice, wilful ignorance, or base calumny, which can accuse the originators of the Constitution of the 3rd of May, 1791, of having been blameworthy revolutionists."

CHAPTER VIII.

THE POLES OF LITHUANIA.

It is usual to speak of Poland as divided into three parts; but, as we have seen, it was divided into five by the Treaties of Vienna, and left partitioned into four by the triple arrangement of 1846, when the appointed protectors of Cracow united to destroy its political existence, and to make the "free city" an integral part of Austrian Poland. Russia possesses two of these quarters,—the Kingdom of Poland, which, except as regards the superior authorities, has an administration almost entirely Polish, and in which Polish is the official language; and the Polish provinces annexed by Russia at the various partitions, including the one which accompanied the formation of the little Duchy of Warsaw after the Peace of Tilsit. The latter class of Polish territory, which comprises Lithuania, White Russia, and the provinces on the Dnieper, is always spoken of by the Russians as having been "conquered;" a distinction being thus made between it and the Kingdom of Poland, of which the government was intrusted to Russia in 1815 under certain conditions. The right of conquest, it is true, is also pleaded now and then in the case of the Kingdom, but it is not strongly insisted upon. As for Lithuania and the rest of the conquered provinces, Russia maintains that she had a right to seize them, inasmuch as they belonged, or partly belonged, to the great Russo-Norman Empire of which the present Tsars claim to have inherited the sceptre. You may argue with Russians about the Kingdom of Poland, and the Emperor Alexander is said to be willing, at some very favourable opportunity, to give special liberties to this portion of his dominions, but Russia will listen to no suggestions on the subject of Lithuania and the Dnieper provinces. "Here," the Emperor has said, once at Wilna and once at Kaminietz-Podolski, "I am standing on Russian soil and recognize none but Russians;" and the most sanguine of the Poles admit that Russia would never, under any circumstances, give up this large portion of the Poland of 1772 without a life-and-death struggle. Even the Russian Liberals, who are in favour of granting Poland a separate Government, mean, for the most part, by "Poland" the Kingdom, whereas what the Poles themselves naturally aspire to is the re-establishment of their native land, with the frontiers it possessed before the partition. Alexander I. certainly contemplated, at one time, the reconstruction of all Poland, and it is said that high words (easily forgiven, no doubt) passed on the subject between him and Karamzin, the historian, who denied the right of any Russian Emperor to alienate territory which belonged to Russia *ab antiquo.* A liberal amateur historian of the present day, Prince Troubetskoi, is of opinion that Russia ought to possess not only the "conquered provinces" actually belonging to her, but also a large portion of the Polish province now under the government of Austria. Prince Dolgoroukoff, the author of *La Vérité sur la Russie,* will not allow that the Poles have any claim to the "conquered provinces," though he would not object to the Poles of the Kingdom having self-government and being represented at St. Petersburg in that happy, but perhaps distant, day when Russia is to be governed constitutionally. Finally, M. Herzen does not take at all the same view of Russian history as the Poles, and, though he admits the right of every nation to choose its own rulers, would be obliged, from an historical point of view, to claim for Russia such a province as Kieff, which belonged for centuries to Poland, and also for centuries before the Mongol invasion to ancient Russia, though never, until the partition, to the "Muscovites." The Polish historians admit no origin for the present Russian Empire other than the Tsarate of Moscow, and they maintain that the Russo-Norman Empire, or federation of dukedoms, was not merely divided but dispersed before Moscow was founded. According to them, the name of Russia was unjustly assumed in the 18th century, while the Russians say that it was justly resumed, inasmuch as Russia, after existing as a federated State which, under the Tartar domination, became broken up, had at last commenced to reconstitute itself into one whole. Either theory can be proved to the perfect satisfaction of any one who has not studied both sides of the question. In the meanwhile, one thing is certain, that all Russians believe in the continuous history of "Russia" from Rurik to the present day, and that all Poles regard the present Russian Empire merely as an unlawful aggrandizement of the Grand Duchy of Moscow.

There is also a religious question in connection with the Russian-Polish, or Polish-Russian, or "Ruthenian" provinces. The Russo-Norman Empire, under Vladimir, received the Christian faith from Greek missionaries at Kieff. Four centuries afterwards, the western portion of this Empire, which, during the Mongol occupation of Eastern Russia, had fallen into the power of the Lithuanians and Poles, adopted the union with Rome. The Poles style the Russians schismatics, while they regard the Greek Uniates of the Russo-Polish provinces as fellow-believers and Catholics. The Russians, on the other hand, pride themselves with reason on having refused to acknowledge the supremacy of the Pope as the price of assistance from the West against the Tartars, and declare that the Uniates were separated from them by menaces and persecution during the period when Russia was attacked on the one side by the infidels of Mongolia, and on the other by the Roman Catholics of Poland. They claim the inhabitants of Western Russia and of Lithuania, which became united to it before both were absorbed by Poland, as members of the Greek Church who have been for a time led away from their true fold. The Poles regard them as Greeks who, having seen the errors of their ways, were brought at last to recognize the Pope as their spiritual father.

As to the question of language in the "Ruthenian" provinces, there can be no doubt that the so-called "Muscovites" have a slight *primâ facie* case in their favour, inasmuch as the alphabet in use among the people is the Cyrillic alphabet, which, with some slight modifications introduced under Peter the Great, is also that of Russia. The Russians say simply that the popular language of these provinces is Russian, or a dialect of the Russian. The Poles call it "Ruthenian," and say that it is a variation of the Polish—a most notable variation, certainly, considering that it is written in entirely different characters. On this point, on the religious point, and, once for all, on the great political point, the Poles and Russians will never agree; and it seems to me that the Poles are wrong to pay so much attention to the minor question, inasmuch as the major one must be decided in their favour by all who believe, what no one with the least sentiment of justice or honour can deny, that the partition which gave the disputed territory to Russia was a shameful and cowardly violation of international rights. The Poles will never make foreigners understand the precise difference between Russia and Ruthenia, and they have themselves a dozen different theories of the derivation and meaning of the name or names. Thus Miçkievicz, as a poet and a Panslavonian, regards "Russ," own brother to the legendary Tchekh and Lekh, as the founder of ancient Russia. Lelewel, as an historian, wishing to establish the anti-Slavonian character of the Russian Empire, shows that Rurik, with his two or three thousand followers, came from Rosslagen in Sweden, and belonged to the tribe of Ross, which, he tells us, gave its name to the territory subjugated by Rurik. Others, apparently with the view of mortifying the Tsar, declare that Russia was once only a dependency of Poland, (which is only true as to a particular province, once called "Russia," now Eastern Galicia,) and that it owes its name to Ross, a river in the

Ukraine. Other insulting etymologists argue that the Russians are so called from the word *rosya*, signifying "dispersed"; or, if that be doubted, that they are, at least, styled *Russi* in ancient chronicles because they had red hair. As they have not red hair, as they were not "dispersed" when they were first called Russians, and as they were never, as a nation, dependent on Poland, these latter derivations are not very valuable. Finally, M. Cyprien Robert, the late Slavonian professor at the College of France, gives Ruthenia and Russia separate origins, and takes a solitary voyage to Illyria in search of a word from which the name "Ruthenia" may have been formed.

The Russian theory as regards the claims of Russia to "Ruthenia," or the eastern provinces of ancient Poland, and to Lithuania, is set forth clearly enough in the following brief but instructive synopsis prefixed to the *History of Russia*, taught in all the Russian and Russo-Polish schools:—

"ANCIENT HISTORY, FROM THE ORIGIN OF RUSSIA UNTIL PETER THE GREAT, 862–1689.

"1. Founding of Russia. A Slavonian kingdom formed under Norman chiefs. Christianity introduced. Lawgiving of Yaroslaff. 862–1054.

"2. Russia divided into federated dukedoms under the descendants of Rurik. 1054–1238.

"3. Division of Russia into two halves, Eastern and Western, under the yoke of the Mongols. 1238–1328.

"4. Formation in Eastern Russia of the Government of Moscow, and in Western of the Government of Lithuania. 1328–1462.

"5. Struggles of the Tsars of Moscow with the Tartars for independence, and with the Poles for Lithuania. 1462–1604.

"6. Government of Moscow weakened by the attacks of pretenders, 1604–1613; and by the union of Lithuania with Poland, 1596.

"7. Renewal of wars between Russia and Poland for the Grand Duchy of Lithuania, with great spread of civilization in Eastern Russia, and new attempts of the Polish Government to absorb Western Russia. 1613–1689.

"MODERN HISTORY, FROM PETER THE GREAT UNTIL THE DEATH OF NICHOLAS I., 1689–1855. EUROPEANIZATION OF RUSSIA.

"1. Reformation of the Tsarate of Moscow by Peter the Great. 1689–1725.

"2. His work strengthened by his immediate successors. 1725–1762.

"3. Consolidation of the Russian Empire, and the union of *nearly* all Russian territory into one whole, by Catherine II. 1762–1796.

"4. Russia takes a decided part in European politics," &c.

Russia, then, claims Western Russia, or Eastern Poland, on the plea that it once belonged to the Empire of Rurik, and Lithuania on the still more extraordinary ground of the aforesaid portion of Rurik's Empire having been conquered by the Lithuanians! With such principles as these, ingeniously applied, there is no country in Europe to which Russia might not establish a title.

All the Russian theories, however, give way before a few simple facts which show at once whether Ruthenia or Western Russia, after its union with Lithuania and with Poland, was really a country of Russians or of Poles. Not to mention the Czartoryskis and a number of the chief historical Polish families, Ruthenia has been the birth-place of the greatest of Polish kings and warriors, Sobieski; of the greatest of Polish patriots, Kosciuszko; and of the greatest of Polish poets, Miçkievicz. Whatever dialect the peasants may talk, and whatever the ancient history of the country may be, it would be difficult for a Russian writer to persuade us that the land of Miçkievicz, Kosciuszko, and Sobieski is not Poland.

To speak of actual affairs in the "conquered provinces," we find that in all of these Russian is the official language, though the functionaries, for the most part, understand Polish, and employ it from necessity when it is found desirable to address a Polish population in a tongue which it really understands. Thus, the proclamations recently issued in Lithuania on the subject of manifestations, national costumes, &c., were drawn up in Russian and in Polish, the latter being intended for use, the former merely for show; for surely no Russian need be cautioned against taking part in demonstrations on behalf of Poland?

The Government would willingly persuade itself and all Europe that Lithuania, as well as Volhynia and Podolia, have become Russian; but they are no more Russian than Posen and Galicia are German. To say that Wilna is not Polish is like saying that Burgundy is not French. The political ethnomaniacs who are always talking about the "rights of nationalities" might, and to be consistent, ought to, propose the annexation of the province of Alsace to some German State, but they could never think of recommending the separation from France of Burgundy, Normandy, or any other territory now thoroughly French, however distinct its origin might be from that of the more ancient provinces of France. In a political sense, the capital of Lithuania knows to its cost that it is Russian. It is also quite true that it is not Polish in an ethnological point of view, just as Normans are not Saxons, nor Saxons Britons, though the descendants of these races in England are all Englishmen.

Whether the Russian Government, in spite of its assertions to the contrary, looks upon Lithuanians as Poles is sufficiently shown by the fact that it licenses a Polish theatre in Wilna—taking care, however, for the sake of appearances, to have the playbills printed in Russian and in Polish, side by side. Whether the Lithuanians *are* Poles is proved by their refusing to enter the theatre, which, at present, like that of Warsaw, is closed.

Without going back to 1812, when the Lithuanians rose in a mass to welcome Napoleon's army and join in the war against Russia; without going back even to 1830, when they took part in the national insurrection, and after which their Polish University was suppressed; without looking beyond the orders and cautions addressed quite recently to the Lithuanians by the Russian authorities, it is impossible for any one who has lived for a few days in any Lithuanian town not to see that the great mass of the people are not Russian, but eminently Polish, and, therefore, anti-Russian. Even in Kovno all the ladies are in mourning, and wear the same black crosses and black and white crucifixes which are so general in Warsaw. No Polish costumes are seen, but orders are seen on the walls proscribing them under severe penalties, and threatening with the terrors of the Russian law all peasants who venture to wear Polish coats, or Polish caps, or Polish belts, or belts with Polish ornaments.

Another order forbids manifestations of every kind, and in particular, the singing of the "insurrectionary hymn."

A third commands all the inhabitants of Kovno who have not yet given up their arms, to surrender them without delay, and warns them that if, after so many days, arms of any kind are found in their possession, they will be severely punished.

A fourth doubles the posts at the barriers and the patrols outside the town, and cautions mothers against mixing or allowing their children to mix in crowds.

There is also a general anti-curfew order, which obliges all persons appearing in the streets after nine at night to carry lanterns.

Soon after the publication of the mural proclamations, the following orders were printed in the *Kovno Gazette.* It will be observed that they are more precise and more severe than any that have appeared in the Kingdom of Poland; that the words "Poland," "Polish," "Pole," are not once mentioned from begining to end, and that in the *chapitre des chapeaux* (Art. 5) "four-cornered caps" are spoken of, as if the writer was not in the least aware that this was the kind of cap to which the name of Kosciuszko is always given :—

"1. From the date of the present order, in the space of a week for the towns, and in the course of a month for the communes and district villages, the landed proprietors, the functionaries of the Civil Service, including the heads of several provincial administrations, the peasants of the Crown, and individuals of all other classes without exception, are to deposit in the towns with the police-masters, and in the districts with the officers of the country police, all arms in their possession, whether fire-arms or arms of any other denomination. The possession of arms after the term specified will expose the possessors to all the rigour of the laws.

"2. All kinds of meetings and manifestations are forbidden; and, in case any one of these manifestations—in which the singing of the insurrectionary hymn in the churches, in the public places, and in the streets, is included—should be made by an assemblage or by the mob, the localities in which they take place, and in which they occasion any scandal or disorder, will, as a punishment, have soldiers quartered upon them at the expense of the inhabitants, who will be charged with all the cost of moving and billeting the troops in conformity with special instructions.

"3. The authorities of the towns and communes who do not give evidence of their solicitude by preventing or putting an end to disorders will be held responsible for their conduct in virtue of the caution which has been addressed to them on the subject.

"4. The Government having positively stated beforehand that it regards manifestations of a pretended religious character as contrary to public order, the clergy will be held responsible, in accordance with the law, for its participation or ostensible connivance in the singing of seditious hymns in the churches.

"5. It is forbidden to wear in public distinctive signs. As such are considered four-cornered caps and coats cut after a particular fashion."

In the centre of the market-place of Kovno, and in front of the town-hall and barracks (which the Russians, with a good taste worthy of them and of the Austrians, have established in an ancient Polish church), a monument has been erected to commemorate the retreat of the French in 1812. It is a column of no particular order of architecture, crowned with a nondescript fruit, half melon, half pine-apple, which is again surmounted by a Greek cross. It is one of the worst monuments in Europe, and quite bad enough to figure in the chief square of Manchester, opposite the Infirmary and close to Sir Robert Peel with his bale of cotton, cheap loaf, or whatever it is. It bears a neat inscription, however, in the style of the admirable one on the Borodino memorial ("Napoleon entered Moscow, 1812; Alexander entered Paris, 1814"), and which is as follows:—"In 1812 Russia was invaded by an army numbering 700,000 men. It recrossed the frontier numbering 70,000."

As a companion to this might be engraved on the walls of the Kovno Church:—"In 1795 Russia took possession of her ancient province of Lithuania. Sixty-six years afterwards it was found necessary to employ force to prevent the Lithuanians from wearing Polish costumes."

CHAPTER IX.

SOME EFFECTS OF THE PARTITION.

PERSONS who speak of the partition of Poland as an accomplished and quite unalterable fact, are not, I fancy, aware of the community not only of sentiment but also of material interests which, even under existing circumstances, unites a great many Polish families, possessing more or less land, in several if not all the politically separated parts. The subdivision of property, which, if the partition of Poland had never taken place, might have been injurious, promises now (from a Polish patriotic point of view) to be of great benefit to the country, while it has really been the salvation of numerous persons who, having had their estates confiscated in one quarter, have yet been able to live on what remained to them in another. Everywhere in Galicia and Posen you will find proprietors who took part in the Polish war of 1830-1, and who have forfeited all their possessions in Russian Poland. Many previous residents in the Kingdom retired after the loss of the major part of their fortune to live on such remnants of it as were still

PEASANTS OF THE NEIGHBOURHOOD OF WILNA.

left to them under the Prussian and Austrian Governments. Others who had gone from Posen or Galicia to Warsaw to join the insurrection came back minus so much Russian property, but, though with diminished means, yet far from ruined. Those who had estates only in the Kingdom of Poland or in the Polish Provinces of Russia, and who were not included in the somewhat vaguely worded indemnity published after the capture of Warsaw, lost everything.

To show the fortunate effect which the division of property, taken in connection with the partition, has had upon Poland—assuming always that the Polish cause is not irretrievably lost—I may mention that but for it the late Prince Czartoryski would have been left penniless after the confiscation of 1831. So would the Sapiehas, of whom the chief, Prince Leon, is now the President of the Galician Diet. So would the Sanguskos; and Prince Ladislas Sangusko, nevertheless, is able to take his place among the Polish magnates in the Upper Chamber of the Reichsrath. It may seem at first sight somewhat of a Court Circular notion to say that the ruin of such families as these would be the ruin of Poland, but it must be remembered that the Polish aristocracy are not "leaders of the fashion," they are leaders of the nation. All of them have risked everything over and over again, and it is, doubtless, this readiness to sacrifice themselves, and the greatness of their actual sacrifices, that have enabled them to preserve the influence they enjoy throughout their tortured country, of which (to apply an expression of M. le Maistre's) they are still "the bones." In the days of Poland's prosperity, when all the high offices of State were filled gratuitously, many of her ambassadors ruined themselves in maintaining the credit of the Polish name for magnificence and hospitality at foreign Courts. When the Duchy of Warsaw was being formed, Prince Radziwill took the command of a regiment of Polish Lancers, recruited and equipped at his own expense, and paid for this new delight with 150 Lithuanian villages, which were confiscated by the Russian Government. But every act of cruelty on the part of the Russian Government is stored up to be avenged when it may be possible; and thus it may be said there is no way of repressing the Poles except by pursuing a system of severity so crushing that they cannot even think of vengeance. This was really the system of the Emperor Nicholas, and after the fearful retribution which he dealt out to the insurgents of 1830-1, there was indeed peace throughout Russian-Poland. It was the peace of the grave; but at least there were no disturbances. The Poles declare now that nothing can keep them down, that nothing can resist their "moral force," and so on; which may be a noble conviction, but is a thorough delusion, nevertheless. The saints and martyrs whom they invoke suffered martyrdom and died; and a prolonged series of Nicholases might in time have put an end to the existence of Poland. Hitherto she has only been afflicted with one; and before the destructive work of the late Emperor commenced the Poles had had time to breathe and to fortify themselves, under his predecessor. But the old system once abandoned—as in many respects it most positively has been—it is impossible that the present Emperor, the emancipator of the Russian serfs, can return to it. He could scarcely, for instance, carry out such threats as were uttered very seriously against Poland by the Emperor Nicholas. Such a menace, let us say, as this Sovereign addressed to a deputation of citizens who sought an interview with him on the occasion of his first visit to Warsaw, after the suppression of the insurrection and the erection of the citadel; and to whose protestations of some feeling, not very easy to imagine under the circumstances, he frankly, and perhaps justly, refused to listen. After advising them to look entirely to Russia for their future welfare, he added (as the reader has already seen), "But on the slightest insurrectionary movement I will reduce the city to ashes, and in that case shall certainly not build it up again." On such a plan as this Poland could doubtless be ruled, though it would be very like the government of the Mongols, who did not molest their subjects as long as they paid tribute peacefully and regularly, but massacred them whenever they became turbulent or fell into arrears. The Mongols, moreover, while sparing the working men, were always remorseless in their severity to insurrectionary chiefs, and this also was the policy of the Emperor Nicholas. Nevertheless, the ruin of the great families of Poland was almost impossible to bring about, owing to the fact that by inheritance and marriage they had all become possessed of estates, great or small, in various portions of the dismembered kingdom.

The general union, so much desired by the Poles, and which they all regard as the first indispensable step towards ultimate independence, is aided by every marriage which links an important family in Galicia or Posen with one in the Kingdom or in any other part of Russian Poland. The feeling in regard to this was shown in a remarkable manner in Cracow, when a member of the Tarnowski married a member of the Zamoyski family. If a "matrimonial union" had been about to be celebrated between an Emperor of Austria and a Russian Grand Duchess, and if Austria and Russia were adored instead of being detested by the Poles, there could not have been more excitement in the usually tranquil, almost lifeless, city of Cracow than was caused by the event which *did* take place.

PARISH CHURCH AT CRACOW.

The fact that each of the families about to be connected had given an illustrious High Constable to Poland in the days of Poland's prosperity and grandeur had something to do with the excitement; so also had the great popularity of Count Zamoyski. Another remarkable point was, that the bride was the niece of the late President of the Agricultural Association in the Kingdom, and also of the late President of the sister society in Galicia. A more significant wedding could scarcely have been imagined, and it must be remembered that the Poles are now in such a state of feverish excitement that they see signs and symbols in what to other nations would be quite ordinary facts. The ceremony took place in the cathedral, where the tombs, monuments, and votive offerings—such, for instance, as the tapestry taken by John Sobieski from the Grand Vizier's tent at the battle of Vienna—suggest, at a glance, all the grandest figures, and all the greatest events, in the history of Poland. All who were at the altar—that is to say, all the men—were dressed in the Polish national costume, not the conventional, semi-Hungarian costume of the present day, but the Oriental caftan and girdle of the ancient republic. The whole scene was strikingly and affectingly Polish, but, as if not to let the illusion go too far, and to recall the Poles who filled the cathedral to the remotest nook from any "reveries" they might be indulging in, the marriage service was interrupted more than once by the bugle calls of the Austrian garrison, who occupy the fortress in which the cathedral is enclosed.

Another bond of union between the three recognized Polish divisions (in the fourth the Russians will scarcely allow the word "Poland" to be pronounced) existed in the relations kept up between the three Agricultural Societies of the Kingdom, Galicia, and the Grand Duchy of Posen. It has been said that the Agricultural Society of Poland was not a political body; but how could an assembly of landed proprietors from all parts of the Kingdom be anything else? That it had no political power, and that it did not occupy itself in a direct manner with political questions, is true enough—but it, at least, represented a political purpose. Four thousand landowners, subscribing 50*s.* a-year each, talking openly of manure, and thinking always of the salvation of their native land—that is what the Agricultural Society presided over by Count Andrew Zamoyski really was. A Government which cannot tolerate such a society must, indeed, be intolerable; but to represent the Agricultural Association as having been merely a farmers' and gardeners' club, without any sort of political character, is to make an assertion which the Russians can easily disprove, and is, therefore, a false step on the part of the Poles, to say nothing more. It is something like saying that the Russians will not allow the Poles to pray for their country, whereas what they object to (though for a long time they did not stop it) is the singing of a hymn which is a more direct provocation to civil war than the "Marseillaise"—a composition, by the way, which I do not think the great friend of Poland would like to hear sung by 2000 or 3000 persons in the Madeleine or Nôtre Dame. It is like setting what the Emperor Nicholas has given below what the Emperor only promised. Finally, it is like accusing the Russian Government of forming a good opera and ballet company at the Warsaw theatre, with the view of demoralizing the Polish youth, instead of getting up performances of translated Corneille and Racine, which the French, like clever, sensible people as they are, refuse to listen to in the original. With so many grievous, unanswerable accusations to bring against the Russian Government, it is a pity the Poles should advance any minor charges which they cannot well substantiate.

It seems to me that in dissolving the Agricultural Association the Russians did not dissolve an unpolitical but a political body, and one of great importance, such as a Government based on illegality could not suffer to exist. The Emperor Nicholas, who was severely logical and logically severe in his manner of ruling the Poles, would never consent to its formation, and when the authorization of the Emperor Alexander II. was obtained (through M. Muchanoff, I believe) it was expected that the Society would consist only of some hundred members. It had not, however, been long in existence when it was found to number 4000. It was not a conspiracy; but it was very like a patriotic confederation, and its influence was not lessened by its putting itself in connection with the Agricultural Associations of Leopol (or Lemberg), Cracow, and Posen, which were represented at Warsaw by duly appointed delegates. To show whether the Lemberg Society had any political character, it will, perhaps, be enough to mention that Prince Leon Sapieha quitted its presidency to assume that of the Galician Diet, and that he has been replaced at the head of the Agricultural Association by Dr. Smolka, the leader of the Polish party in the Reichsrath.

In considering to what extent and in what manner the dismembered country is still united, I must not forget the Holy Places, such as Czenstochow, in the Kingdom, and Calvarya, in Galicia, which, at certain seasons, are points of meeting for thousands and tens of thousands from all parts of Poland. When I was at Posen a large party of ladies had just started on foot for Czenstochow. Persons go there constantly from Cracow, and it is even visited by pilgrims from as far off as Volhynia and Lithuania, to say nothing of railway pilgrims in multitudes from Warsaw. The miraculous virgin of Czenstochow bears on her right cheek the marks of two sword-wounds received from the Swedes, which, it is reported, the most cunning painters and restorers are unable to efface. This, then, should be the Virgin pre-eminently adored by Polish patriots, who, moreover, remember that Czenstochow was the last refuge of the Confederation of Bar. Every morning you may see four or five acres of peasants lying flat on their faces before the crucifix which stands on the hill in front of the monastery—a field of many-coloured rags, from which suddenly thousands of heads spring up, followed by thousands of bodies. I have not seen Czenstochow, however, on one of its grand days; but, fortunately, I was at Calvarya when the most important festival of the year was about to be celebrated. This was the annual Indulgence, which in the month of August gives the little village of Calvarya the dimensions and population of a large city, and the appearance of an immense camp. Calvarya is built on hills which, if they were not in the vicinity and almost beneath the shadow of the Carpathians, would be called mountains, and the eminence on which the monastery stands is said, in position as well as in form, to present a striking resemblance to Mount Calvary.

During the season of the Indulgence the great encampment has what may be called its commercial quarter, consisting of streets of wooden booths and huts of the most primitive construction, which are shut and abandoned at other periods of the year. Some of these edifices are composed of nothing more than a few boards fastened together, so as to form a square roof with four wooden beams to support them at the corners. They look like gigantic tables, but they are intended to serve the purpose of houses and shops, and they are certainly light airy habitations for a hot summer. Upwards of 60,000 persons took the Sacrament last year at the Indulgence of Calvarya, and it is calculated that more than a third of the entire number of pilgrims, spectators, and dealers of various kinds do not communicate. Altogether, there must have been nearly 100,000 persons in and about the place, for the most part peasantry, and the number would probably have been greater but for the comparative lateness of the harvest, which is usually finished before the Indulgence commences, but which was delayed last autumn in many parts of Galicia by the rainy weather. The pilgrims arrived, village by village, each group with its leader and its standard, the standards emblazoned with figures, and serviceable, moreover, for worldly purposes, as without them it would be difficult, after reaching Calvarya, for a peasant who once became separated from his company to find it again. On arriving at its destination each village party plants its flag in the ground to mark its halting-place, so that the day before the Indulgence the heights are covered far and wide with these religious banners. The peasants are all in their holiday attire and wear "four-cornered caps" and "coats cut after a particular fashion," such as the Russian Government, with its peculiar notions on the subject of dress, would be shocked to behold. They, moreover, carry long thick staves, which, considering the hundreds of miles many of them have to walk, is surely pardonable. Finally, each company sings religious chants along the line of march, and, what is still more remarkable, many of them went back last year singing the patriotic hymn, which, it may be said, was taught them at Calvarya, where thousands of them heard it, and afterwards joined in it for the first time. A great number of copies of the "Address from the Inhabitants of Warsaw" were also distributed, and a sermon was preached to them, which must have had a greater effect than either the address or the hymn. In the courtyard before the monasterial church are two long rows of confessionals, one on each side, and in front is a balcony, from which the monks give absolution and preach to the immense crowd assembled beneath. The subject of the sermon last year was the duty of sacrifice, and the preacher impressed upon his congregation that a time had arrived when all class interests and all personal interests must be forgotten. "Every one," he said, "must be prepared to suffer." "I," who am thus addressing you," he concluded, "may be taken from this place to a prison. If so, I shall glory in suffering for my country, and shall pray that it may not be in vain."

The Russian and Austrian Governments will, no doubt, say that this was very dreadful, and that, according to their favourite accusation against the Poles, it was "mixing up politics with religion." But for "politics" read "patriotism," and who can say that the sacrifice of the individual for the good of his country is not a religious idea? This is precisely the patriotism of the Poles, many thousands of whom are constantly risking their liberty individually, and are ready to give up their lives, in the hope and belief that by so doing they may help to gain liberty one day for Poland; doing this, moreover, with the conviction that for the present they cannot possibly prevail over their enemies, and that no one will, under any circumstances, assist them from abroad.

As Calvarya was founded by Zebrzydowski, one of the most celebrated of the Palatines of Cracow, and maintained by subsequent donations from the Czartoryskis—as, moreover, the Mount of Landskrona, in its immediate neighbourhood, was the last stronghold of the last band of heroes who resisted the Austrians and Russians after the insurrection of Kosciuszko—the Poles could not help having their patriotism excited by the associations of the place, even if they had learnt to guard against such a dangerous sentiment. A fortnight after the Indulgence a mass was announced at Calvarya for the repose of the late Prince Adam Czartoryski, and his portrait, together with his heraldic emblem, the Royal or Grand-Ducal "Horseman of Lithuania," was placed in the church or chapel founded by him. The Government, with rare tolerance, permitted the celebration of the mass, but the police objected strongly to the Lithuanian cavalier, and could not be persuaded for some time that it was not the portrait of Kosciuszko on horseback!

It must not be supposed, from what I have said about the patriotic demonstrations at Calvarya, that the Catholic clergy in Austrian Poland are in the habit of pronouncing themselves, directly or indirectly, in favour of Polish independence. They are an obstacle to the Polish cause in Galicia, as they are its chief support in the Kingdom and in the Grand Duchy of Posen. It is quite impossible to shut up the churches in Warsaw so as to prevent the singing of the patriotic hymn when the Russian "schismatics" desire it. The Catholic religion forbids such a thing! But under a Roman

Catholic concordat-loving Government the case is quite different. How it is possible to disobey a Power which supports the Pope? No; the Church first and Poland afterwards, or perhaps not at all.

I admire the Poles singing their patriotic hymn and thinking always of the recovery of their ancient independence; and I can understand the Russians, unless they mean to give up Poland forthwith, doing all they can to prevent this hymn being sung. But what are we to think of a clergy, who on the same subject have one rule of conduct for Catholic Austria and another for "schismatic" Russia, and who do their utmost to strengthen or weaken a Government according as it does or does not acknowledge the Pope? The Poles must not be persecuted by heretics. But let them be massacred by direction of a Catholic Government, and the Pope only interferes (as in 1846) with a recommendation to the priests to warn the faithful against the crime of sedition! The Abbé Lescœur has recently published a book on *The Catholic Church in Poland under the Russian Government*, which is far more calmly and impartially written than most works of the kind. Thus, beyond a charge brought against an ecclesiastic, who from a Greek Uniate became a Greek, of having kicked a woman's teeth down her throat, it contains no very cutting personalities, while it is, of course, highly complimentary to all who have left the

Greek Church to become Roman Catholics. But, while going out of his way to attack our barbarous Protestant rule in Ireland, not only in a religious, but also in a political and commercial point of view ("Ireland produces, England consumes," is one of his conclusions), the author has not one word to say against the Austrian Government in Galicia. Much sympathy, indeed, the Poles would obtain from their Church, if Russia and Prussia were Roman Catholic instead of "schismatic" Powers! It would have protested against the cruelties of the Emperor Nicholas as violently as against those of the Emperor of Austria and of the King of Naples. After actively preparing the way for the partition of Poland a century and a half beforehand by its persecutions in Little Russia, the Catholic Church now injures the existing Poles by defending them awkwardly and suspiciously against all tyranny but the tyranny of Roman Catholics. A high-minded Catholic gentleman, the Count de Montalembert, has denounced the Austrian Government and its criminal share in the massacres of Galicia and in the absorption of Cracow repeatedly, and in the most eloquent terms, from the Tribune and through the press; so also has an English Catholic peer, Lord Beaumont, in the House of Lords; but the Catholic clergy of Galicia, in accordance with their instructions, have always sided with the Austrian Government, whatever atrocities it may have been committing.

The Church, however, cannot possess the sympathies of the Poles and of the tyrants of the Poles at the same time, and accordingly, in Galicia, where it is an instrument in the hands of the Government quite as much as the Russian Church is in Russia, it is losing all moral power except over the peasants, on whom the influence it exercises is of an anti-patriotic and degrading kind. In the other parts of Poland the teaching of the clergy tends to bring classes together and to prepare the way for a general union. In Galicia, where it supports established power, it is an impediment to Polish unity, and therefore and above all, to Polish independence.

CHAPTER X.

THE POLES IN THE UKRAINE.

One of the most remarkable proofs of the increased liberty enjoyed by Russians, generally, during the last few years, is found in the very different tendencies manifested, with more or less freedom, by various journals and reviews of recent foundation.

Many Russians, and, as it seems to me, the wisest among them, think that if Russia only attends to her own affairs for many years to come, she will have plenty to do without troubling herself about the interests of her Slavonian relations in Austria and on the Danube. Such is apparently not the opinion of M. Aksakoff, a well-known writer of the Panslavonian persuasion, and editor of a weekly journal, which, among other Slavonian cities, is to give the latest intelligence from Cracow and Lvoff, or Lemberg. I can fancy how much obliged the Poles of Cracow and Lemberg will be to the Moscow editor for studying their wants; and it is rather strange that Prince Sapieha, or Dr. Smolka, have not yet proposed a vote of thanks to him in the Galician Diet.

But if a certain sect in Russia believe it is the destiny of their country to form and dominate an immense federated Slavonian Empire (a creed which the Emperor Nicholas would not allow to be preached out of regard for Austria, now abandoned and loathed by all Russians), there is also a party, it seems, which would rather proceed to federation by a contrary process, and which already regards "Little Russia" as something quite distant from Great Russia and from Poland. There is something significant in the mere existence of such denominations as Great Russia, Little Russia, New Russia, White Russia, Red Russia, and Black Russia. All land that bears the name of Russia, however coloured or qualified, is claimed by the Russians, even though a portion of it by some historical accident happens now to be under the sceptre of Austria; but at the same time, Great Russia is eminently Russian, whereas White Russia has Polish-Lithuanian traditions and sympathies, while Little Russia is emphatically anti-Polish, and yet by no means inclined to confound its history and existence with those of the Russian provinces generally.

Little Russia is the name given to that portion of the Ukraine which detached itself from Poland and placed itself under the protection of Peter the Great's father, in the middle of the seventeenth century, and which afterwards rose under Mazeppa to defend itself against Peter the Great, when Russia, instead of protecting, had destroyed its liberties as guaranteed by treaty; and which was finally "pacified" at the battle of Pultava, though its agricultural population was not reduced to serfdom until the reign of Catherine. On the whole Little Russia may be said to have stepped from the Polish frying-pan into the Russian fire; but, though no one is allowed to hint anything against the fire, everyone is, of course, encouraged to say as much against the frying-pan as possible. I do not know whether the Little Russians are pleased at having been deprived of their liberty by Russia, but it is certain that they remember with indignation the religious persecution to which they were subjected by the Poles. Bogdan Khmelnitzki, the leader of the successful revolt of the Ukraine against Poland, is one of their greatest heroes; while Mazeppa was, until quite lately, cursed regularly every Sunday and holiday in all the churches of the Empire—of course by the express command of the Russian Government.

The grounds on which Little Russia claims, at least in a literary point of view, to stand apart from Russia generally are, that it has a different language and a different history. Its language or dialect is a shade nearer to the Russian Proper than the Ruthenian spoken by the peasantry in Volhynia, Podolia, and a portion of Kieff; while the Ruthenian, on the other hand, is a shade nearer to the Polish than the Little Russian. Its history, too, belongs partly to Poland and partly to Russia. As for its literature, that is only just beginning to exist. The greatest author it has produced, Nicholas Gogol, belonged to the Eastern or Russian Ukraine, and of course wrote in Russian. The late Schevtchenko, the greatest tale-writer and poet that Russia has possessed since Gogol's death, wrote, however, in the dialect of the Polish Ukraine, and his poems in the Little Russian or Ruthenian dialect, were, so to speak, to have been the chief colouring matter of the *South Russian* (for which read *Little Russian*) *Review*, started at the beginning of the present year, under the auspices of M. Kostamaroff, the esteemed Professor of History at the University of St. Petersburg, and author of a very successful life of Bogdan Khmelnitzki. The fate of Schevtchenko, who possessed an equal genius for poetry and for painting, bore a strange resemblance to that of the Ukraine itself. He was born a serf, and was liberated from serfdom by Wielgorski, the Russian composer, and two Russian authors, Joukovski and Gregorovitch, who commissioned him to paint their portraits, and gave him his ransom-money as the price of the work. After he had received his liberty he foolishly thought that he was free to express his thoughts in print; and for falling into this error was sent into exile by the Emperor Nicholas. Thus Russia liberated him, and Russia also enslaved him.

Schevtchenko was born not in Little Russia—not in that portion of ancient Poland east of the Dnieper, which placed itself under Russian protection in the seventeenth century—but in the adjacent province of Kieff on the other side of the river, which was forcibly annexed to Russia at the second partition of Poland in 1793. Accordingly, he was a "Ruthenian," and his writings will enable us to judge how far the Russian theory is true, that the modern Russian and ancient Ruthenian languages are the same, and that the inhabitants of the Ruthenian provinces of Kieff, Volhynia, and Podolia are Russians, in spite of the fact that they escaped the Tartar domination, and at the period of the second partition had enjoyed an uninterrupted union of four centuries and a half with Lithuania, and through Lithuania with Poland. The writings of Schevtchenko, then, are *translated into Russian*—a sufficient proof that his Ruthenian dialect and the language of the Russian Empire are not, by any means, identical.

If a committee of ethnologists decided to-morrow that the Ruthenian provinces were not Slavo-Russian but Slavo-Polish, Russia would, of course, not give them up for that; therefore, from a political point of view, it is useless for the Poles to argue the question. The great point to remember is, that these provinces are all included in "the Poland of 1772," and that Russia is bound by the articles of the Treaty of Vienna to govern the inhabitants as Poles, and to give them "a national representation and institutions." Nevertheless, it is a curious fact that the *South Russian Review*, while maintaining that the provinces of Kieff, Volhynia, and Podolia have a Russian agricultural population, which is to the educated Polish population in the proportion of eleven to one, announces among its contributors a member of the so-called Russian population whose writings are unintelligible to the great body of the Russians.

In addition to articles on the history and prospects of Little Russia, notices of Little Russian pictures and music, and tales in the Little Russian or Ruthenian dialect (with copious glossaries appended to each), the *South Russian Review* has published some very curious papers on Poland before the partition, and especially on the relations between peasants and proprietors in the Polish and Lithuanian provinces of the ancient kingdom. What is most curious about these productions is, that they are founded upon Polish and Ruthenian documents contained in the archives at Kieff, and edited by Russian authors. According to the said Russian authors, they are complete, conscientiously prepared summaries or reports. According to the Poles, they are full of such suppressions and perversions that, on the whole, they may be regarded as little better than forgeries. Probably they are not mere fabrications, but contain about as much truth as we might expect to find in a history of the Roman Catholic Church by Dr. Cumming; or of the Reformation by M. Veuillot.

Such Russians and Germans as care about justifying the partition of Poland are fond of calling attention to the miserable position of the Polish peasant prior to that operation, as if to suggest that it was performed for the benefit of the "masses," and to destroy the influence of the aristocratic class, which never did anything for the country except make and administer its laws, fight its battles, and maintain its reputation in Europe for learning, politeness, and general civilization at a period when Russia and Prussia were not known even by name. Poland's great crime is to have had serfs whose position, however unfortunate, was at least determined by law, and who, among other exemptions, were free from military service; and for this she was punished by the surrounding Powers in whose dominions a system of absolute slavery existed, and who forcibly interfered to prevent the promulgation of the Constitution of

1791, which provided for the gradual emancipation of the Polish peasantry! Doubtless the Poles are more sensitive than any other European people on the subject of their past history, from the fact that their natural progress has been violently checked for the last ninety years—an interval during which all the other nations have been advancing, while Poland has been retrograding in everything except its national spirit and the national literature in which that spirit is embodied. It is natural that the Poles should resent with bitterness any approach to a calumny on their past life, even when the calumny, if generally believed in, would not in the least affect the question whether the neighbouring despotic Powers had or had not a right to put an end to Poland's existence. It should not be forgotten that the Sovereigns who partitioned Poland recognized no liberty of any kind on the part of any class of subjects. The Poles, however, are not content to be regarded as having been simply a little better than their almost barbarous neighbours; and as to the serf question alone, it is quite certain that the Poles took a first great step towards the complete emancipation of the peasants, in 1791, twenty years before the work of emancipation was commenced in Prussia, fifty-seven years before the peasants were liberated in Hungary, Galicia, and other parts of the Austrian Empire, and seventy years before the partial abolition of serfdom in Russia. M. Kostamaroff, whom I have already mentioned as one of the chief contributors to the *South Russian Review*, proposed in its pages that the archives at Kieff should be thrown open to all men of letters, that they might judge for themselves whether, and, if so, in what respect, the commission had rendered itself liable to the accusations brought against it by the Poles. This would of course be the fairest, and indeed the only possible, way of settling the dispute. The suggestion, however, has not been adopted, and, in the meanwhile, Polish writers maintain that the selections published by the Russian Commission from the archives at Kieff are full of passages which do not at all accord with historical documents of unquestionable authenticity in the hands of certain Polish families, and among the archives at Leopol in Galicia.

The Polish and Lithuanian archives described in the library of Kieff consist of 6715 "books of Acts," and of 377 separate "Acts." They were taken from Wilna during the great plunder of Poland's historical, numismatic, literary, and artistic treasures, of which the insurrection of 1831 was made the pretext, and were deposited by order of the Emperor Nicholas at Kieff. It would have been barbarous to burn them, but to confide their partial publication to irresponsible Russian editors was something far worse. After taking part in such a murder as the destruction of Poland may well be considered, Russia would only have acted wisely in making all possible efforts to cause her crime to be forgotten. Instead of that, she follows up the act of assassination by rifling the victim's pockets and founding upon the papers stolen from them a lying biography, or, at least, an injurious one, of which, in spite of the honourable advice of M. Kostamaroff, it is not permitted to test the truthfulness.

A reply to the charge of perversion and falsification was published a few months since in the *South Russian Review* by M. Youssephovitch, assistant curate of the university of Kieff, and chief of the commission entrusted with the publication of reports and selections from the archives. M. Youssephovitch says, that as to the charge of falsifying documents to suit the supposed views of the Russian Government, he can have no motive for so doing; that as chief of the commission he receives no salary from the Government, but is left independent and only answerable for what he publishes to his own conscience, which would not allow him to alter the sense of grave historical documents; that the contest between Russia and Poland is at an end; that there can be no reason now why Russia should attack the Poles; that no Russian writer says a word against them, and that all the Russians were heartily glad when the present

Emperor restored the use of the national language in the public offices and schools of the Kingdom; that at Wilna a commission, similar to the one sitting at Kieff, is directed exclusively by Poles [this, however, is only an archæological commission]; and, finally, that it is not his fault if the documents which he has made public do not show what the Poles would wish them to show, though, as for that matter, what nation, he asks, has not left traces of vice and crime in its history? He at the same time offers to print any ancient documents referring to the subject on which his publications are said to have thrown a false light that may be sent to him for that purpose by Poles; but he does not say a word about throwing open the archives at Kieff to the inspection of strangers.

Another sign that Little Russia, or South Russia, does not (naturally enough) wish to have its past and future life mixed up indifferently with that of Russia in general, was given about a year and a half ago by the university of Kieff on the occasion of a farewell dinner to its curator, M. Pirogoff, the eminent surgeon.

A subscription for an appropriate memorial was got up at the banquet, a thousand roubles were forthcoming on the spot, and the books were to be kept open for four years, when the entire sum subscribed, with accumulated interest, are to be given as a prize for the best essay on university education in the west of Europe and in Russia; the essay to include a special history of the University of Kieff, and of the two Lyceums of Odessa. The Academy of Kieff, the parent of the actual University, is remembered as the most ancient educational establishment in Russia, and the people of "South Russia" naturally do not wish its history to be confounded with that of the universities in various parts of the Muscovite-Russian Empire founded only the other day.

In the meanwhile, whatever be the ultimate fate of South Russia, that portion of it which belonged seventy years ago to Poland, and to which Poland's right was at that time unquestioned, had the same, or nearly the same, measures of disarmament applied to it which were put in force when the state of siege was first proclaimed in Lithuania. There was this difference, however—that whereas in Lithuania every one was disarmed, it was expressly stated that in Kieff, Volhynia, and Podolia, only the Poles were to give up their weapons. Jews "worthy of confidence" might keep a gun, and guns were to be left, when the Governor of the province thought it necessary, in the hands of the peasantry, to enable them to destroy wild beasts. This reminds one of Galicia, where numbers of proprietors are not allowed to keep fowling-pieces, even in the shooting season, though the peasants may fire away at anything all the year round.

Finally, all persons — including Polish proprietors favourably known to the Governor of the province, who by special exception are allowed to carry guns—are to have their names inscribed on the police books; and, with the exception of Russian nobles, officials, and merchants, and of "trustworthy Jews," to find responsible persons who will guarantee the propriety of their conduct as arms-bearers. The Governor-General of Volhynia and Podolia, who is at the same time the military Governor of Kieff, expresses some surprise that it should have been found necessary to have recourse to the above measures in provinces where the Roman Catholic (*i. e.* thoroughly Polish) population numbers only 485,000 out of a general mass of 5,250,000. His Excellency, apparently, forgets that the Polish element is the influential and thinking element in these provinces to such an extent that, under a representative system such as that of England, all the deputies chosen in Volhynia, Podolia, and Kieff, would inevitably be Poles; that, whatever dialect or *patois* the Volhynian or Podolian peasants may speak, the books issued from Zitomir, the chief town of Volhynia, and Kaminieç, the chief town of Podolia, are exclusively Polish; and, finally, that the millions of peasants who are classed as Russians, chiefly because they are Greeks, were not led back into the fold of the "orthodox" church, but were driven into it with bayonets and sharp sticks.

CHAPTER XI.

PRIVATE LIFE IN POLAND.

"How do people live in Poland?" the reader may feel inclined to ask.

It is easier for a traveller of the last year or two to say how they die there. "*Mourir pour la patrie? Oui, je comprends cela,*" a certain Pole, who had deliberately taken up his residence abroad, is reported to have said: "*Mais y vivre? Jamais!*"

They don't dance in Poland; they don't sing much (unless it be the patriotic hymn, which they sing on all possible occasions); they don't go to the theatre or to concerts; they don't give brilliant parties of any kind; and it is only at weddings that ladies put off their mourning, and for one day only appear in white. A Polish gentleman, at whose house I was staying in the country near Posen, was building a new conservatory, a billiard-room, and thought, at first, of adding a ball-room; "but it was scarcely worth while," he said. "The Poles had given up dancing, and would not be likely to begin again for a very long while."

"Used you to dance a great deal, formerly?" I asked a young lady in another part of Poland, who was of opinion that dancing would totally disappear among the Poles as a national custom, inasmuch as they would soon begin to forget their steps (as if Polish young ladies did not dance naturally).

"A great deal," was the reply, "but not very often; we live so far in the country. We used to begin very early, and dance till about five. Then the musicians could play no longer, and everybody pretended to go. However, when they had all put on their morning clothes, and were about to start, it always happened that some one suddenly struck up a mazurka, and we began again, the shutters were closed, and we generally went on dancing until twelve. Then we had an early dinner, and at last the party really broke up. Nothing of that kind, however, since the 27th of February." *

This unhappy country, now the saddest in all Europe, was at one time the gayest. A Polish gentleman of the neighbourhood of Cracow used to say that his great-great-grandfather's wedding lasted a week, and ten barrels of wine were drunk; his great-grandfather's five days, when

* The day (1861) on which the soldiers, for the first time during the present reign, fired on the people at Warsaw.

three barrels were drunk; his grandfather's three days, when one barrel was drunk; his father's twenty-four hours, and a hundred bottles were drunk; his own occupied an evening, and nothing was drunk but a little champagne at supper; his son was married very quietly, and the guests had twelve cups of tea. Let us hope that the grandson will return to champagne and to good Hungarian "born in Hungary and bottled in Poland." "*Optimum vinum,*" say the Poles, "*in Hungariâ natum, in Poloniâ ducatum.*"

I suppose no one expects me to say what the Poles eat in the way of national dishes, to describe the savory *bigos,* dear to hunters, of which a poetical description may be found in Mięķiewicz's "Pan Tadeusz," or to analyze the more than refreshing *cholodieç,* in which the principal ingredients are cream, slices of cucumber, ice, and fragments of game—the whole constituting a remarkable fine soup for a hot summer's day.

"But what is the conversation of the Poles like?" it may be asked.

To me it was deeply interesting; but it was always on the same subject.

And are all classes affected in the same way

CLOTH MARKET AT CRACOW.

by the present tragic position of their native land?

In the towns, yes; but in many parts of the country the peasants probably care for very little beyond their daily wants. Nevertheless, in Lithuania the Russian Government forbids them to wear Polish costumes, from which it may be concluded that they *would* wear them if left to themselves. Among the inhabitants of towns, and also among peasants in the neighbourhood of towns, the patriotic feeling from high to low is universal. A wedding took place at an hotel where I was staying in Cracow. I was wondering what the company would do to amuse themselves. They did nothing all the evening, and then sang the National hymn. This was not the marriage of a proud, "factious" aristocrat (familiar type to the imagination of Russian and German pamphleteers), it was the marriage of a waiter's daughter, and the guests were waiters, innkeepers, and small tradesmen, with their families.

In Warsaw the feeling against Russia is so strong that music-publishers and librarians will not have any Russian music or books in their shops.

In Cracow I bought an Austrian map, the

"Ethnological Chart of the Austrian Empire." When it was sent home to me I unrolled it, and found a slip of paper wafered on to it, inscribed as follows:—

"This map was made by a false German, who has German-coloured our Polish districts and towns."

I pointed out to the person who brought it to me that I could not remove the paper, and that if I tore it off there would still be four large wafers remaining on the map, which would slightly disfigure it. The shopman quite agreed with me on that point; but said that his master, seeing that I was an Englishman and took an interest in Polish subjects, was determined that I should not be deceived by "false Germans;" that he would rather the notification as to their falseness were not removed, but that I was, of course, at liberty to take the map or leave it.

The reader may be sure that I took it, and that I mean to keep it and do not mean to remove the notification as to the falseness of German map-makers when laying ethnological colour round Polish towns. I suppose that there are no shopkeepers anywhere else in the world who would object to sell a map from patriotic motives, if they fancied that it represented their country in a disadvantageous light. The bookseller in Cracow, no doubt, said to himself,—"They may turn our palaces into barracks, our chapels into tobacco-warehouses, the tombs of our patriots into forts, and they may affect to regard us as Germans; but, at least, they can't make us sell a lying publication which declares that we *are* Germans in the face of the whole world."

Poor fool! If he had known anything about the principles of political economy he would have been aware that, having bought his map in the cheapest market, all he had to do was to sell it in the dearest. It was not his affair to see whether Cracow and Leopol were marked as German or as Polish towns. It would be almost as absurd for a shipbuilder to inquire whether the vessels he was building, or an ironfounder the cannons he was casting, were for the service of his country or of his country's enemies. Was there no one to tell him that if there was a demand for certain German ethnological maps that demand would be supplied, whether he liked it or not, that he might as well supply it as anyone else, and that it was even better he should do so in the interest of Poland, than that he should refuse and throw the trade into the hands of foreigners?

I met just such another fool in Warsaw, who would not sell me a history of Poland, on the ground that he could only procure the histories authorized by the Government, and that they were not true.

Another imbecile of the same type was a circulating-library keeper, who, finding that I was studying the modern history of Poland, gave me one day, without my having asked for it, a translation, which he had taken the trouble to make himself, of the speech to the Diet in which Alexander promised to extend the Constitution of 1815 to all the Polish provinces in the possession of Russia. This was no part of his business, and brought him no profit. In a commercial point of view he was therefore a fool; but if there are many fools of the same kind, their folly will one day make Poland a fine country.

This patriotic feeling, which, in all sorts of little and great things, the Poles are constantly showing, is caused no doubt, or, at least, has been greatly increased, by the suffering they have undergone; and do not let anyone imagine that they suffer less acutely in Austria and Prussia than in the more uncivilized Russia because they are not tormented there in precisely the same manner. We and other independent nations are so fortunately situated that, apart from massacres, we can form no idea as to what the Poles have to endure under their foreign Governments.

"I don't think we have any particular complaint to make that would be very intelligible in England," said a Polish gentleman to me in Cracow; "they don't shoot us in the streets if we keep quiet. The police don't interfere with us. The press is tolerably free. Books of all kinds are openly sold in the shops. But we are governed by foreigners. The misery of that you can no more understand than a rich man can enter into the feelings of a poor man—an utter impossibility, unless he has at some time been really poor himself."

I afterwards noticed a great many very palpable grievances which the Poles of Galicia had to put up with; but the foreign yoke is the evil of evils.

"The rule of the foreigner," says M. de Maistre (a man not fond of anarchy), "is a misfortune without parallel. No punishment, no torment of the heart can be compared to that." Indeed, I never heard the Poles, unless they were pressed on the subject, complain that they were overtaxed, or say very much about any special hardships caused by foreigners being set in government over them. This was not because they did not feel them, but because in the midst of general injustice it does not occur to them to lay stress on particular cases. If we hear of a woman being forced to marry a man whom she hates, and whom she has long had the best reasons for hating, are we afterwards to conclude that she is living happily with him because we never hear of his publicly ill-treating her? Is there no other way of torturing a wife but by the vulgar Russian-in-Warsaw mode of throwing knives at her head? The scribes of the German Chancelleries know better that that. They can render the life of a Pole intolerable without causing the least sensation in Europe, and without furnishing a pretext even for the composition of a newspaper paragraph. When I arrived in Cracow and looked for the mound raised by the Poles in honour of Kosciuszko, I was ashamed to ask whether it could be the green hill just outside the city, on which the Austrians had erected their principal fort. It seemed to require such a combination of stupidity and irreverence to turn the tomb of the Polish hero into a post from which to bombard the ancient Polish capital that I fancied I must be wrong, and did not wish to be thought capable of imagining anything so preposterous. When, at length, I put the question, and expressed my astonishment at the answer, "You cannot have been very long in Poland," my informant remarked, "if you are surprised at that. The Austrians take strange liberties with us. Their manner of arranging Kosciuszko's tomb is only one of them."

If this contempt for the feelings of the Poles is really only part of a system, it is, of course, quite natural that they should not call attention to particular instances of it. Otherwise, I do not

see why the Austrians should not take all the salt they can get from the mines of Wieliczka and Bochnia, impoverish Galicia by excessive taxation, give all the important offices in the Administration to Germans, and still not insult the Poles. I think the Austrians might not only not lose, but might even gain, by such a change. The Poles are just the people of all others in Europe who would be likely to put up with a certain amount of injustice if no indignities were offered to them.

Have the Austrians never heard of a certain class of liars of whom it is said that they never tell a falsehood except for their own advantage?—a very respectable class of liars, indeed, far superior to those who scatter falsehoods abroad from malice or mere wantonness. Now, as there are liars and liars, so there are tyrants and tyrants; and it is surely not too much to ask in the present day that tyranny shall not be so practised as to wound the victim to the heart without securing any particular advantage to the tormentor. The Prussians exercise their tyranny in a less openly offensive manner, and never injure their Polish subjects without a view to profit, immediate or remote. They do not desecrate Polish tombs, or turn Polish chapels into tobacco-warehouses, like the Austrians; neither do they erect trophies on spots where Polish insurgents have been slaughtered by their troops, like the Russians. They ignore the Polish language, they will not tolerate the teaching of Polish history, they will not allow a Polish college or a Polish theatre to be opened; if a Polish estate is for sale, they will buy it for something more than the market price and sell it for something less to a German; they will seize Polish newspapers without just cause, they will imprison Polish editors in the hope, if they cannot ensure their condemnation, that they may at least injure their journals during their absence from them; they will even *invent* conspiracies, so as to make their measures for repression appear justifiable;—but they do all this with a direct view to their own advantage, and for the furtherance of the great scheme of "Germanisation" in the Grand Duchy of Posen. Let them have their meed of praise, such as it is.

While, however, we in England are calmly speculating as to which of three varieties of tyranny practised in Poland is the worst, there are many Poles who have actually tried all three, and who say, as Fuller said after reflecting on different modes of death, with their advantages and disadvantages, "None please me." Count Prozor, the representative of a powerful family, and one of the most influential men of the Court of Stanislaus Augustus, was first of all seized and imprisoned by the Prussians. Having, after a time, been set free, he went to settle in France, but soon changing his mind, returned to Poland, where he was seized and imprisoned by the Austrians. In 1802 he was liberated, but was soon afterwards sentenced to exile by the Russians. He did not make the journey to Siberia, being pardoned by the Emperor Alexander; but in 1825, while still detained at St. Petersburg, he was accused of having taken part in the conspiracy which broke out in that year, and passed the last few years of his life in the fortress of Peter and Paul. Finally, he was proved to have had nothing whatever to do with the conspiracy; and, having been once more set at liberty, escaped all chance of further persecution by dying.

This noble old man, when he was eighty years of age, used to boast that he had lived as Poland had lived—he had passed half his life in prison, and had been dismembered like his country.

"Prussia," he said, "took my youth; Austria, my health; Russia, my intellect; but they cannot take my soul."

CHAPTER XII.

THE NOVGOROD MEMORIAL.

It must have astonished a great many persons last autumn to hear that Russia was about to celebrate her thousandth birthday. But it was not the completion of ten centuries of existence as an Empire that she commemorated at Novgorod. It was simply the accomplishment of that period of time since the foundation of an ancient and long since defunct Russia, of whose inheritance modern Russia has contrived to possess herself. These two Russias are no more identical than Austria, the actual representative of the German Empire, is identical with the Germania of Tacitus; or than Prussia would be identical with the German Empire if the Prussian Sovereign were to unite to his Kingdom a number of German duchies and adopt the title of Emperor of Germany. In the year of our Lord 862, on the 26th of August (7th of September, new style), precise hour in the day not known, Ruric the Norman arrived among the Slavonians of Novgorod, by express invitation, to teach those discontented republicans the blessings of monarchy. The Scandinavian chief did what chiefs in his position have always done. He came as a friend, remained as a foe, and taught his confiding hosts the art of governing in a very practical manner, ruling them with a rod of iron. In spite of protests and attempts to throw off the Norman yoke, Ruric and his immediate descendants established their sway, and extended it over nearly all the territory west of Moscow now included under the name of Russia. They even descended the Dnieper from Kieff, the capital of this Norman or Varangian Empire, formed among Slavonians on Slavonian ground, and set their descendants the example of attacking Constantinople long before there was any pretext for doing so on behalf of Christianity. Igor, the son of Ruric, and his Russian followers were Pagans when they made war upon the Greek Empire, from which, about half a century afterwards, Russia received the Christian religion.

There are a dozen different derivations of the words "Russia" and "Russian," to the most admired of which I have already called attention. I believe, the one now most generally received (and universally by the Poles) is that of Lelewel, who sets forth that Ruric came from Rosslagen in Sweden, that he was the chief of the tribe of Ross, and that the couple of hundred thousand conquerors belonging to that tribe, who, by successive influxes, established themselves in "Russia," gave their name to the country which they subdued. But whether the Norman invaders—the Varangians or "Varings" of Rosslagen—settled in a territory which was called Russia before they entered it, and afterwards adopted the name of the conquered race, like the Norman invaders of England;* or whether they brought with them the name of Russians and imposed it on the people they subjected, like the Norman invaders of France; in either case the origin of Russia as an organized State is to be found in the conquest of certain Slavonian cities by bands of Scandinavian warriors. Of these cities Novgorod and Kieff were the chief; and it was in Novgorod, a thousand years ago, that the Normans of the tribe of Ross, under Ruric, first established themselves.

Under the descendants of Ruric, Russia was divided into appanages, governed by Princes who owed allegiance to a Grand Prince, the head of the eldest branch of the family. The Grand Prince resided successively at Kieff, at Vladimir,

* This would appear to have been the opinion of M. Augustin Thierry, who speaks of "the Varangian conquerors of the Russian towns," though these Varangians were themselves called "Russians."

and at Moscow; until, in the thirteenth century, the Mongol-Tartars devastated Russia and forced the Prince, or Duke of "Muscovy," to become a tributary of the Khan.

In the meanwhile—and even before the Tartar invasion—the other principalities or duchies had broken the political link which formerly bound them together. Secession had taken place on a large scale, and in manifold directions; and after much fighting one against the other, the duchies, already separated from Muscovy and from the Grand Duke, were either annexed to Poland or to Lithuania (to be united to Poland at a later period); or, like Pskoff and Novgorod, became independent republics.

On the whole, it may be said that Western Russia became Lithuanian (even the two republics being subject to the influence, and to some extent under the protection of Lithuania), while Eastern Russia, or Muscovy, fell beneath the yoke of the Mongols.

Thus, a portion of the Empire of Ruric became Polish and a portion Tartar—that is to say, tributary to the Tartars, though not Tartar as to its internal government. When the Tartar yoke was thrown off, the Muscovite despotism, which had grown up under the auspices of the Khans, easily prevailed against the free but unwarlike and ill-organized republics of Novgorod and Pskoff. Then the Grand Dukes, after taking the title of Tsar, turned their arms against Lithuania, and the great Russian and Lithuano-Polish war commenced; in which Muscovy, gradually advancing, and only receding to advance still further, gained possession successively of Smolensk; of Little Russia; of Kieff and the course of the Dnieper; of that portion of Poland which fell to her lot at the various partitions; and finally of the Duchy of Warsaw, erected into a constitutional kingdom in 1815, and reduced, after the insurrection of 1830–1, to the position of a Russian province with a Russo-Polish administration.

It is usual to attribute the success of the Russians over the Poles to a perfidious and unscrupulous policy. Until the moment of the first partition, however, the Russians in their perpetual wars with Poland owed the advantages they gained to no remarkable dexterity of their own, whether moral or immoral, but simply to the factiousness and folly of their enemies. At the end of the sixteenth century the Poles were within 150 miles of Moscow. The Poles have always said that conquest was not one of their "national ideas," but they would have subjugated Muscovy all the same had they been able to do so. That most able monarch, Stephen Batory, made the attempt, and probably would have succeeded had he been faithfully supported by his nobility, who, however, were always so suspicious of absolutism being imposed upon them, that they went on mistrusting their own kings until they ended by falling under the absolutism of foreigners. The Poles held Moscow in their possession in 1612, and although the crown of Muscovy had been offered to a Polish Prince by the Council of Boyars, the Polish Prince did not resign his title to it when, in consequence of his not complying with the conditions on which it had been proposed to him, the offer was withdrawn. Indeed, the Russians only regained possession of their capital by rising against the Poles under Minin, the cattle-dealer, and Prince Pojarskoi, just as the Poles, nearly two centuries afterwards, rose against the Russians, under Kilinski and Kosciuszko. The capture of Smolensk and that of Moscow were "national ideas" enough, or Sigismund III. would not have erected a column in the middle of Warsaw to celebrate those exploits. Smolensk, which only belonged to Lithuania by right of conquest, was taken, lost, and retaken by the Russians in regular warfare; the Ukraine and the left bank of the Dnieper became Russian, because the Poles drove the Cossacks to seek the protection of Alexis Mikhailovitch (Peter the Great's father); Kieff was ceded to Russia for money by John Sobieski; and it was not until the first partition in 1772 that Russia transgressed the laws of international morality in her dealings with Poland. In that year, however, Catherine II., whose troops, at the request of the Polish Government, had occupied the country since 1764, suddenly refused to quit it, and treacherously claimed a mass of territory to which Russia had not the shadow of a title.

However, under actual circumstances, the modern Emperors of Russia may well consider themselves the representatives of Ruric, for, with the exception of Eastern Galicia (which the Russians claim more loudly and more openly every day), they possess all the provinces over which the descendants of Ruric have ever ruled. They may not be the rightful heirs, but they certainly hold the estate, and the validity of the title is denied by Poland alone of all the nations in Europe—for the Poles still form a nation by their literature, their political aspirations, and their general unity of sentiment and purpose.

Contrary to the custom in all civil processes, Russia seized the territory she coveted first and undertook to prove her right to it afterwards. When the partition of Poland was perpetrated, we had as good a claim to a portion of France, through our Norman kings, and France as good a claim to all England, through her Norman dukes, as Russia had to a single square inch of Polish soil. The so-called Russian provinces had been united for upwards of four centuries to Lithuania, and through the union of Lithuania to Poland had become Polish by civilization. Moreover, Catherine, in a formal "declaration," made in 1764, eight years before the first partition, set forth that, in taking the title of "Empress of all the Russias," she had "no intention of arrogating any right, either for herself, or for her successors, or for her Empire, to the countries and territories which, under the name of Russia or Ruthenia, belong to Poland and to the Grand Duchy of Lithuania." In fact, she had no more right to the said territories than the Sovereign of Great Britain has to Brittany in France; and the Bretons, though of the same race as the people of Wales, would, of course, fight us to a man if we ever presumed to appear among them as the defenders of their nationality, just as the inhabitants of the Russian or Ruthenian Provinces of Poland fought under Kosciuszko against Russia.

It would be a grave historical mistake, then, to regard the Novgorod Column as commemorating the thousandth year of the existence of the Russian Empire, inasmuch as the Russian Empire has only existed as a unified State since the fifteenth century. It is a development, or rather an amplification, of the Grand Duchy of Muscovy, the chief of the federated principalities governed by the descendants of Ruric, of which the political federation was virtually destroyed as long ago as the thirteenth century; though the religious union between them was maintained in Eastern Russia throughout the Tartar domination.

Nevertheless, the Novgorod Column celebrates a most important event, for the arrival of Ruric, in the year 862, was certainly the beginning of Russian history. Modern Russia is Muscovy aggrandized; but, at the same time, the Grand Duchy of Muscovy was formed, and the city of Moscow founded, by a descendant of Ruric through the eldest branch of the family. Without Ruric there would have been no Russia; neither "Muscovy" nor the "Empire of All the Russias." We know what the effect was of 60,000 Normans (more or less) landing in England; and we may judge from that how the character of the peaceful, agricultural Slavonians, inhabiting Novgorod, Kieff, and the immense tract of country lying between those two cities, must have been changed by the 200,000 Scandinavian warriors who established themselves on their territory as conquerors and rulers. The Norman chiefs who settled in Russia were cruel and perfidious. They poisoned the allies whom they suspected or feared, as William the Conqueror poisoned his relatives, the Counts of Brittany; and they blinded and otherwise tortured their vanquished enemies as remorselessly as did the Christian Normans in Western Europe. But they brought with them a genius for military and political organization which, as Miękievicz testifies in his lectures, was the secret of the ultimate success of the Russians of Muscovy in their continual struggles against the Tartars; and, for good or bad, they put Russia in the way to become what she now is. With less power of resistance, Muscovy might have sunk into a Tartar State, instead of a Christian State paying enforced tribute to the Tartars. That it became even the latter was the fault of Western Europe and of the Pope, who abandoned it when it refused as a condition of aid to acknowledge his supremacy.

The Poles maintain that the Modern Russia or "Muscovite" Empire is something quite different from Ancient Russia or "Ruthenia," and are indignant with the Russian Government for resorting to the unstatesmanlike artifice of saying "it's the same concern," &c. It matters little to the West of Europe what the Russian Empire is called, or what its precise origin may have been. The Poles, however, attach the greatest importance to these questions; and whereas the word "Muscovite" is only used in France, Germany, and England by ingenious writers who are afraid of employing the word "Russian" twice in the same sentence, everything in Poland is "Muscovite" that belongs to the Russian empire, and it is intentionally so designed to show that the Poles regard "all the Russias" as unlawful acquisitions on the part of the Moscow Tsars.

According to the Polish view of Russian history, the numerous principalities into which the Russo-Norman Empire, founded in Slavonia by Rurik and his companions, broke up, were already separate States at the period of the Mongol invasion. Then, being called upon by all-powerful circumstances to choose between spiritual subjection to the Pope and political subjection to the Tartars, ancient Russia (or "Ruthenia," as the Poles, for the sake either of greater clearness or of greater confusion, insist on styling the country, though it is termed "Russia" and "Ruthenia" indifferently in mediæval Latin chronicles) made an effort to maintain its independence without adopting either of those courses; but unavailingly. At last Western Russia became united to Lithuania, Poland, and the Catholic Church; while Eastern Russia remained Greek Catholic, and had to submit to the domination of the Mongols. Eastern Russia or Muscovy, became consolidated under the rule of the Grand Dukes of Moscow, who at last succeeded in breaking the Tartar yoke; since which period the entire inheritance of the sons of Rurik has been falsely and perfidiously claimed by the Tsars of this Tartar-bred State; not a Ruthenian nor a Slavonian State, but merely the development, under Mongol auspices, of a Ruthenian colony founded in the twelfth century, among tribes of Ouralian origin; a State which, in its sub-Mongol abasement, lost all notions of liberty and legality such as continued to exist in the independent and *quasi*-republican principality of Novgorod and in the other Russian or Ruthenian principalities annexed to Lithuania and to Poland; a State in which the ancient Ruthenian, Slavonian language, became so corrupted by an admixture of Tartar words as to be unintelligible to Ruthenians and Slavonians in general.

Then, putting ethnology on one side, the Poles call attention to the fact that Muscovy did not owe its growth, or rather its aggrandizement into the modern Russian Empire, either to Norman feudal principles or to Slavonian patriarchal, and more or less democratic principles; but simply to the Mongol principle of autocracy, to which the Muscovite people had become so familiarized during two centuries of servitude that they would allow their Tsars either to massacre them at home, or to lead them to death on the battle-field abroad, without ever daring to utter one murmur of complaint. Russia, they say, calls herself a Slavonian Empire, but she has hitherto brought nothing but slavery and death to the Slavonians whom she has subjected, from the destruction of the Republics of Novgorod and Pskoff to the three partitions of Poland and the absorption of the Duchy of Warsaw.

Russian writers, on the other hand, of all shades of opinion, maintain that ancient Russia, though already divided into separate but federated principalities, lost its political cohesion finally through the invasion of the Tartars, when, but for the strengthening and binding influence of the Christian religion ("*religio*" in its original sense) it would probably have become dispersed and absorbed among the surrounding nations and tribes. Nevertheless, for two centuries it formed the real bulwark of Christian Europe against the Tartar hordes, though if the Russians had basely consented to accept their alliance, repeatedly proposed, they might well have avenged themselves on the Western Catholics who abandoned them, because they refused to acknowledge the supremacy of the Pope as the price of assistance against the barbarians. In the meantime, while Christian Russia was struggling as best she could against the cruel persecution of the Mongols, Poland not merely looked on, but profited by Russia's weakness to deprive her of an immense portion of territory, subjecting the Russian population thereof to the tyranny of a Polish aristocracy, and forcing upon it the "union" decreed between the Roman Catholic and Greek Churches at Florence in 1440. Then Russia, having dwindled for a time between the Mongols and the Pope, into the Duchy of Moscow, issued at last, triumphant and strong, from her long and painful servitude, drove back on one side the Tartars, on the other the Poles and Lithuanians, allied with the Swedes, and gradually extended herself first into the Tsarate of Muscovy, and finally into the Russian Empire, considerably enlarged and improved, but not complete as long as the East Galician or Red Russian portion of it remains under the sceptre of Austria.

The ethnologists of Europe do not require to be told (whatever the origin of Moscow may have been) whether or not the Russians of the present day are Slavonians by descent, by traditions, and by language,—by mental and physical temperament, and by manners and customs, from superstitions to favourite drinks, and from popular songs to cookery. It is quite true, on the other hand, that the higher classes in Poland possess widely-different notions on the subject of liberty and legality from those which have *hitherto* prevailed among the classes corresponding to them (as regards social position) in Russia, who for centuries have been made to feel that in important matters there is no law for them but the absolute will of the sovereign. Nor because the Russians and Poles speak mother tongues between which considerable affinity (though nothing approaching to a twin-like resemblance) exists; nor because the Russians, like the Poles, are great believers in fantastic religious legends and in the efficacy of pilgrimages; great singers of plaintive melodies in minor keys; great consumers of black bread, salted cucumbers, cabbage and beetroot soups, corn brandy and mead; and great haters of beer-consuming Germans,—certainly it does not follow from these Slavonian peculiarities, common to both nations, that the stronger of the two ought to oppress the weaker. "*Sois mon frère, ou je te tue,*"—"Acknowledge my dominion as Slavonian, or I will annex and tranquillize you, as I did White Russia, Black Russia, and all the rest of them," is the real language of Russian Panslavonianism to the Slavonian world in general, and especially to Red Russia, supposed to be suffering just now from the tyranny of the Galician Poles.

About the ultimate fate of Eastern Galicia there can be no doubt, inasmuch as she is represented on the Novgorod monument, which is valuable as showing the world what Russia really will be when she has finished constituting herself. Daniel, Duke of Galicia, crowned King of Russia (or Ruthenia) by the Pope in the thirteenth century, when all Eastern Russia (or Muscovy) had already been subjected by the Tartars, is the personage through whom modern Russia claims a province which united itself voluntarily to Poland in the fourteenth century. Daniel, Duke of a province which never was Russian in the modern meaning of the word, and which numbers among its illustrious children Sobieski and Kosciuszko, figures on the Novgorod monument in company with certain Lithuanian warriors who, by having conquered a portion of ancient Russia in the days of the Tartar domination, have, it seems, given modern Russia a right to possess all Lithuania.

Gedemin, the Lithuanian, could he rise from the dead, would be astonished to find that he, too, was a Russian, and as such has a place on the Novgorod monument. And why not Batu-Khan and Tamerlane? it may be asked. Their possessions in Russia and elsewhere belong also in the present day to the Russian Empire. Batu and Tamerlane were not, it is true, members of the Orthodox Church, but neither was Gedemin. He was an unprejudiced and very tolerant pagan, converted for a moment to Catholicism by a promise from the Pope of assistance against the Teutonic Knights, but again a pagan when he found that the assistance was not forthcoming. Prometheus might also be claimed as a Russian on account of his long and painful connection with the Caucasus, which is now quite as much Russian, and by the same title, as Lithuania.

"The history of Russia," a thorough Russian might argue, "is the history of the provinces which compose the Russian Empire, not merely from the moment at which they became Russian, but from the remotest period." Such a doctrine, which, applied to Austria, would make the history of that empire include the history of Venice, is manifestly false and absurd; but it is one which prevails in Russia, and which must be borne in mind by every one who wishes to understand the historical monument of Novgorod. This memorial, (of which the admirable design has been reproduced in our illustrated papers) is in the form of a bell — in memory, no doubt, of the "great bell of Novgorod," which was held in such veneration in the days of Novgorod's liberty, and which was carried away to Moscow and hung in the Kremlin (where it still remains) when the city was subdued and sacked by the Tsar Ivan. A band of bas-reliefs encircles the lower part of the bell; around the middle portion are arranged six groups of colossal figures; and the memorial is crowned by a Greek cross held by a personification of the Orthodox religion, at whose feet kneels a personification of the Russian people, protected by a shield on which the two-headed eagle is emblazoned.

Of the groups of colossal figures, the first represents Rurik of Rosslagen arriving sword in hand among the Slavonians of Novgorod and laying the foundation of the Russian Empire (862). Certainly, the thousandth anniversary of such an event was well worth celebrating. Whatever may have been the middle history of the principalities governed by Rurik's successors, the chief Russian families at this moment, and nearly all the leading men who have appeared in that part of Slavonia which was invaded in the ninth and tenth centuries by the Russo-Normans, have been descended from the conquering race. Nothing is known of the history of the country now called Russia before Rurik arrived in it with the able governors and irresistible warriors who extended their dominions in a few years from the Baltic to the Black Sea; and, but for the infusion of this powerful military and political element, who can say that the feeble Slavonians east of the Dnieper would ever have been able to drive back the Tartars, first in the fourteenth and finally in the fifteenth century, or to resist the attacks of the

Swedes and the Poles, who at the beginning of the seventeenth century established themselves, the former at Novgorod, the latter at Moscow?

The principal figure in the second of the colossal groups is the Russo-Norman, Vladimir, under whom Christianity was introduced (988); the principal figure in the third is Demetrius of the Don, a Prince of Russo-Norman descent, who, for a time, freed Muscovy from the Tartars (1380); in the fourth Ivan III., also of the house of Rurik, who founded the Muscovite-Russian Tsarate (1462); in the fifth, Michael Fedorovitch, the first Tsar of the House of Romanoff, descended from Rurik by the mother's side (1613); in the sixth, Peter the Great, the founder of the Russian Empire.

The bas-reliefs include the figures of 107 persons who have contributed to strengthen or to civilize Russia. Among the "promoters of civilization," specially so-called, are the Byzantine Apostles Cyril and Methodius; Nestor the chronicler; several "wonder-workers" and martyrs who suffered under the Tartars; Jonas, the Greek metropolitan of Kieff, who defended orthodoxy against Isidor, the Latin or Greek-Uniate metropolitan appointed by the Pope, after the Council of Florence; and, finally, Innocent, the late Archbishop of Odessa—some of whose discourses, by the way, have been translated into English, French, and German, and whose sermons to the army of Sebastopol gained great celebrity in Russia during the Crimean war.

Among the political heroes are "Silvester the priest of Moscow, the virtuous rebuker of Ivan the Terrible" (who naturally put his adviser to death).

The list of Russian "warriors and heroes" includes a certain number of ancient Norman and Lithuanian chiefs, and, belonging to more recent times, Yermak, the conqueror of Siberia; Minin and Pojarski, the liberators of Moscow from the Poles; Palitzin, the monk who defended the Troitza Monastery against the Poles; Ivan Sousannin, who sacrificed himself to save Michael, the first of the Romanoffs, from the Poles (known to musicians as the hero of Glinka's *Life for the Tsar*); Bogdan Khmelnitzki, who transferred the sovereignty of the Ukraine from Poland to Russia; Souvaroff, and a great many more generals and admirals, the series terminating with Paskievitch, the conqueror of Erivan and the establisher of "order" in Warsaw, followed by such names as Lazareff, Korniloff, and Nachimoff. The commanders of 1812 are, of course, not forgotten. The two principal ones,

Barclay de Tolly and Kutouzoff, had already had statues erected to them in St. Petersburg, but as they are placed in the open air, without their hats, the Russians consider that they have been badly treated, and have recorded that opinion in the following epigram :—

"Barclay de Tolly and Kutoùzoff
In Moscow froze the Frenchman's nose off.
Russia, her gratitude to show,
Put them out hatless in the snow!"

At Novgorod these generals, it is to be hoped, are allowed to wear their helmets.

The earliest of the "writers and artists" belong only to the reign of Catherine. Nearly all the poets, dramatists, and novelists whose names are inscribed on the monument are known abroad by their reputation, if not by their actual works, many of which, however, have been translated into German, French, and English—those, for instance, of Lomonossoff, Kriloff, the fable-writer; Karamzin, the historian; Griboiedoff, the comedy-writer; Poushkin and Lermontoff, poets and novelists; Gogol, the novelist and comedy-writer, &c. It is characteristic of Russian civilization that not one philosophical or scientific writer can be found whose name is thought worthy of being placed on the Novgorod memorial, though during the last half-century the country has produced a great number of remarkable writers in other departments of literature.

The painters represented are Bruloff, and Schevtchenko the painter and tale-writer of "South Russia"; the composers, Glinka and Bortnianski.

The Novgorod monument, whatever else may be said of it, commemorates the foundation of a State which certainly has not existed 1000 years, but whose progress during the last 400—counting from the establishment of the Tsarate of Muscovy in 1462—has, just or unjust, been quite unparalleled in modern or ancient times. If Russia (or "Muscovy") has owed this progress to wickedness and nothing else, then wickedness has had an unusually long triumph in the east of Europe, and the reign of Beelzebub in those parts ought now to be drawing very rapidly to an end. But, in any case, Russia can make out no historical claim more ancient than that which she derives from the perfidious violation of the integrity of Poland in time of peace to either Poland or Lithuania—which was to Poland simply what Scotland is now to England. It appears from the Novgorod Memorial, that "Poland" (*i. e.* the Kingdom of Poland) is not regarded even now as forming part of the Russian Empire, and it is more than probable that at a fitting opportunity Russia would willingly enter into an arrangement for granting a certain independence to this portion of the ancient Polish kingdom. But she will keep to Volhynia, Podolia, the province of Kieff, and all Lithuania, as to Moscow itself; though it is quite clear that she has no more right to Wilna than to Warsaw, unless, indeed, she rests her claim solely upon the Treaties of Vienna—in which case it is an unbecoming piece of mockery on her part to put the name of Gedemin on the Novgorod Memorial, as though to make the world believe that this Grand Duke of Lithuania, intimate ally of Poland and enemy of Russia, was somehow or other a Russian!

CHAPTER XIII.

THE POLISH QUESTION IN RUSSIA.

"WHAT do the Russians say to the general claims of the Poles?" I have sometimes been asked. They said nothing to the claims of the Poles, as far as I could tell, the first time I visited Russia in 1856. They believed that the Polish question was at an end, which, indeed, was a very general opinion in Europe until the beginning of 1861, when the "demonstrations" and massacres of that year proved the contrary. Of course there were plenty of political men who knew what the exact state of Poland was, and that it had been thought prudent to keep 100,000 men there during the Crimean War. But, as a rule, no one seemed to bestow a moment's thought on Poland. Everyone in Moscow and St. Petersburg was talking about the coming emancipation of the serfs, and the reforms of all kinds said to be in preparation, and by which it seemed at the time that both Russia and Poland would profit. Poland, moreover, was perfectly quiet, and whatever wrongs might have been done to her she seemed at last to have been completely conquered, and to have accepted her position as a Russian province. I met Russian officers, it is true, who had been at Warsaw, and who said they had never once been invited to a Polish house, and that the enmity between Russians and Poles was as great as ever; but the general impression seemed to be that the Polish game had been played out and lost, and that the fate of Poland was mixed up indissolubly with that of the Russian Empire. This notion had, to some extent, been confirmed by the fact that the Poles had fought side by side with the Russians against the allies in the Crimea, and against the Turks in Asia Minor, and that very few indeed had deserted. I found that almost every one who took any interest in literary matters had a copy of the Countess Rostopchina's poem on Poland; * but many Englishmen admired Byron's verses on George the Fourth's visit to Ireland, without caring much for the sufferings of the Irish at that period, and the Countess Rostopchina's lines may have become popular, not only on account of their poetical merit, but also because they attacked in a very vigorous manner a redoubtable tyrant, against whom no one dared whisper a syllable in print.

I made a point, however, when I was in Russia, a year or two ago, of ascertaining, as far

* *The Forced Marriage* (See *Appendix* No. 3).

as I could do so, what the Russians really thought about the position of the Poles. Curiously enough, the first sign I met with of any interest in the matter was a picture at the annual exhibition of the St. Petersburg Academy of Arts. The work represented the halt of a party of exiles. The scene is on the road to Siberia—a grey, snow-laden sky above, and desolation and Cossacks all around. In the foreground, on an uncovered cart, to which he is chained by the legs, lies the inanimate body of a prisoner, who has neither the figure nor the features of any of the other exiles, for the most part ordinary criminals; and who, if physiognomy be any guide, has never committed the slightest action of which he need be ashamed. His forehead, nose, chin, and the general contour of his face are of the most noble type, and the artist has succeeded in giving an expression of remarkable dignity to the dead or dying man, though he is stretched out in an horizontal line, and has both eyes closed. But no,—one eye is partly open; for the officer in command of the escort, a low, cunning, callous, brutal-looking personage, who is puffing away at a short pipe, is at the same time lifting up the eyelid of the expiring Polish gentleman, to ascertain whether he is really dead, or only counterfeiting death, so as to be left behind before his time. The political exile, however, for he can be nothing else, has a glassy eye, which will convince the officer of the inutility of taking him any further on his journey. On his thin white hand, hanging lifeless at the side of the cart, is a signet ring—some family memorial which he has contrived to keep to the last—and, as a final humiliation, this is passing into the possession of a born thief who, crouching beneath the vehicle, and suddenly catching sight of jewellery, flies at it like a cat at a bird. The horses have been unharnessed from the cart; the officer was only taking one last critical look at his expiring prisoner, and the Cossacks in advance are already beginning to move on into the gloom of the steppes. On one side of the road a group of women and children, who have accompanied their husbands and fathers thus far, and who will now have to leave them for ever, are weeping and wailing. On the other, close to the departed, soon-to-be-forgotten exile, a Russian peasant, with a sore and sorrowful expression of countenance, is examining a terrible wound which the fetters have already made in one of his legs. This is, doubtless, one of those unhappy serfs who, until the publication of the recent *oukaz* of emancipation, could be sent by their proprietors to Siberia, with or without cause, provided only the latter paid a certain sum for their equipment and travelling expenses.

But, "*où la liberté va-t-elle se nicher?*" It appears that in Russia an artist may paint and exhibit what a writer will not venture to describe.

It is a curious fact that the critic of the *Contemporary*, in speaking of M. Jacobi's "Halt of a Party of Prisoners," confines himself exclusively, but in a very studied manner, to its external aspect. He takes a picturesque view of the general scene, and says that one of the exiles wears a ring, relates the imaginary surprise of some imaginary spectator at seeing this ring on the finger of a convict, and asks, what can be the meaning of it? It is a question which anyone who has seen the picture could answer. No work in the Exhibition attracted nearly so much attention, and the young painter was rewarded for it by the Academy with a well-merited gold medal of the first class.

Of the Russian journals and reviews (I speak of independent ones started by private persons and maintained without any sort of assistance from the Government) the first that published anything on the subject of the agitated condition of Poland in 1861 was the organ of the Slavennophils, edited at Moscow, by M. Aksakoff, under the title of the *Day* (*Dyen*).

The reader already knows that, in the Polish provinces, where the peasantry speak "Ruthenian," and the proprietors, merchants, tradesmen, and townspeople, and the more or less educated classes in general, speak Polish, the Russian Government puts itself forward as the protector of the "Russian" people. On the subject of these provinces

M. Aksakoff, like all Russians that I have ever met with, shares the views of his Government. "Here," he says, "we stand for a people, with a people, and in the name of a people; for the free rights of a people, for its liberty and independence, for the persecuted against the persecutors. The question is clear, and we are strong in the knowledge of our right, and in the approval of our social conscience. In one of the numbers of this journal we called the Polish claims to Kieff, Smolensk, &c. *mad.* We keep to that designation because they deserve no other. They are not only quite mad, but immoral in the highest sense of the word, inasmuch as they rest upon possession gained by force, and are directed against the freedom of the people.

"The same moral foundations, rights, and duties exist also, of course, for the Greek, in connection with the Ionian Islands, and for the Pole as concerns those Polish provinces where the people is either of Polish descent or speaks the Polish language, professes the Catholic religion, and, in general, does not separate itself, and its historical fate, from the Poles as a nation. Judging with all severity the Polish claims to Kieff and Smolensk, we should sin against logical sense were we to deny the legitimacy of their patriotism, in regard to Posen, Cracow, and Warsaw. If the Austrians and Prussians have not had conscientiousness vouchsafed to them sufficiently acute to enable them to understand in what relation they stand to the Polish people, *we* can boast of the special mercy of God in that respect, so that we are made to feel every falling-off from the mora law; to feel every, even the smallest, departure from rectitude, and, accordingly that much of it which our historical lot has assigned to us in connection with Poland."

He then continues as follows:—

"Indeed, the German newspapers are filled with the most cutting censures upon Russia for her weakness of action in Poland.* They require from us that indiscriminate energy which, undoubtedly, a German would show in our position. But of energy for evil purposes Russia is not capable. That, however, is nothing. Even if we wished to put it forth, such energy would, fortunately, not bring us those sweet fruits which it brings to others; to taste them would not be

* This was perfectly true. In Posen, when the intended celebration of some great Polish anniversary had been prevented by the Prussian troops, many German newspapers took that opportunity of telling the Poles that they must not imagine they would be allowed to behave in Prussian Poland as the Russians allowed them to behave in the Kingdom. When the Austrian Government found that the Galicians persisted in singing the patriotic hymn, they ordered the churches to be closed wherever it was sung; and this at a time when it was—not permitted, but at least tolerated, in every church in Warsaw.

permitted to us by our social conscience. We have plenty of material strength; a strength resting on sixty millions of population, to which is opposed the weakness of five millions. But so important is the moral principle of justice to so moral a nation as Russia, that for this material strength, with all its greatness, to be of use, it is necessary we should have the consciousness of undoubted moral right on our side.

"There is no doubt that the fall of Poland was prepared by the constitution of Polish society, by the falseness of the nobles, and by Catholicism; by Poland's betrayal of Slavonian principles, by the pride and impatience of the Polish nationality, and the jealousy it awakened among other nations of the same family. The existence of Poland in her ancient form, upon the principles manifested in her history, was, according to all probabilities, no longer possible. As a troublesome and aggressive neighbour she hindered the free development of Russia, and the historical Nemesis has avenged upon Poland all the wrongs she committed upon the Russian people in the beginning of the seventeenth century. We will suppose all that to be just; but the *incidents accompanying the end of Poland* which terminated her political existence will die a natural death, while they have renewed the life of Polish nationality, and have imparted to it that moral strength which it shows at present.

By the latest examination of history it is proved undoubtedly that the whole plan for the partition of Poland was originated by Frederic 'the Great' (so styled), who managed at the same time to direct affairs so cleverly that the blame fell with all its weight on Russia, which was less in fault than either of the other Powers. We all know that Russia, at the partition of Poland, only re-annexed her ancient Russian provinces and took Lithuania with them, and that the so-called Kingdom of Poland fell to us by the decision of the Congress of Vienna. Of course Russia could have performed the work of re-annexation by other and more direct means: either upon the demands of the persecuted people of those Russian provinces, or by simple war against Poland. But all this is of no great importance in the presence of Russia's undoubted claim upon these lands.

"As for the annexation of the Kingdom of Poland, Russia granted it a constitution; and Polish nationality, by the way, owes its very existence to that incapacity of ours, which, as we have said, forms our *moral merit* in history. If any fault can be charged against us, it is to be found in our having supported the ambitious claims of our neighbours, and having consented to the subjection of a free Slavonian race to foreigners. But, on the whole, Russia was less in fault than either of the other Powers, as regards the destruction and partition of Poland, though, as a moral country, she feels more deeply than either of them whatever injustice there was in the affair.

"From this it is clear, that for the peace of our national conscience it is absolutely necessary to give freedom and power to the moral principle, and to manage to get to the truth as to our relations towards the Poles. Of course we do not venture to take upon ourselves to decide the Polish question: it is connected with the question of Government rights, with the demands of European politics, and with different other questions, for the most part not to be approached by a private individual;—but we are examining the subject from a moral point of view, and having already expressed ourselves in our newspaper upon the Polish claims to White and Little Russia, we think it our duty to complete these opinions. Probably many will reproach us with our 'idealism'; let our readers decide that for themselves.

"According to our personal conviction, we ought, as we have already said, to get to the truth of our relations towards the Poles so as to know and understand what they really need and want. It seems to us that amongst other means to this end, the most powerful would be straightforward—thoroughly straightforward—literary discussion.

"Unfortunately, the experience of ages shows that passionate desires, though without foundation, seldom yield to simple conviction. A powerless man, but full of fire, does not, as a rule, yield before any, not even the most evident proofs; he seeks to find out by experience his own capacities for action; and it is really only by experience that he becomes convinced of the injustice of his impulses, and finds out his real position and vocation.

"We will allow ourselves a supposition. Supposing we were to step out of Poland and take our stand on our own Russian boundaries? Firmly protecting the latter, we could then be patient and impartial witnesses of the internal struggles and labours of Poland. Undoubtedly, that would be not only morally pure, but even generous on our part. Continuing our supposition, let us ask, would the Poles have enough strength to create anything good and lasting, and would their neighbourhood be injurious to us? However difficult it may be to answer this question, still let us examine it a little more closely.

"If, in reality, the words of Napoleon about the Bourbons are applicable to Poland; if they have forgotten nothing and learnt nothing, then, of course, their new existence would not last long. Ultramontane fanaticism, the aristocracy of the nobles, and the narrow national pride shown by them even now in Galicia and the province of

Chelm,* if they can give strength for resistance, cannot, however, lay the foundation of anything. . . . . .

"If the Poles, carried away by their political ambition, should overstep their boundaries and invade us, they would meet not only unremitting resistance from the people, but would give us a full moral right to punish their unlawfulness, and destroy the cause of wrongful bloodshed.

"But if the Poles are capable of being re-born, of repenting of their historical mistakes, and will take their stand as a peaceful Slavonian people, then, certainly, the Russian people would be glad to see in them kind, friendly neighbours.

"However, we think that, in any case, Poland herself, after some years, would try to re-unite itself—this time willingly and sincerely—to Russia. The wound on our body, so long and so painfully sore, would then, at last, be healed. Our social conscience would no longer be troubled by doubt, and the moral principle would fully triumph.

"Is it possible that this end cannot be attained by a peaceful and reasonable path? Can it be that the Poles, having forgotten the rule '*Respice finem,*' . . . . . . is it possible that they

* The peasants of Eastern Galicia and of Chelm, in the Kingdom of Poland, are Ruthenians by race and Greek Uniates by religion. Their misfortune apparently consists in not having been compelled by force, like the Ruthenian peasants of the Polish provinces, to enter the Russo-Greek Church.

can only be brought to reason by *incidents*, and that no other proofs can reach them! We are convinced that, early or late, there will be the closest, fullest, and most sincere union of Slavonian Poland with Slavonian Russia. The course of history leads undeniably thereto. And would it not be better, in the sight of such an unavoidable historical conclusion, to look forward and remove all causes of animosity and misfortune, and willingly confessing and repenting mutually of our historical sins, join together in a brotherly and intimate union against our general enemies—ours, and of all Slavonians?"

M. Aksakoff having denied the claims of the Poles to the Ruthenian provinces, and having also expressed his conviction that nothing so much as free discussion could aid the solution of the Polish question as between Russia and Poland, M. Grabowski, a Pole, addressed two long letters to the editor of the *Dien*, in which he contraverts M. Aksakoff's arguments on the subject of the said provinces, and attacks the Russian Government severely for its general policy and treatment of the Poles. The Censor in Moscow could not give his *imprimatur* to M. Grabowski's articles, upon which they were submitted to the Minister of Public Instruction, who also thought it impossible to allow them to be printed. At M. Aksakoff's special request, however, they were shown to the Emperor, who, having read them, ordered at once that they should be permitted to appear.

The publication of M. Grabowski's articles caused a great deal of astonishment among readers of newspapers, and still more among journalists, as until then Poland had been a proscribed subject except to writers who were prepared to defend the attitude and excesses of the Russian Government. Consequently, until the appearance of the *Dien* in September, 1861, no independent Russian organ had published a single article on the disturbed state of Poland.

In September, or October, 1861 (I forget which), the *Contemporary*, a review, published fortnightly at St. Petersburg, and which (until it was suppressed the other day) had a very large number of readers, printed an article on Poland, in which the writer declared that the Russians were quite in a false position in the Kingdom, and that as regarded the disputed nationality of the border provinces, the inhabitants themselves ought to be consulted.

The *Russian Messenger*, the most conservative of all the independent Russian journals and reviews, but which is strongly in favour of such reforms as have been proposed everywhere by the Russian nobility (*i. e.* the formation of a general representative assembly, abolition of class privileges, the introduction of trial by jury, &c.), had, when I was last in Russia (from September, 1861 until February, 1862), published nothing on the subject of Poland. I believe, however, that the important party represented by this journal thought the Kingdom of Poland could not be governed unless representative institutions were given back to it; and I always heard it said by Russian Constitutionalists that the dissolution of the Agricultural Society was an impolitic measure, inasmuch as it deprived the Government of a means of ascertaining the feelings and wishes of the influential classes of the nation. But the Constitutional party, like the Slavennophils, deny altogether the right of the Poles to the Ruthenian and Lithuanian provinces, though, as every one knows, these provinces are distinctly recognized as Polish in the Treaties of Vienna.

Nevertheless, if this Constitutional party should ever succeed in attaining the object of its wishes —that is to say, a Government resembling as much as possible that of England—the Polish question, even in the Lithuanian and Ruthenian provinces seized at the three great partitions, would soon settle itself. If the future liberty of Russia is to be of the English and not of the

Prussian pattern, the Poles, wherever they are found, must be allowed to establish Polish schools, and to teach Polish history as written by Polish historians. Then the Polish language would assuredly prevail over all the Ruthenian dialects of the peasantry, just as the Russian language has prevailed over them in Little Russia. The peasants desire everywhere to learn the language spoken by their superiors. As I have before remarked, the Welsh peasant, the Irish peasant, and the peasant of the Highlands, go to school to learn English; and in the same way the peasant of the Polish provinces of Russia, whatever may be his native *patois*, will wish the language of his education to be Polish.

Again, were a representative assembly for the whole Russian Empire to be formed to-morrow, the deputies from the Polish provinces, would, if the educated classes alone voted, be Poles to a man —for all the educated classes in these provinces are Poles by civilization, whatever they may be by ancient descent.

Finally, if religious liberty were proclaimed, it is probable enough that the peasants of the Polish provinces, who were driven by force in 1833, to join the Russo-Greek Church, would, once left to themselves, return to the union with Rome. If not, the Poles would at least find themselves deprived of what is now a just subject of complaint on their part; and in this there would be a clear gain for Russia.

In any case, Russia cannot do justice to herself without doing justice to the Poles; and at the Assemblies of 1862, when so many provinces petitioned the Emperor to endow Russia with a constitutional system, the Russian nobility, in pleading their own cause, were also, whether they wished it or not, pleading the cause of Poland.

CHAPTER XIV.

CONSTITUTIONAL MOVEMENT IN RUSSIA.

FROM absolutism to communistic radicalism there is but one step, and some notion of what Russian radicalism is in its most silly form may be obtained from a document entitled *An Address to the Young Generation*, which was widely circulated last year in Moscow and St. Petersburg. The author, a writer named Mikhailoff, who had previously made himself known by some curious articles on the emancipation of woman, was discovered, arrested, tried, and sentenced by the Senate to twelve and a-half years' exile to Siberia, with hard labour in the mines, being half the ordinary legal punishment for the treasonable offence of which he had been convicted. The Emperor afterwards reduced the term of exile to six years and said nothing about the hard labour, which it was understood would not be enforced. Nevertheless, so much sympathy was felt for the author of the *Address to the Young Generation*, that a subscription was opened in the two capitals for his benefit, and a large sum collected. The print-shops were full of his portraits, no album of *cartes de visite* was considered complete without that of Mr. Mikhailoff, and there was even a demand for his articles on the emancipation of woman. Many a worthier man than Mr. Mikhailoff has been sent to Siberia, without any notice being taken of his absence from his usual abode, and this novel and almost ostentatious enthusiam for an exile who had certainly not been banished without cause, could only be explained by a general desire to testify want of sympathy for those who had banished him. One of the largest contributors however, to the testimonial to be presented to Mr. Mikhailoff on the occasion of his temporary retirement to the wilds of Siberia, is understood to have been the Emperor. At least, the Governor-General of St. Petersburg gave a thousand roubles, which he could not have offered without the Imperial permission, and which everyone said came from the Emperor himself; the chief object in making the gift having doubtless been to deprive of all significance the reflection upon the Government implied in getting up such a testimonial at all. It was suggested at the time that, instead of conferring the crown of political martyrdom on Mr. Mikhailoff, the Emperor would do well to treat him as revolutionary wild Irishmen are habitually treated in England—that is to say, to forgive him, and at the same time allow his absurd and immoral address to be published in the newspapers. It contains, perhaps, a certain infinitesimal portion of truth; but this is quite lost in the false, criminal, and utterly destructive views which it sets forth in every line. The Communistic tone of the address is such as must surprise an English reader; but the most simple, envious, and generally base form of socialism, after being scouted from England and taking refuge in France, and after being at last discarded even by the paradox-loving Proudhon, has still—indeed, now more than ever—hosts of admirers in Russia, where it is chiefly esteemed on the ground that it is original and native to the Russian soil.

The Communists one meets with in Russia are not, as with us, cobblers and tinkers out of work; you may find among them rich proprietors and plenty of officers of the Guard, riding chargers and wearing uniforms which together must have cost them something over a thousand pounds. As the Communists of the Guard do not sell their valuable chargers in order to buy carthorses for the peasants, and as the Communists of the landed interest divide their estates, not according to Owen, or St. Simon, or Fourier, but in conformity with the official regulations on the subject of emancipation, one cannot help thinking that there is something negative rather than positive in

Russian Communism, and that it simply means reaction, and protest against the system which placed all the property of the country at the mercy of one sovereign will.

Mr. Mikhailoff's address commences with an attack upon the Emperor for not emancipating the peasants during the Carnival of 1861, as though some connection existed between liberty and masquerading. It accuses him of not having given them "the kind of freedom which they had imagined and which was necessary for them" (that is to say, freedom to dispossess the proprietors of their land, without offering them any species of compensation), and of having "robbed them of their joy" by postponing their liberation until Lent. Moreover, the "people's party," which evidently includes Mr. Mikhailoff—for he himself describes it as "the most educated, most honest, and most able portion of Russian society"—was not consulted about the emancipation, but, on the contrary, was "treated with utter scorn" by the Emperor. "None of the people," we are told, "took part in it; journalism did not dare to squeak; the Emperor threw the people their freedom, as one throws a bone to a hungry dog, to quiet him for a moment and to save one's own calves.

"All this," continues the writer, "cannot and must not be forgiven. The people do not exist for the Government, but the Government for the people. The Romanoffs have evidently forgotten that they were chosen by the people (and did not fall from heaven) because they were thought more fit to govern than any Polish or Swedish kings; * and if they do not justify the expectations of the Empire, off with them! We do not want a power which offends us, which impedes our intellectual development, the civic and economical development of all the country. We have no need of a power whose motto is dissipation and self-interest. We need no Tsar, no Emperor, no Anointed of God, no ermine mantle covering hereditary incapacity, but a simple earthly man, understanding human life and the people by whom he is elected. We need no Emperor anointed in the Cathedral of the Assumption, but a chosen elder, receiving wages for his work. The emancipation of the serfs and the events of the last four years have shown that the new Government, as at present composed, and with the rights by which it now profits, is good for nothing."

The writer goes on to say that there is not one class which Imperial power does not offend, and that the last great offence was given when Im-

* Michael, the first of the Romanoffs, was elected by the nation (accepting with the crown a constitution) after the expulsion of the Poles from Moscow in 1612, and while Novgorod was still in possession of the Swedes.

perial power thought it was laying the foundation of a great Russia.

"We do not deny the importance of the fact expressed in the manifesto of the 19th of February," he continues, "but we do not see its importance where the Government sees it. The emancipation of the serfs is the first step either to a grand future or to immense misfortunes to Russia. It is for us to choose. The emancipation is important, because it has sown the seeds of general discontent towards the Government. We wish to remind Russia that the time has now come for her to treat the Government as the peasants of a certain estate in Tamboff treated their German stewards. When the manifesto of the emancipation was read to them, they harnessed horses to a cart, told the stewards very politely to get into it, and when they had driven them to the limits of the estate, said to them, also very politely, 'We are much obliged to you for having governed us, but now go: God be with you, and never come back here!'"

The Government has weakened its own power by weakening that of the proprietors, and Catherine understood what she was saying when she declared she was the principal proprietor in the Empire. In all Russian history despotism has only benefited the people once, "and that was when the reigning Emperor said 'Let the serfs be free,' and 100,000 proprietors bowed their readiness to obey his autocratic will." But this was the last flash of expiring despotism. Discontent is now in every breast, and everyone is expecting something to happen. If Alexander II. does not understand this and does not "yield to the people" while there is yet time, so much the worse for him.

The young generation are called upon "not to forget that we address ourselves principally to you; that in you only we see those who are capable of sacrificing personal interest for the happiness of the country at large," and, finally, "of saving Russia." They are to "tell the people that they have well-wishers, who wish them to possess land, and not that they should always be dependent upon proprietors, who wish to diminish their tributes and payments of all kinds, to establish truth on the judgment-seat, and to release the people from a superabundance of nurses and guardians."

Nor are the soldiers to be forgotten. They are to be told that they, too, have their well-wishers, "who desire them to have higher pay and shorter service, and to free them from the stick." The young generation are to explain this fully to the people and the soldiers, and must "not forget to add that the impediments to all this are the Emperor and his ministers, for whom it would not be profitable."

Some persons, we are afterwards told, "wish to make of Russia an England. But does Russia, by her geographical position, and her natural riches, resemble England? Would the English, if they had lived on Russian soil, have been what they are now? We have been the monkeys of France and Germany, quite enough, without aping England."

Mr. Mikhailoff little knew that he might be accused of "aping" Cobbett in recommending the employment of "a chosen elder receiving wages for work done" instead of an emperor. But it is only what is best in England that the foreign revolutionists, speaking generally, have learned to hate.

"As for the revolutionary attempts of 1848, they were failures only as regards Europe; and it by no means follows that a new order of things cannot be established in Russia. Are the economical and territorial conditions of Europe the same as ours? Do and can agricultural Communes exist there as here? Can every peasant and every citizen there be a landed proprietor? No: but in Russia they can. We have so much land that we have enough for tens of thousands of years. We are a nation behind other nations, and that is where our salvation lies. We must thank our fate that we have not lived the life of Europe. Her misfortunes and difficulties ought to be lessons to us. We do not want her aristocracy or her proletarianism, her formation into kingdoms, or her imperial power. We are like new settlers; we have nothing to break down. Let us leave our field of people at rest as it is, but we must weed out the rank grass which has sprung up from seed blown to us in the shape of German ideas of economy and government."

As Germany has her petty princes and France her Napoleons, while "America" is governed after quite a different fashion; so Russia can and must be organized quite differently from either America or any of the European States. "We do not want to divide our land according to foreign taste, or as land was divided before land became scarce in ancient times. We can act according to our own ideas in this matter, and that is why we are not afraid of the future, and go boldly forward to face revolutions. We even wish for them. We have faith in our young strength. We believe that we are destined to open a new era in history; that we have our own word to say, and are not called upon to follow Europe. . . . . If, in order to carry out our instinctive ideas and to divide the land among the people, it should be necessary to kill a hundred thousand proprietors, we should not be afraid to do so. And there is nothing frightful about it. Remember how many men we lost in the Polish and Hungarian wars for the caprice of Nicholas, without any advantage, and to the disgrace of the whole country. And is the nobility better than the working forces of the country? No: until now it has been their enemy."

Mr. Mikhailoff then asks what the aristocracy really is; whether it could get on without the labouring classes, and whether the labouring classes could not get on very well without it, supposing that it and all the court were suddenly to perish. "What," he inquires, "can a grand duke want with one hundred and thirty horses, when a better and more useful man can drive very well with a pair? Why should fifty millions a-year be spent on the court, when for a tenth part of the sum, men could be employed who would understand and work for the good of the country?" Finally, he recommends young men to form revolutionary circles, each among his own friends, and points out what a fine thing it would be if each of them could make only ten converts to the bloody creed preached by Mr. Mikhailoff. And if a few should be killed, why then they will have shared the fate of "the victims of the 14th of December" (December 26, 1825, new style), and, after all, they must die some day or other!

There is not an idea in Mr. Mikhailoff's "proclamation" (except, perhaps, the very original one that the Emperor "robbed the people of their joy" by not emancipating them during the Carnival) which had not been already expressed either in the writings and speeches of our western revolutionists or in M. Herzen's work *Du Développement des Idées*

Révolutionaires en Russie. After hearing the opinions, views, and the line of conduct expressly recommended by Mr. Mikhailoff, there are probably not many Englishmen who will think that he was a particularly fit object for a quasi-national testimonial, however much they may regret that his feeble malignity should have exposed him to a severe punishment.

Some time before Mr. Mikhailoff's affair, subscriptions had been got up in various parts of Russia, half privately, and also quite publicly in the assemblies of the nobility, in aid of young men prevented by the newly-imposed fees from continuing their studies at the Universities. This became so much the fashion at last, that proprietors of places of public entertainment took the hint, and at the Moscow Hermitage (a sort of Russian Cremorne) a *fête* was actually given last winter on a scale of unusual magnificence "for the benefit of the poor students." Love of learning had doubtless something to do with this movement, and personal sympathy for the students (after the utterly illegal and barbarous treatment which they had suffered at the hands of the soldiers and police) still more; but in many places it evidently proceeded from a strong feeling against the general policy of the Government, and, like the subscription for Mr. Mikhailoff, meant simply opposition. These negative evidences of a desire for some kind of reform were followed at the beginning of last year by positive demands from the nobility of various provinces for the formation of a representative assembly; the nobility of Moscow recommending, at the same time, the introduction of trial by jury, the abolition of the censorship, the full publication of the budget, and the immediate termination of the troublesome and alarming emancipation question, by assigning forthwith to proprietors and peasants their respective dues, and by making over to the latter, as absolute property, the land of which they have, hitherto, only enjoyed the usufruct. In Moscow, as soon as it was known that certain questions of provincial finance had been disposed of, and that speeches and propositions were to be made on subjects of vital importance, political amateurs flocked to the Assembly as eagerly and in as great numbers as theatrical amateurs do to the Opera House the nights that Lébédéva dances. On the whole, I still believe that the "Muscovites," as a body, care more for ballets than for Constitutions, and that an act of gross illegality committed by the Government would not raise their indignation so much as a solitary whistle directed by an idiotic theatre-goer against their favourite *danseuse*. Nevertheless, the galleries of the Assembly Hall of the nobility were crowded every day, and the speeches applauded, hissed, and discussed in all possible tones, so that the President every half-minute was obliged to request the silence of the auditory, which he did in the politest, and also in the most ineffectual, manner.

Downstairs, where, strictly speaking, the Moscow nobles ought alone to be admitted, but where it was easy to get introduced, were proprietors who had no estates in the Moscow province, and some of whom had come from a great distance and at great personal inconvenience, simply to see what Moscow meant to decide, and to influence the Moscow electors. All these visitors belong to the Liberal party, and are in favour of an address recommending the formation of a Legislative Chamber, to be composed, not of functionaries and Imperial nominees, but of representatives chosen by the provinces. It is quite certain that the Institution of the Committee of Ministers (which, by the way, had assembled and performed business for two years before its existence was formally and officially announced) has not only given no satisfaction, but has produced no impression of any kind on the Russians. All that you can get any of them to say about it is, that it is an old affair, that it is a thing of no consequence, that it may do no harm, but that it certainly can do no good, and so on. In support of their assertions they point to the similar committee, called in the official translations "*de rédaction*," to which was intrusted the comparison of the various provincial projects, and the preparation of a final general project for the emancipation of the serfs. "The members of this committee," they say, "were clever, ingenious, hard-working, conscientious men, for the most part functionaries highly educated, but not practically acquainted with the details of village life in Russia. Their scheme for improving the condition of the peasants is like a piece of watchwork, only it is like watch-work that won't go. A General Assembly formed from among the proprietors, and with a certain amount of representation secured also to the peasants, might have produced a scheme capable at least of being put into practice." Indeed, centralization and bureaucracy find no favour in the eyes of Russians of any class (except, of course, the bureaucrats themselves); and the most intelligent of the proprietors say calmly, but decidedly enough, that what they require above all is such an amount of "self-government" (the expression has been quite adopted in Russia) as the peasants already enjoy in their village communes, and consequently an entire change in the Administration, and in the recently-established committee system, which leaves important reforms affecting the whole Empire to bodies of officials nominated at St. Petersburg.

There are committees for reforming everything in the Empire, from the army to the censorship, and from the banking system (or rather the absence of it) to the distribution of taxes; but, in the meanwhile, the Empire itself is not consulted, directly or indirectly, as to its own wants, and, as the committees are not allowed to meet together, it is thought probable that in many instances they may be working at cross purposes.

In the meanwhile there is not one class in Russia which is not discontented—as far as mere discontent can possibly go—with the existing system. The peasant possesses neither the personal liberty promised to him, nor the free use of land which, though never promised to him, he always expected to obtain. The proprietor, after being assured by the Emperor that his right to the whole of his land was inviolable, finds himself obliged to cede, as a general rule, two-thirds of his estate to peasants who do not perform the conditions on which it has been granted to them, and concerning which the proprietors were never seriously consulted beforehand. The functionaries are all insufficiently paid, and the best of them are highly dissatisfied with their position—on account, perhaps, of the growing conviction that it is mean to take bribes, while the fact still remains that officials must live, and that the Government does not give them nearly enough to live upon. The merchants are absurd enough to blame the Government for the unfavourable rate of exchange, and for the utter stagnation into which Russian commerce has sunk. The educated non-nobles, together with many noble young Radicals and Communists, complain that the Government consults the nobility alone on changes which equally interest the other classes. The personal enemies of emancipation are still full of bitterness against the Emperor for having diminished their incomes. Indeed, whatever other wants the Russians may have just now, it is quite certain that all classes complain very much of want of cash. Some few take a high ground in their lamentations, and say that Russia has no longer any influence in the councils of Europe; but a great many proprietors go straight to the point, and tell you that they received no money last year from their estates, and that they are not at all sure that they will get any this year. The merchants say that no one pays them, that no one *can* pay them (if you have no commercial dealings with them), and that it is not easy for any merchant in Russia to avoid bankruptcy.

In the meanwhile, however, the great people of Moscow are evidently not on the verge of starvation. I hear stories of the ladies in some of the provincial towns having sworn a solemn and touching vow to have no more than three silk dresses in their wardrobes, and of the number of dinner parties being limited to so many *per* family throughout the winter; but the well-born and highly well-born nobility still contrive, somehow or other, to live in the old style. Numerous families have, it is true, sent away a large number of useless servants —emancipated, and with perfect liberty to get employment, which they cannot obtain. But, to speak only of public and striking facts, it is certain that there is no diminution this year in the number of magnificent sledges and admirable horses seen in the streets of Moscow; that the Orlovsky trotters, of which the horse-fancying nobles are so justly proud, are as rapid and as spirited as ever, and receive evidently their proper allowance of corn (though oats, I am told, with many a sigh, are this year twice as dear as they were last); and that you can only get a box at the opera as a favour, the subscription-list being completely full, and at prices which would make many a Western *impresario* tear his hair with envy and rage.

The great theatre of the day, however, is the Assembly, and the places are all taken at an early hour to witness the really exciting performances of the 360 nobles of Moscow. The nobility of the provinces includes a large number of individuals, but only 360 are electors; the others have a right to be present and even to make speeches, but cannot vote.

The tumult in the hall is excessive. There are thirteen tables, one for each district, furnished with ballot-boxes, writing materials, and secretaries; around which thirteen little assemblies of great talkers are formed. The great crowd of electors, however, is gathered round the table at the head of the room, where the Marshal of the Government (*quasi* sheriff of the county) presides. At this table the orators read their written orations; not one of them makes a speech in the proper sense of the word, and I naturally ask whether the Government requires, as a measure of precaution, that every one who addresses the Assembly should first put his words upon paper. Nothing of the kind. Every one may say what he pleases, only the Moscow nobles are literally "unaccustomed to public speaking," and cannot speak in public. "You should hear us at Tver and Vladimir," say some visitors in black, proprietors in provinces where the nobles are notoriously liberal, and where they appear already to be cultivating Parliamentary habits; "there we make speeches an hour long, and some of the speakers have really something to say."

When an address or written speech is unusually tiresome, there is a general movement towards the refreshment tables and the smoking-rooms. There is some resemblance, then, after all, between the Moscow Assembly and the British House of Commons.

When I have been some time in the smoking-room, a newly-made acquaintance asks me whether there is anything else I should like to see. I reply that I should like to see a Russian country gentleman,—not a General who has estates, nor a functionary who has estates, nor a St. Petersburg man of society, who, like the others, knows his estates only by what they produce; nor an habitual absentee of French or English sympathies and tastes, nor an ignorant boor, who has estates and nothing else—but a Russian gentleman, occupying himself, above all, with the cultivation and improvement of his land, understanding the wants of Russian agriculture, attending, also, to the wants of his peasants, interesting himself in all that concerns the welfare of his country, and looking to the Government, not for personal advancement, but only for that legitimate protection which at present it does not afford. My friend cannot at the moment remember the address of any such person, and thinks he might have some trouble in finding him in the Moscow Assembly. He divides the Russian nobility into the educated and liberal, and the more or less educated and illiberal, and says that among the better half there are English Russians, and French Russians, and St. Petersburg Russians, and Russian-University Russians, who have passed good literary and scientific examinations, but who are scarcely equal to the management of an estate as under the new conditions it ought to be managed; that, as for

Russian Russians, they are scarce, and he wishes there were more with so much earnestness that I begin to fancy, and at last find out, that he himself is one of them. At the present moment, however, what he chiefly regrets is that there is no sort of *esprit de corps* among the nobility—not only of Russia generally, but not even among that of the Moscow "Government." Some of the young men think it chivalrous to preach communism and democracy, and to claim the right of representation for peasants who have scarcely yet ceased to be serfs; other very antiquated ones think only of their recent losses, and, if they dared to do such a thing, would not be ashamed to petition the Emperor to re-establish serfdom. Between these extremes men of all shades of opinion are found. Individuals do not agree, and naturally the districts will be at variance in the answers to be returned to the Minister's five questions. There is not a noble in the Assembly who is not discontented, and yet the Assembly cannot find out as a body what it is that the nobility wants.

Some one says, half in earnest, that if the debates become too tumultuous, and are prolonged beyond a certain time, it is just possible that the Government may close the Assembly. And if so, I ask, could the nobles of Moscow do a bit more than the students of St. Petersburg did when the

University was shut up? It is impossible to deny that they would find themselves in precisely the same position. The outside public, not being absolutely idiotic, cares nothing for the nobility. Certain members of it are undoubtedly very accomplished, estimable, and patriotic men; but as a class it has done nothing for Russia, except in time of war, when nobles, peasants, and all classes have always been ready to sacrifice themselves for their country, or for the Tsar, who is their country personified.

While the Assembly was sitting a discussion was kept up in the Moscow journals on the subject of the nobility, and the propriety of maintaining it as a separate caste, with all its existing exemptions and privileges. To describe the arguments on both sides in a few words, I may say that *Nashe Vremya* (*Our Time*), was in favour of keeping up the nobility as a class apart, on the ground that such a class was necessary in the country until a *tiers état* should have formed itself. The *Russki Vestnik* (*Russian Messenger*), which is nothing if not Conservative (but in the English sense of the word), maintained that a respectable *tiers état* would never form itself as long as the nobility existed as a privileged order, and that all privileges of nobility ought to be abolished, when a true aristocracy, owing its power to its natural position and to the leadership which it ought to assume and to be able to keep, might flourish side by side with a gentry (the small proprietors of the present day), and a self-respecting middle class, whose members would not be incessantly striving by means of State service to become "nobles," but would be content, when they had raised themselves above some of their equals, to remain and give importance to the general body.

After a sitting of three weeks the labours of the Moscow Assembly of the Nobility may be said to have amounted to this: The Assembly voted an address, *proprio motu*, to the Emperor on the critical position of the country, and it replied at length to five questions proposed to it by the Minister of the Interior.

The following is a translation of the address:—

"The Moscow nobility, full of sincere love for its native land, has had the good fortune to prove it more than once by its services to the Empire in moments of heavy trial. The memorable year 1812, and the arrival of the august Monarch whose name you bear in the ancient capital, when the enemy had unexpectedly crossed the precincts of the Empire, are still fresh in our recollection. With confidence in the sympathy of Moscow, the Emperor Alexander appealed to our nobility, and called upon it to save the country. The voice of the Emperor penetrated the hearts of his loyal subjects.

"In a few hours money, troops, and the whole

of Russia were at his disposal. Our nation came out gloriously from the struggle, and the Empire became stronger than ever. But then it was threatened by an external enemy; it is threatened now by a not less menacing danger from within. In every rank of society there is some sort of departure from law, and, in their true meaning, the laws are not observed. Neither persons nor property have any protection against the will of the Administration. Classes have risen one against another, and the enmity between them grows greater and greater in consequence of individual discontent, together with a general fear of a pecuniary catastrophe from a Government financial crisis, indicated already by the instability of the unit of reckoning, an utter absence of credit, and, finally, by a multiplicity of false rumours which convulse the public mind. Such, in a few words, is the present state of things, and the Moscow nobility thinks it its duty to address the Emperor on the subject. The corner-stone on which all these evils rested—the right of holding serfs—has been taken away and destroyed, but much has yet to be done in order to reset the shaken edifice of the State on substantial foundations. To eradicate the bad, and to march in front, after its Emperor, in the path of peaceful reforms, such as shall satisfy the existing wants of society, restore a full measure of order, and avert, even in the future, all possible disturbances,—

this is the desire of the Moscow nobility; and it addresses its Emperor in all confidence, and submits to his gracious inspection the following measures as calculated to rescue the country from its present difficult position:—

"1. A greater extension to appointment by election in the Government service, and also to local self-government. At the same time, there must be a more strict fulfilment of the law, not only by the subordinates, but also by the superior officials, with strict responsibility before the law for every one in the Government service, each one being held accountable for his own actions.

"2. Protection for the rights of person and property of all the citizens (*sic*) of the Empire, through the introduction of oral evidence in judicial proceedings, and of trial by jury.

"3. The termination of the present antagonistic attitude between nobles and peasants, through the compulsory and immediate apportionment of the land, when the regulation-charts are given in; the Government making itself responsible for the *obrok* and for the redemption money, with a guarantee of 80 per cent. on the entire sum.*

* The regulation charts (*oustavnie gramota* in Russian, *charte réglementaire* in French) show what land on each estate is given up to the peasants for their use, and as property purchasable by fixed annual payments, and what land is retained absolutely by the proprietor. All the regulation charts ought to have been given in a year ago, but it was difficult to get the

"4. The publication of the Government debt and of the Government revenue and expenditure, so that the public mind may be quieted as to the prospect of a financial crisis.

"5. The freest discussion in print concerning reforms of all kinds, in connection with the forthcoming economical and administrative reforms.

"These are the measures to promote the welfare of our country.

"Your Imperial Majesty has more than once addressed in full confidence your faithful nobility, which has always answered with readiness to its Emperor's call. More than once, Emperor, you have said to us, 'I trust in you—trust in me;' and the nobility has always, in entire faith, awaited the completion of the good beginnings of its Tsar. In the present difficult moment it is ready again to stand staunchly by the Russian throne, and with all its force to co-operate with its Emperor in the fulfilment of his good intentions. With this view the Moscow nobility begs your Imperial Majesty, most loyally, to choose from among its body a committee for the consideration

peasants to sign them. The *obrok* may be looked upon now merely as the legal rent to be paid by the peasant for the land made over to him for his use. Former serfs who have no land will pay no *obrok*. Many proprietors assure me that those who have land will not pay it either. To force them to do so is very nearly impossible.

of the principles which ought to lie at the basis of the future laws on election; also of laws on the taxation of land, on the establishment of land-credit institutions, and on the necessary reforms in judicial proceedings. As these questions interest and concern all the territorial and other classes, the result of the committee's labours should be examined in a General Assembly, convened from all the provinces, at Moscow, the heart of Russia; the views of the persons chosen from all classes in the Empire being afterwards submitted to the inspection of your Imperial Majesty."

I heard this address read, and can testify to the excitement it produced, and the immense applause it received in a crowded assembly. When balloted for, it obtained 306 white balls, the entire number of nobles qualified to vote amounting to 362. The introduction caused prodigious enthusiasm among the old generals, many of whom seemed quite ancient enough to have served in the campaign of 1812, and the description of the actual state of the country called forth murmurs of sympathy from all parts of the hall. Nor were the eminently loyal passages less approved; and if the Moscow nobility—ladies as well as gentlemen—could "save the country" by clapping their hands, the country is already saved, and Russia is henceforth firmly established as a constitutional State.

It must have surprised many persons in the West

of Europe to find that political machinery already existed in Russia, by which large bodies of land-owners could communicate their views to the Crown. It has existed, however, since the reign of Catherine, though little advantage has been taken of it until during the last twelve months. Under the Emperor Nicholas the Russian nobles seem to have gone quietly enough to Siberia when they were sent there. Nor did their order make any endeavours to procure the substitution of a system of legality for the mere arbitrary rule which was a standing menace to all. There seems to have been no *esprit de corps* among them; at least, they never manifested any, except, perhaps, in certain conspiracies, between which and total political inaction no medium appears to have been known. The Assemblies of the nobility, instead of reaching new developments, became more insignificant with each succeeding reign, and under the Emperor Nicholas they might as well have not existed for any political importance that they possessed. The nobles still met and elected "marshals," whose duty, theoretically speaking, it was to represent the wants of their constituents to the Sovereign, but who, in practice, were only expected to give good dinner parties and balls. After the emancipation of the serfs, however, it became vitally important for the nobility to examine the new position in which this important measure placed them. A new class of free peasants, possessing a perfect system of self-government in their village communes was being formed beneath them; a class, numbering 23,000,000, in presence of which the nobility, with its merely nominal privileges, must in time lose all *prestige* unless endowed with a sufficient amount of political power to enable it to keep its natural place at the head of society. It had to choose, moreover, between retaining certain exemptions and exclusive rights of no real importance, but which are calculated to excite the envy of those not belonging to the nobiliary order, and resigning these "privileges" while demanding "franchises" for the great body of the nation, upon qualifications quite irrespective of title and birth.

The triennial assembly of the nobility of Moscow was to be held in January, and the Minister of the Interior, Mr. Volouieff, knowing what the nature of the discussions would be, endeavoured to give them a direction of his own, by proposing certain special questions and warning the members against considering any others. However, to very narrow questions very wide answers may be returned, and Mr. Volouieff's precautions proved quite unavailing in the face of the determination of the Moscow nobility to make themselves heard. He begs them not, on any account, to present an address; and they present one which, with all its expressions of loyalty, is couched in such language as no legally-recognized representative assembly in a constitutional country would like to use in approaching its Sovereign. They hear doubts expressed as to the existence of any *esprit de corps* among them and vote the said address by the immense majority of 306 over 56. The Government, through a journal of its own, published in Moscow, *Nashe Vremya* (Our Time), invites, and urges them, in a series of articles, to keep all their privileges; and they reply by asking that the right of representation (the only privilege worth mentioning which the Russian nobility still possess) may be extended to all classes. Finally, the Government seems to be of opinion that the majority for the address may be deprived of its importance if a larger minority can be secured against the answers to the five questions, and invites voters on the latter subject to inscribe their names on paper bulletins and throw them into the ballot-boxes, instead of the usual white and black balls; the consequence of which last step is to swell the Constitutional majority to such an extent that it is found unnecessary to ballot at all, and the answers are adopted by acclamation.

Then, a gentleman from Smolensk, who is also qualified to vote in the province of Moscow, begged hard, but in vain, to be allowed to read a paper signed by himself and twenty of his personal friends, in which the Emperor is complimented in an ironical strain on the sacrifices he has made for the serfs at the expense of the proprietors. "The Gospel teaches us," says one passage in this extraordinary production (chapter and verse not cited), "to deprive ourselves, if necessary, of our coat in order to clothe the poor. You have done more than this, sire, you have deprived us of two coats, and have given them both to the peasant."

A memoir by Mr. Bezobrazoff was not only listened to and applauded, but put to the vote, and adopted, not finally, but simply as worthy of discussion. What appears to have pleased the Assembly in it was the general freedom of the views expressed, the author's notions of what is good for *his* class being very different indeed from those he entertains in connection with the wants of the merchants and peasants. Ultimately, however, it was decided that the propositions contained in Mr. Bezobrazoff's paper could not be entertained by the Assembly at all, and, in spite of much hard fighting on the part of the author, it was rejected.

It was expected at one time that the address from Zvenigorod, adopted unanimously by the nobles of that district, would be also voted by the Assembly of the province; but, after the large majority gained by the other address (from the district of Podolsk), it was thought useless to put it to the vote. It is worthy of observation that, whereas the nobles of Podolsk were struck by the similarity of Russia's position in 1862 and in 1812, those of Zvenigorod were equally impressed with the parallelism existing between the Russia of to-day and Russia after Moscow had been occupied by the Poles in 1812. The conclusion of the Zvenigorod address was as follows:—

"The nobles, after examining the questions proposed by the Government, have come to the conclusion that they must all, and especially the first two, be looked upon not as local provincial questions, but as questions of State; and as they do not concern the interests of any one class, but of all the country, the only advice the nobles can offer to the Government at the present juncture is, that it should resort to the measure which has always been adopted in Russia in extreme cases, both by the people and the Crown—namely, the formation at Moscow, the natural centre of the country, of a National Representative Assembly, chosen from all classes and from all parts of the Empire. Our national history teaches us that important political and civil changes in the life of the people have been effected through the joint exertions of the representatives of all classes chosen in local assemblies. Thus, in 1613, when Russia, after the expulsion of the Poles from Moscow, found itself exhausted not only by the foreigner's invasion, but also by internal disturbances which had accompanied the invasion throughout; when it found itself without a Tsar, and without a Government, a Zemskoi Sabor * was gathered together at Moscow, when it raised to the throne, by the will of the people, of whom he was the representative, the ancestor of the reigning house of Romanoff, Michael Feodorovitch. So also the Empress Catherine II., desiring to give new laws to her people, assembled a committee composed of the representatives of all the classes in the Empire.

"Even if the five questions now proposed were decided, that would not satisfy the demands of the country; for, in consequence of such an important change as the emancipation of the serfs, it is absolutely necessary that there should be an alteration of the laws in many respects, and the questions connected therewith are not five but many more, and equally important. Is it just, for instance, that among the classes composing the landed interest, unequal rights should exist? The peasants liberated from serfdom may assemble whenever the village commune requires it, while the nobles and persons of other classes are not allowed to do so. Is it just, too, that the agricultural classes should not all take part in choosing those persons whose

* An historical expression, which is now in every one's mouth in Russia, and which may be rendered in English, "Assembly of the Country," — representing all classes and conditions.

actions and decisions concern them all?* This distinction, depriving some of that natural right by which others already profit, plants between classes an animosity which may bear bitter fruit. For that reason, the nobles think it their bounden duty to state their conviction that the existing evil can only be rooted out after the Zemskoi Sabor, representing the views and wishes of all classes, shall have fully examined and considered the wants of the country, so that new institutions and laws, suited to the actual condition of the Empire, may be formed. It is not to be doubted but that, in such a widely-spread Empire as Russia, different requirements will be expressed in different localities, and the Zemskoi Sabor, in deciding questions concerning the whole Empire, ought to frame laws so as to make them, as far as possible, applicable to all possible events; therefore, the nobility considers it absolutely necessary that before the Zemskoi Sabor begins its labours, an assembly, composed of representatives of all classes, be formed in each province, whose duty it will be to examine in what the local wants caused by the recent changes consist, and in what manner they are expressed. Thus, valuable

* The justices of the peace, or peace-arbiters, specially appointed for the decision of disputes between peasants and proprietors, but whose functions in time are intended to have a wider range, are at present chosen in each province by the governor from a list presented by the nobles.

and absolutely necessary materials will be prepared for the consideration of the Zemskoi Sabor."

After the adoption of the address from the Podolsk district, attention was called to the fact that the Government, in its redemption operations,* pays the proprietor in bills bearing interest, which the Government itself refuses when they are offered in repayment of money advanced by the Crown on mortgage. It was resolved that a memorial should be drawn up on the subject, and submitted to the Minister of the Interior, but that no mention of it should be introduced into the address to the Emperor on the general state of the country.

But the most remarkable, and certainly the shortest, speech of all those delivered at the Moscow Assembly was an oration in half-a-dozen words, pronounced by a certain member. A great discussion was going on as to the propriety of the nobles retaining their privileges. Suddenly, the member in question rose on behalf of the minority, and commenced, "The Emperor Nicholas, in his wisdom," when a roar of laughter burst forth from all parts of the hall. The speaker started afresh, and had got as far as "The Emperor Nicholas," when

* If a commune of peasants can pay 20 per cent. on the arbitrarily-fixed value of the land assigned to it for cultivation, the Government will advance the remaining 80 per cent. The proprietor receives a quantity of paper, and the peasant a quantity of land.

cries of "Silence!" were raised, and what the late Emperor Nicholas thought on the subject of the Russian nobility (among whom there is scarcely a family of importance that did not, during the last reign, have some one of its members sent to Siberia) remains a secret with the said speaker, who was not allowed to speak.

Just when the deliberations of the Assembly were drawing to a close—after a meeting of three weeks' duration—it occurred to Mr. Bezobrazoff that the address to the Emperor had been adopted only for discussion, and that to be adopted finally it must be balloted for again. He observed, at the same time, that its propositions were far from being in conformity with the spirit of the Russian monarchy, of which one of the essential conditions was that nobles alone should possess the right of electing certain officers, and of addressing representations to the Crown. The project of calling together a Zemskoi Sabor, representing all classes, was not only in flagrant disaccord with actual principles of government, but was in itself bad, inasmuch as the lower classes had not yet attained a sufficient degree of development to be able to profit by electoral rights.

Mr. Bezobrazoff was replied to by Mr. Pavloff (ex-member of the central committee for the preparation of the scheme of emancipation), Mr. Naoumoff, of Podolsk (author of the address to the Emperor), and Prince Alexander Shtcherbatoff (marshal of the district of Vereia). They explained that the address had been adopted by the Assembly, and must be sent to the Emperor; and that, as regarded the nobles retaining their exclusive privileges of representation, it was to their own interest to resign them, or rather to extend them; that the nobility, by its exemptions and privileges, had sufficiently excited the jealousy of other classes already, and that it must aim now at union with, and not separation from, the classes below it.

"Let it remain as it is," said one of the speakers, "if it wishes to be crushed between the Crown and the people."

Prince Shtcherbatoff argued, in the same sense, that there was no salvation for the nobility unless it made itself the representative of the general interests of the country, and admitted the deputies of all classes to the deliberations of the new Assembly which must shortly be formed. It was also shown that the Zemskoi Sabor was not foreign to the spirit of the Russian Government, but, on the contrary, that it was an historical institution in Russia, and in times of difficulty had always been referred to.

Mr. Bezobrazoff still maintained that the best elements of Russian life entered into the nobility; and that its power was joyfully acquiesced in by the people.

Count Orloff Davidoff observed that the supporters of the address seemed to think they had got hold of something very like the English constitution, but that one of the best things in the English Constitution—the House of Lords—was omitted. This nobleman (who was one of the leaders of the Opposition at Moscow, to the scheme of emancipation*) afterwards suggested something in the style of the Swedish Constitution, and argued that it was absolutely necessary to keep up the nobility, as a class, apart.

In proof of the rapid progress made by the Russians, not during the last few years, but during the last few days of the meeting of the Moscow nobility, it may be observed that the very men who, at the commencement of the meeting, had lamented their inability to speak in public, found that they could speak with great effect as soon as it became absolutely necessary for them to answer, extemporaneously, the arguments adduced against their written propositions. All the most animated speeches were made on the subject of the nobility, considered as a privileged class, and the only nobles who spoke at any length in favour of preserving

* It ought to be remembered, however, that no one in Moscow opposed the personal emancipation of the peasants. A minority of the nobility were in favour of emancipating the peasant with his land; the great majority were in favour of the proprietor keeping his land, and of making the peasant merely a free agricultural labourer.

such an order were Count Orloff Davidoff (who, by the way, was educated, not in Russia, but at the University of Edinburgh) and Mr. Bezobrazoff.

It having been decided that the address had been legally adopted by the Assembly, Mr. Naoumoff (apparently the leader of the Constitutional party in this improvised Parliament of Moscow) proceeded to read the answers to the Minister's five questions. The answer to the first, and infinitely the most important (on the subject of "service by election"), after some preliminary remarks, presents the following proposition :—

"The spirit of election is inherent in the spirit of the Russian people. It has been worked out in its history, and all classes of society profit by it even now, though in unequal degrees."

It is then pointed out that, though corporations of merchants and communes of peasants possess on many points the right of self-government, the will of an irresponsible Administration too often counteracts the good that might result from such a system, and that neither they, nor even the nobility in their assemblies, take part in the formation of Government laws. The class of free peasants who manage their own village affairs without being interfered with by the Administration, has lately been increased by 10,000,000 (counting male serfs lately emancipated alone) and, as few peasants are qualified to exercise judicial functions, it is suggested that in exercising their right of electing judges, they should be allowed to choose them from among any class, instead of being confined, as at present, to their own.

After a sketch of the development of electoral privileges in Russia, comes a proposition for forming a General Representative Assembly, "even if it be allowed only a consultative voice," and for admitting landholders and other proprietors not actually belonging to the nobility to the Provincial Assemblies on the same footing as the existing class of nobles.

The "general conclusion" is as follows:—

"As those questions concern the whole Empire, and not any particular locality, therefore not one province alone, but not even all the provinces of the Empire working separately, can assume to decide them fully and in all their bearings. All they can do is to prepare materials by investigating local requirements and wants.

"The Moscow nobility, then, think it absolutely necessary to ask the Government to hear the voice of Russia, and to summon deputies from the provinces to participate in the formation of a decisive law on the subject of elections, the law of rural taxation, and to examine in all its aspects the question of land banks, the necessity of the whole country electing representatives in due proportion, so as to do away with the predominance of one class over another, protection being secured to the chosen representatives, so as to give increased value to their opinions and votes. It is only in such a manner that a legislation, the materials of which will have been elaborated by the people whom it concerns, can satisfy the general requirements of society, and not prove practically in disaccord with the conditions of actual life.

"Finally, the Moscow nobles think it their duty to express their most loyal gratitude to His Imperial Majesty for the confidence reposed in them in the present instance, and venture to trust that they will not be deprived of it on future occasions."

Having been adopted by acclamation, the five answers were signed by Mr. Voiekoff, the marshal of the Moscow province, and the thirteen marshals of the Moscow districts, as representing the entire Assembly. The opposition of two or three (to which the minority in favour of nobiliary privileges had now dwindled) continued to protest, and even went so far as to behave uncivilly to Mr. Voiekoff, after which the Assembly broke up.

The answers were forwarded to the Minister of the Interior, to be submitted by him to His Imperial Majesty. The address was sent to the Emperor direct, but its receipt was never acknowledged.

Before taking leave of the Moscow Assembly, I may observe that the views expressed by it with such remarkable unanimity, Radical and revolutionary as they would have been considered a few years ago, are now those of the Conservative party in Russia. With the exception of a certain number of confirmed bureaucrats, indifferent to all political creeds, the Government, as upholding the existing system, has no supporters. The Conservatives, however, wish for a strong Government, reposing upon the confidence of the nation, which the actual Government is far from possessing, and which it can only gain by passing good laws, and then enforcing obedience to them.

By the side of this Conservative exists a dangerous and destructive Communistic party, who out-Proudhon Proudhon, and are the sworn enemies of superiority of every kind. According to the meanest men of this party, the time has not yet come for establishing deliberative assemblies in Russia, simply because the nobles, as forming the only enlightened class of any magnitude in the Empire, would alone be able to make their voices heard. The fact that the nobles wish the representatives of all classes to be consulted, and to admit all landed proprietors to the same electoral rights as belong now to the nobility alone, does not, from the above point of view, alter the question in the least. The most enlightened men in the Empire would still take the lead.

Soon after the convocation of the Moscow nobility, the nobility of St. Petersburg, and of various other provinces, were called together by Imperial summons, to express their opinion on the subject of "land credit institutions" and the best means of establishing them. At St. Petersburg, as at Moscow, the Assembly took a wide view of the question submitted to its consideration, and ingeniously argued that land societies and banks could not be established without confidence in the Government, and that confidence could not be reposed in the Government until it granted a constitution. This process of reasoning being tacitly accepted by all the nobles of the St. Petersburg province, the real subject of discussion at the Assembly became representative institutions, the question of land banks being thrown quite to the background.

The St. Petersburg was as different, externally speaking, from the Moscow Assembly, as the one city, half-western in its appearance, is unlike the other, so thoroughly Russian. In the free and easy Moscow there was an utter absence of methodism about the parliamentary proceedings. Visitors were admitted into the body of the hall, and were only excluded from the central arena in which all the political fighting took place. The electors stood, sat, walked to and fro, talked all at once, laughed, declaimed, rushed into violent gesticulation, and, in short, went far to give one the idea that if it only were held in the open air, the meeting of the Moscow nobility would be not unlike the war council of some early German tribe. It was a primitive, picturesque scene, and although a great deal was said that could not, amid the murmuring of three or four hundred voices, possibly be heard by a general listener, there was meaning in the bustle that was going on, and the result of all the familiar conversation was something approaching very closely to unanimity. Three hundred and sixty proprietors dispersed over an immense province like that of Moscow must, after all, have a good deal to say to one another when they meet only once in three years, especially at such a critical time as the present. Moreover, the debates were conducted with due order and system as soon as a regular proposition was brought before the Assembly; but, until then, the utmost liberty of speech and action was allowed to every one, and to every one at the same time.

In St. Petersburg, on the other hand, there was a careful observance of parliamentary forms—

to such an extent that the Assembly was rarely addressed by more than two persons simultaneously, while, on the whole, the members behaved as if thoroughly acquainted with parliamentary usages, and as if Russia had been a parliamentary country from the beginning, and never anything else.

In Moscow, the "floor of the house" was scattered over with chairs, which the noble electors seemed to take pleasure in pushing about as much as possible. In the St. Petersburg Assembly, there were no chairs, but rows of benches, covered with red cloth, and symmetrically disposed so as to form three sides of a square, the fourth being represented by the table of marshals—nine marshals of districts, and the "grand marshal" of the province (Count Schouvaloff). The latter dignitary presided, and tinkled a little bell when he had any communication to make to the Assembly, and, generally, as a signal for silence. The praiseworthy notion of arranging the assemblies, so as to render it possible to speak in them with a fair chance of being heard, is said to have been started and first carried out at Tver, where the nobles are not Constitutionalists "of the morrow," and where, moreover, numbers of them hastened to give liberty and land to their peasants at a time when the emancipation of the serfs was far from finding favour in the eyes of many of those proprietors who are now so clamorous in their demands for an emancipation of the rest of the population.

The St. Petersburg nobility, it is true, was by no means slow in responding to the Imperial proposition for "ameliorating the condition of the peasants," and it is, perhaps, in a similar spirit of loyalty that it has shown, during its recent deliberations, a determination not to press any fundamental changes in the system of government on the Emperor, as long as there seems to be a chance of something in the nature of the reforms now everywhere demanded being proposed by His Majesty himself. All the Assembly did in this matter was to postpone its rough project of a constitution for a twelvemonth; and this year—unless, in the meantime, extraordinary and almost impossible concessions are made by the Crown—it ought to be brought forward again at the provincial elections, when, to a certainty, it would be adopted by an immense majority.

To return to the external part of the St. Petersburg Assembly: no one was allowed to enter the body of the hall, except those who had a right to sit there and vote. Visitors were admitted (by tickets only) to the galleries, and the first symptoms of applause manifested by them were instantly checked by the President. The public seemed inclined to applaud a good deal the first day; and one gentleman, who was particularly enthusiastic in expressing his admiration of a certain speaker, was rewarded for his pains by being cordially thanked and almost embraced by a lady, overflowing with animation and gratitude, who chanced to be sitting next to him, and who turned out to be the said speaker's wife. Perhaps it was on the motion of this almost too successful orator, that plaudits were afterwards strictly interdicted among the public.

In the centre of the gallery, facing the table of marshals and immediately opposite the President's chair, was a place of honour, reserved for a personage whom the Russians have every right to regard as a good judge of parliamentary proceedings—namely, the British Ambassador. Lord Napier was a frequent visitor at the Assembly (as who in St. Petersburg that took the slightest interest in Russian political movements was not?); and, if the correspondent of one of the Belgian newspapers is to be believed, he was accompanied every day by a newly-invented functionary called a "*traducteur-sténographe*"—for which read, simply an attaché who understands Russian. Fortunately, it was easy to ascertain what the St. Petersburg nobles wanted, and what they were determined not to have, without the aid of any sort of stenography, inasmuch as the principal speeches delivered at the Assembly could be obtained in writing from the speakers. One "memoir" read at the commencement of the meeting was lithographed, and was known in Moscow as well as in St. Petersburg to every one, except exclusive readers of official journals, the day after its presentation—indeed, to some few the day before.

The minor observations made by numerous short-winded speakers on such special subjects as liberty of the press and trial by jury, however true, were not new, except, of course, that they were all very new indeed for St. Petersburg, or rather for a St. Petersburg public assembly. It was rather novel, too, to see princes, counts, generals, and courtiers of various kinds, striving who could go the furthest in the path of reform, and to hear them loudly declaiming what a very few years ago they would not have dared (or perhaps even have cared) to whisper. If one said that the press ought to be free, another rose and added, "Yes, free in all respects." Then came a suggestion that freedom of the press was worth nothing and meant nothing, unless press offences were tried before a jury. "The jury, by all means; but what is a jury without advocates?" "And what are advocates, unless they possess full liberty to say all they think fit on behalf of their clients under the approval of the judge?" "And what are judges unless they are made independent of the Administration?"

Thus, one question led to another, until at last it

became evident that in the opinion of the Russians there was not one good institution actually existing in Russia; that moderate or partial reforms were past thinking of, and, in short, that the whole edifice of the State was unsound.

When some one mentioned the now tolerably well-known fact (it appears to have been cited repeatedly at every meeting of the nobility which has been held this last winter in Russia), that the first of the Romanoffs was elected to the throne by a general representative assembly, the remark was made that "If a representative assembly could do nothing better than *that*——." The end of the observation is sufficiently obvious.

The arguments advanced against the formation of an "Assembly" or Council of the Country* by Mr. Nicolas Bezobrazoff, were similar, if not precisely the same, as those which he made use of, without success, at Moscow and elsewhere. This loud-toned and eloquent, and, by force of repetition, somewhat tiresome champion of the privileges of an official nobility which no one respects is, of course, a disbeliever in the natural influence of a genuine aristocracy. "Keep up our nobiliary chart," he exclaims, in the Assembly of every province where he possesses an estate. "As for a

* "Assembly of the Country" (*Zemskoi Sabor*). In St. Petersburg the same thing is called "*Zemskaia Douma*,"—*douma* signifying "council."

system of general representation, the country is not ready for it, and does not desire it; while, on the other hand, it would be delighted to see the nobility maintain the privileges which still belong to it, and which it will be only too glad to exercise for the good of all classes."

An immense majority of the St. Petersburg nobles showed that they were not by any means of Mr. Bezobrazoff's way of thinking; but an ironical smile of assent passed over the faces of all present whenever, in mentioning the Emperor Nicholas (which occurred several times), he coupled very pointedly with the name of the late Tsar the amusing official epithet of "never-to-be-forgotten."

Either Mr. Bezobrazoff or some other speaker on the same side, in considering the propriety of admitting the representation of all classes to a deliberative assembly, observed, amid general laughter, that such a scheme would give the merchants and peasants entirely their own way, inasmuch as they could vanquish the gentlemen of the assembly by brute force, and, coming half-drunk into the council chamber, would simply pitch into them, and turn them out! With what love (according to this view) the inferior classes in Russia must regard the nobility; and how enchanted they must be that for *their* benefit it should retain its exclusive privileges!

To come at last to the serious business of the

St. Petersburg Assembly, which consisted, first, in replying to the Government on the subject of the Bank question; and secondly, in listening to, discussing, and virtually adopting two "memoirs" presented by Count Schouvaloff, marshal of the St. Petersburg province, and Mr. Platonoff, marshal of the district of Tsarskoe Selo, the latter of these bearing, in addition to the author's signature, those of Prince Schtcherbatoff (brother of the Prince Schtcherbatoff who took a leading part in the debates at Moscow), Prince Paskievitch (son of the former Viceroy of Poland), and Count Strogonoff (son of the director of the education of the heir to the throne).

The reply on the subject of the Bank question was to the effect that its further consideration ought to be entrusted to a committee chosen from among the St. Petersburg nobility, to whom should, in the first place, be submitted the labours of the Government Committee (formed in the Ministry of Finance), which for some time past has been engaged in the preparation of an extensive banking scheme.

Count Schouvaloff's "memoir" is in three parts. In the first he sets forth the absolute necessity of terminating all disputes between peasants and proprietors, by placing the former at once in the position which, according to existing Government regulations, they cannot occupy until after the expiration of nine years,—nine years of antagonism and hatred (according to Count Schouvaloff), and of anything but freedom to the peasants if things are allowed to continue on their actual footing.

No. 2 shows how the dues, in the shape of *obrok* or *corvée*, which the proprietor has now a right to claim and to get, the best way he can, from the peasant for the land made over to him, may be replaced by a land-tax, the tax being made inseparable from the land even in case of its returning to its original proprietor—the proprietor to be, of course, indemnified by the Government in accordance with principles laid down in the official regulations.*

No. 3 recommends that the assemblies of the nobility be changed into assemblies of landed proprietors of all ranks, and points out that to exclude non-nobles from the assemblies "would not only be an injustice to them, but would, moreover, deprive the nobility of indispensable co-operation." It also advocates "the prompt organization of a system of local self-government" in all the provinces.

As regards the Bank question, Count Schouvaloff's "memoir" commences by admitting that "the establishment of land banks is one of the most essential wants of the present time."

* It is certain that some such project as this is being prepared in the office of the Minister of the Interior.

"But also," it continues, "it cannot be doubted that the first conditions of their existence depend on confidence being felt that the capital invested in them will be employed for the purpose proposed, and such confidence cannot be expected until all doubt is done away with, as to the absolute security of property rights, and until the changes brought about by recent changes in the holding of property are satisfactorily and decisively completed." It further sets forth that the nobles of St. Petersburg "do not allow themselves to entertain a thought as to diminishing the rights granted to the peasants on their estates," and at the same time they "cannot but express a full hope that they may receive the equal and firm protection of the law."

Mr. Platonoff's "memoir," the reading of which produced the greatest enthusiasm, and made the author at once the most popular man, and (so to speak) the leader in the Assembly, commences as follows:—

"The participation of the citizens in the administration of their country was anciently admitted in all well-regulated States, as the surest means of ascertaining the requirements of the people, and of arriving at a thorough discussion of any proposed measure of legislation, or important matter of State. From the days of John IV.* deliberative functions were vested in an

* Familiarly known as John or Ivan the Terrible.

'Assembly of the Country,' composed of persons elected by all the provinces of Russia. The participation of all classes in matters of State is more particularly apparent on the election of Michael Feodorovitch Romanoff to the throne of Russia. The Assembly of the Country of 1613 saved the Russian Crown from falling to pieces. Although the Assembly of the Country has not been summoned since the reformation of the Council of Boyars, in the early part of the eighteenth century, by the Emperor Peter I., who changed it into the Executive Senate, yet the oukaz of that Emperor, dated the 22nd of February, 1711, ordains that two deputies from each province be attached to the Senate; and designated commissioners for questions.* It was only on the death of Peter I., that the participation of citizens in the discussion of legislative measures and other important matters of State was definitely laid aside, and continues so to this day. But that setting aside must be considered as the principal cause of the imperfection and insufficiency of previous and present legislation. With the increase of the population of the Empire, and the development of industry and education, the existing mode of legislation becomes more and more satisfactory, and the necessity of an alteration in the old system more striking. With whatever

* That is, that questions were referred to them for their opinion.

wisdom men skilled in theory may frame projects of laws, those laws should, previous to their final confirmation and promulgation, be carefully examined in all their details and fully discussed, especially with reference to their applicability to the wants and requirements of the people: otherwise they may entail great calamities on the Empire. The dignitaries seated in Council of the Empire, at present charged with the consideration of projected laws, can only examine such projects with advantage in their bearing upon the general interests of the country, but they are unable to foresee the action of such laws on 70,000,000 of inhabitants, differing in their origin, rites, customs, and degree of civilization, and scattered over the entire surface of the largest Empire in the world. In order to attain this object it is necessary to have an assembly of men specially prepared for the purpose and thoroughly acquainted with the varied local requirements of the Empire, just as in ancient days deputies from all the provinces of Russia were gathered together in an 'Assembly of the Country.' . . . . . The Russian nation submits with love and reverence to the supreme power, but, at the same time, it cannot bear without murmuring the oppression of those by whom that power is represented. Every perversion of justice committed in the name of the Emperor, the absolution of persons in the enjoyment of his confidence, irregularities not suppressed, persecutions and abuses—all these destroy the confidence of the people in the Government, shake their loyalty towards the Sovereign, and even undermine his supremacy. For these reasons, not only with a view to the national welfare, but also in order to secure more firmly the power of the Sovereign, it is necessary to discover some trustworthy method of ascertaining the wants of the people, to put an end to the absolution of persons representing the Government, and to open a legal channel by which the voice of the people may reach the throne safely and seasonably. This can only be attained by allowing the citizens to participate in the administration of the country, and by establishing a general popular representation by gathering in one Assembly of the Country deputies elected by the Empire in general. The establishment of a general system of representation is also necessary, in order to unite all the portions of the Empire in one firm and durable political body. Many provinces, more or less distant from the supreme Government, deprived of the means of expressing their requirements, and subject to the action of laws inconvenient in application, and sometimes oppressive, are naturally anxious to emerge from that position.*

* To say nothing of Poland, it is well known that in Little Russia (that portion of the Ukraine which placed itself under Russian protection in the latter half of the seventeenth cen-

Under such circumstances, it is urgently necessary to blend the inhabitants of all the portions of the Empire into one indivisible nation, into one firm political body. We repeat that the only way to effect this is to establish a general representation, by gathering together in an Assembly of the Country deputies from all the provinces of the Empire, who shall make known to the Sovereign the requirements of the people, and at the same time collectively discuss all projected legislative measures and important matters of State before their final confirmation. Without such a general popular representation is established we may fear for the stability of the Empire, and foresee its speedy dissolution."

As to the plan of representation,—

"The district assemblies should consist of a certain number of deputies, determined by law, sent from all the towns, and unions, and parishes in the district. The Assembly of the Country should be composed of a certain number of persons elected by all the district assemblies. In general, the popular representation should be regulated so that the more enlightened citizens should have a predominance of votes, according to their numbers,

tury) a strong party exists which demands a separate government for this portion of the Empire. The tendencies of the Little Russian party are even represented by a review, founded a year since under good auspices, at St. Petersburg.

above those citizens of lower condition, whose civilization has not reached an equal degree of development. It has always been so in the best-regulated States, and on this basis, according to our opinion, society should be constituted in Russia. It may be said, without any injustice, that the citizens of a well-regulated State, in the diversity of their natural capacities, moral qualities, degree of education, and material means, cannot be useful to society to an equal extent, and therefore justice demands that they should not enjoy the same political rights, and that in the true interests of the State they should not participate to the same degree in matters relating to the community. Wise legislators, in forming a citizen society, have always endeavoured to give a majority of voices to educated and well-intentioned citizens."

In conclusion,—

"The object of this short memoir is to show the absolute necessity of subjecting to the examination of a General Assembly of the Country all projects of laws before their confirmation by the Sovereign. In presence of the existing tendency towards the attainment of a certain amount of political independence, if not towards secession from the general composition of the Empire, the only way to unite the country in one firm, indissoluble political body is to institute a system of popular representation. But the representatives can and must have the right of inquiry into these matters of State, which, being produced by pressing circumstances, will bear no delay in their solution. These rights can only legally be resuscitated in Russia by the will of His Majesty the Emperor. To revert to the words used by His Majesty in the Imperial manifesto of the 19th of February, 1861, it is said therein that the most beneficial laws cannot make people prosperous unless they themselves labour to prepare their own welfare under the protection of the law. We confess that a great deal lies before us, and we also feel that our august Monarch is solicitous for the welfare of his subjects, and that there cannot be so much as the shadow of a doubt but that our petition for the extension of that welfare will not be rejected by him."

Thereupon it is suggested that the draft of an address, "perfectly clear and definite," be prepared, so that the wants of the country may be explained to the Sovereign "with exactness and perspicuity"; but this address was not to be submitted to the St. Petersburg Assembly until its next meeting. In fact, Mr. Platonoff (or "Alexander Platonovitch," as he is familiarly called all over the Assembly) was prevailed upon by his friends not to allow even his preliminary "memoir" to be balloted for, in spite of the general and enthusiastic applause which it called forth during the reading. It was quite understood, however, that Alexander, the son of Plato, was to return to the charge, not only with his "memoir," but with a project in detail to follow; and in the meanwhile he had hearty congratulations offered to him on his success as an orator, and was, moreover, to have received a decidedly substantial token of esteem in the form of a banquet, for which the subscription list was opened in the hall of the Assembly immediately after the termination of the political business of the meeting.

The circular letter containing the five questions which the Government submitted to the consideration of the nobility had been presented at about the same time (end of 1861) to the marshals of twenty-two provinces, in which triennial elections of marshals were about to take place; and when, at the end of December, assemblies of the nobility were held in the towns of Toula, Novgorod, Pskoff, Smolensk, and Saratoff, such answers were returned to the Minister's five questions as amounted simply to a demand for a constitution. The nobility ought at the same time to have been assembled in certain of the Polish provinces incorporated with Russia. Here, however, the views of the proprietors were already sufficiently known. Not only were no questions put to them, but they were not even allowed to meet for the purpose of choosing a marshal. In one of the districts of Mohilew, where it was thought the nobles might be allowed to assemble, an address to the Emperor was adopted, praying His Majesty to substitute a Polish for the actual Russian administration, and to govern Mohilew as a Polish and not as a Russian province. Thereupon the marshal of the district in question was arrested (as the Marshal of Podolia was arrested for the same offence a year afterwards) and the Assembly of the nobility abruptly closed.

Of the five truly Russian provinces whose nobility first replied to the Minister's five questions in a liberal spirit, little expected from them, and far less hoped for by the Government, Toula showed itself the most daring. The nobles of Toula answered with an address, of which the most remarkable portion is contained in the following proposition, brought forward in the first instance and adopted unanimously in one of the district committees, and finally balloted for in the General Assembly, when it received 344 white balls against 110 black :—

"On the Institution of a Committee for the Preparation of Projects of Law.

"The law of the 19th of February (March 31), lately put in force, has proved in many respects in disaccordance with the conditions of village life, and unsuited to its regulation. Insurmountable difficulties are met with when it is attempted to carry it out, producing constant unsettlement and causing incalculable harm to agriculture, which forms the chief source of the riches of the Empire. The interests of landed proprietors suffer, and at the same time the new law is received with discontent by the peasants, whose murmurs have at last become so loud that the Emperor himself thought fit to address severe remonstrances to the peasant-deputies during his recent travels, as has been made known through all the newspapers. Thus the laws made for two classes have proved unsatisfactory to both, notwithstanding the immense sacrifices made by the nobles for the benefit of the peasants.

"The appointment of judicial examiners* ought to have been the first step towards the attainment of that important Imperial aim, the separation of judicial from administrative proceedings. But in the course of more than a year and a-half the

* Performing functions analogous to those of *juges d'instruction* in France, or coroners in England.

institution has borne no fruits, and exists, it may be said, only on paper. The causes of this are not numerous, but they suffice to paralyze the new laws at their very birth, by subjecting judges to the Administration—just what it was desired to avoid—and leaving judicial inquiries under the control of the police.

"From all this it is evident that with us the best of beginnings remain without fulfilment, or else lead to injury and to the discontent of those for whose advantage they are intended.

"Similar results must be expected from other reforms now in preparation in the departments of Finance, Justice, and the Administration; which, instead of the wished-for benefit, will bring with them general dissatisfaction, so dangerous to the Empire and so fatal to the establishment of confidence in the Government.

"The principal, and we may say the sole, cause of this want of accord between the laws published and the demands of the very life of the people lies in the manner in which the laws are formed. Various committees are appointed, committees which are not on harmonious terms with one another, having no general centre, and which do not prepare their work under that strict direction in the absence of which the time at which the Government is to proclaim its new laws becomes a matter of chance. Moreover, these temporary laws, however choicely composed, are far from answering their purpose. They are the production of persons who are useful as one of the elements in bodies intrusted with the preparation of such laws, but to whom cannot be left the sole decision of important questions affecting all the Empire. One-sidedness, a habit of routine, an exceptional knowledge of official affairs, assurance as to the superiority of some one theory over another, without any knowledge of the necessities of the life of the country, owing to their non-participation in the interests and requirements of that life,—all this is shown, first and foremost, in their work, which they doubtless perform dutifully, but in such a manner as to implant ruinous convictions that the interests of the Government differ substantially from the interests of the people. The admission to the Council of 'experts' and deputies, as has sometimes happened of late, has scarcely any significance; either they are appointed by the will of the Administration or they have no official character and are overwhelmed by the official majority. The law reforms which are being prepared under the new order of things must prove more unsatisfactory than ever; or, for accomplishing them, a greater knowledge of local interests and a more thorough understanding of the new and different natural positions of all kinds created by the emancipation of the serfs will be required.

"The above considerations compel attention to the closely-approaching future, which may too easily be darkened by grave disturbances if the reforms undertaken are not carried out in such a manner as to satisfy not only the demands of abstract theory and of bureaucratic routine, but the real demands of Russia, for whose profit they are undertaken.

"Upon the nobility, as the only class which possesses the right of consultation and of representing its wants, devolves the duty of pointing out the defects they observe, and the means of remedying them. At the same time, the new law for the abolition of serfdom brings them already into closer connection with the other classes through their personal interests, which no longer depend exclusively on the payment of *obrok*, or on task-work performed by the peasants, but on all sorts of commercial enterprises by which the proprietors must endeavour to recompense themselves for the losses they have sustained. Every new law will now concern the nobles more nearly than before, and they desire no sort of class privileges, but general protection by good laws for every one and all, and to procure new strength for the Government, so that general happiness may be brought about through a confirmation of faith in its proceedings and in their adaptation to the interests of the country.

"With these views, and to attain the proposed aim, we submit the following measures :—

"I. The institution of one general committee, to which shall be given the exclusive right of forming projects of laws, and of altering and completing existing laws when the Government thinks it necessary.

"II. The said committee to be divided into sub-committees for civil, financial, police affairs, and so on. The sub-committees to originate projects of law each in its own department, and to present them to the inspection of the general committee in full assembly.

"III. The committee to be made quite independent of the administrative powers, so that its projects of laws and its alterations and completions of existing laws may be presented directly, and without change, to the Imperial inspection.

"IV. The committee to be composed—

"(*a*). Of members appointed by the Government, in number not exceeding one-fifth of the entire number of members; and,

"(*b*). Of elected members, five from each province, chosen for three years; at the expiration of that term fresh elections to take place.

"V. The elected members to be chosen on the following bases :—

"1. District Assemblies.

"District Assemblies are to be composed in the following manner, the members being landed proprietors and inhabitants of the district:—

"(*a*). From every volost* of peasants 'temporarily obliged,' † and of Crown peasants, one candidate is chosen; two candidates elected in two neighbouring volosts to decide by lot which of the two shall sit as deputy at the District Assembly.

"(*b*.) Merchants of the third guild, and members of other classes in towns, choose one deputy for every thousand souls for the District Assembly.

"(*c*.) Merchants of the first and second guilds choose one deputy for every five capitals ‡ declared.

"(*d*.) All nobles possessing at present the right of voting in the Assembly of the Nobility are members of the District Assembly on the same basis.

"The deputies of the merchants and other classes in towns and the deputies of the peasants can be chosen from any class.

"The District Assembly meets under the presi-

* A *volost* is a village, or assemblage of villages, containing 1,000 "souls," or male peasants.

† Peasants "temporarily obliged" are the former serfs who have still certain prescribed work to perform (replaceable by money payments) for their late proprietors.

‡ The declaration of a certain capital, which is taxed accordingly, is the first qualification for merchants wishing to become members of guilds.

dency of the District Marshal of the Nobility, and it elects members for the Provincial Assembly.

"2. Provincial Assembly.

"The Provincial Assembly consists of ten members from each district, chosen by the District Assemblies from among landed proprietors, inhabitants of the district. Members of the Provincial Assembly may be persons of all ranks under the following conditions:—

"(*a.*) They must have finished their studies either at one of the Universities, or at the School of Jurisprudence, or at the Academy of the General Staff, of the Artillery, of the Engineers, or of Medicine, Commerce, or Divinity, if they possess only 50 deciatins * of land.

"(*b.*) If they have finished their studies at the Middle Schools or Cadets Corps, they must possess 300 deciatins of land, or house property equal in value to the above-mentioned extent of land; or they must belong to the first or second guild of merchants.

"(*c.*) If they have not finished their studies they must possess 1000 deciatins of land, or house property equal in value to the said 1000 deciatins.

"The Provincial Assembly meets under the

* One *deciatin* = three acres, nearly.

presidency of the Marshal of the Nobility of the province, and elects five members to sit in the General Committee, for which the same qualifications are required as for belonging to the Provincial Assembly.

"In such a manner may be done away with the great defects of the present system of forming projects of laws, and the whole country will take a legitimate share in the work on which the happiness of Russia depends. The idea will be realized which Catherine the Great sought to carry out nearly one hundred years ago, and which even then did good by leading to projects concerning provincial organization, town corporations, and a system of ecclesiastical supervision, —to laws on these and other subjects, which remain till now the best that Russia possesses."

It is a curious thing that Russian noblemen use the ballot-box at their elections, while Russian peasants, in their communal assemblies, vote openly, each man standing up for his own opinion. Vote by ballot, however, is a "privilege" which the nobles of the country are not at all anxious to retain. At Toula the supporters of the above proposition, after voting for it secretly, as the law directs, insisted on signing it publicly; and it was presented to the Emperor as proceeding from all the nobility of four districts in the province

(Krapivensk, Novosilsk, Ephremoff, and Kashira), and from various nobles of other districts, whose names were appended.

To do the nobility of Toula full justice, I must now mention that Toula has not always been a nest of Liberalism, and that the Emperor's invitation to form local committees to consider the best means of emancipating the peasants was received there with a worse grace even than at Moscow. And yet, if the annals of Toula be searched, it can be shown that some twenty-five years ago the nobility of the province petitioned the Emperor Nicholas to be allowed to give liberty to their serfs, and were reprimanded for daring to speak of such a thing! Why did the Toula proprietors wish to free the bondsman in 1838, and to keep him in fetters in 1857? Simply because the emancipation of the serf in Russia is not a question of personal freedom at all. No one of late years has ever objected to the serf going free, provided only he *would* go. That communes of serfs should have liberty given them to cultivate two-thirds of their masters' estates for their own use, at a rent fixed arbitrarily by the Government—that is what the nobles of Toula, Moscow, and so many other Governments thought unjust, and protested against to the best of their ability. To put the matter in a simple business light, Toula is a province where land is very valuable, and where serf labour is not valuable at all. On some estates the serfs were looked upon as positive incumbrances, and land has sometimes been sold in Toula for much more than its ordinary value in that province, merely because it had no peasants attached to it—so unprofitable did it appear to keep serfs who had to be supported when they were infirm and old, and who could not be beaten into doing a good day's work even when they were young and healthy; so unprofitable, above all, was it found to pay them in allotments of excellent land for labour which free peasants would have performed far better for a comparatively small money wage.

However, the would-be emancipators of 1838—the opponents of emancipation coupled with the transpropriation of the proprietors' land in 1857—are leading political reformers in 1863. Hitherto, unfortunately, their suggestions for changing fundamentally the system on which Russia is at present governed have met with but little success in high quarters.

At Tver, where the nobility had already proclaimed their conviction that the welfare of Russia demanded an immediate reform of the Government and the introduction of a representative system, "the Bank question" was regarded from the same point of view as at St. Petersburg. "Give us first a constitution," said the nobles of Tver; "then we shall have confidence in the Government, and it will be easy enough to establish whatever banks may be necessary."

After the nobility of Tver had forwarded their address to the Emperor, the "justices of the peace" of the province met at their assizes and adopted another address, in which they informed His Majesty that, from their own experience in endeavouring to carry out the provisions of the law of emancipation, they had become convinced of the necessity of remodelling it entirely, and that this duty could only be entrusted to an assembly formed of the representatives of all classes and conditions, as had already been recommended by the nobility of the province. They, at the same time, assured His Majesty of their determination to enforce the observance of the existing law to the best of their ability, though persuaded that to be effective it must be reformed in various particulars.

The newly-appointed justices of the peace are all landed proprietors, and are, therefore, not likely to be revolutionists. As they propose to endow the peasants with land in freehold, they can scarcely be accused of being hostile to the liberated serfs; nor, as members of the nobility, whose views as a body they share, can they be suspected of any wish to sacrifice their own order, except, indeed, as a privileged (and for that reason, politically powerless) class. Nevertheless the only answer vouchsafed to the address of the peace justices of Tver came in the form of an order for their arrest. They were imprisoned in the fortress of St. Petersburg, on a charge of "refusing to carry out the law of the 3rd of March," and were ultimately liberated without having been brought to trial.

CHAPTER XV.

EMANCIPATION OF THE SERFS.

It is now nearly eighteen years since the nobles of the ancient Polish and Lithuanian provinces in the west of the Russian Empire were called upon to give an account of the quantity of land allotted to the peasants on each of their estates, and of the amount of labour and produce required from them by the proprietor. Committees, composed of landed proprietors and Government officials, were formed; and to them were presented so-called "inventories," giving full particulars respecting the peasant-land on each domain, and the obligations which it had to support. The object of this proceeding was to bind the nobility of the western provinces to the local traditional custom which fixed the proprietor's dues (as a general rule) at a third of the land ceded by him to his peasants; and its alleged motive was a suspicion that the Polish and Lithuanian nobles might be inclined to visit upon their serfs the wrath they felt at not having been adequately supported by them in their attempt to extend the

Warsaw insurrection of 1830–31 over all the ancient Polish provinces of the Russian Empire. Nevertheless, it was not until 1844, when all the leading proprietors of the western provinces (such as the Czartoryskis and the Sapiehas—to mention two well-known historical names out of a large number) had had their estates confiscated, for the last dozen years, that the Russian Government came forward as the peasant's friend, and imposed upon the Polish proprietors of modern West Russia, or ancient East Poland, its aforesaid system of "inventories."

The "system of inventories" was established provisionally in most of the western Governments for six years, from 1846 to 1852; and on the expiration of the term, it was decided to prolong it and at the same time to extend the system to those of the western provinces where it had not yet been introduced. Nevertheless, the experiment had not been successful. It had placed both the proprietor and the peasant in an anomalous position, and, while giving the latter rights, had left him a serf, and, therefore, unable fully to profit by them. The committees were re-assembled, and, being consulted as to the possible modification of the Government measure, answered, with one accord, that the real difficulty could only be met by the abolition of serfdom. This was at the end of 1854, a few months before the death of the Emperor Nicholas;

and in May, 1857, nine months after the coronation of Alexander II., the nobility of the three Lithuanian provinces of Wilna, Grodno, and Kovno were invited to meet in assembly to consider anew the question of the peasants. The solution promptly recommended by them was, that the peasants should be emancipated personally, and that the proprietorship of the estates should be guaranteed to the nobles—that is to say, that the peasant should be permitted to dispose freely of his time and labour, and that the noble or proprietor, having no longer any claim on him for work or for dues of any kind, should be no longer called upon to allow him any portion of land. This solution (which, by the way, had been proposed twenty years before by the very intelligent proprietors of the rich-soiled province of Toula, and peremptorily rejected by the Emperor Nicholas) would, undoubtedly, have found favour in the eyes of all the nobility of Russia. It will be remembered that the land-owners of Moscow were afterwards held up to general odium as determined opponents of serf-emancipation, and as though serfdom were an "institution" which they really desired to preserve. But, though they may have been ungenerous in not wishing to give up a large portion of their estates to their peasants on conditions which the latter were not likely to fulfil, yet they never took the planter's view of the question usually attributed to them, and all personal rights over serfs were voluntarily resigned by the nobility in all the provinces of the Empire, without any pressure on the part of the Government being needed.

But if the personal emancipation of the serf without land would just have suited the very intelligent proprietors of Toula, and, indeed, of Russia generally, it did not at all accord with the policy of the Government, and Russians of all classes seem now agreed that, so far from contenting the peasant, it would, in all probability, have driven him to desperation. Political economists in the west of Europe can easily show that land ought not to be given to the peasant, and that it is better for him to be a prosperous farmer than a small proprietor without sufficient capital to cultivate his land according to the most approved methods. To convince 22,000,000 Russian peasants, however, of this great truth—22,000,000 peasants who care nothing for agriculture as a science, and who are actually in possession of land which they and their ancestors have held for centuries—this might be more difficult. M. de Molinari, in one of his interesting letters on the subject, published last year in the *Economiste Belge,* proves that the Russian peasant is ignorant of the first principles of economical science, and (as if to punish him for it) declares that he ought not to have a particle of land given to him. Boris Godounoff attached him to the soil. Let Alexander II. detach him therefrom, and the emancipation question is settled. This would be emancipation certainly—but accompanied by what the peasant would regard as confiscation.

"He knows nothing about it," the economist replies. "If he thinks any portion of his master's land belongs to him, when he has once ceased to work for it, he makes a mistake. The Government should consult the truth and not the prejudices of a peasant who does not even understand his own interest."

The object, however, of the Imperial scheme for "ameliorating the condition of the peasants," was to ameliorate their condition in such a manner that its amelioration should be perceptible to them; not to benefit them so stealthily that they themselves should not know it. Mr. Victor Porochin, formerly Professor of Political Economy at the University of St. Petersburg, thinks, with M. de Molinari, that, in the abstract, the liberated serf has no right to any portion of the proprietor's land, but considers it a "necessary act of expropriation" to make over to him his cottage, his kitchen-garden, and other appurtenances. Other of the St. Petersburg economists, such as Mr. V. P. Bezobrazoff (who must not be confounded with M. N. Bezobrazoff, the obstinate defender of nobiliary privileges in the Moscow and St. Petersburg Assemblies) and Mr. Kalinowski (who read a paper on the subject of the emancipation last year at the *Société des Economistes* in Paris), go much further than Mr. Porochin, and hold that the peasant has decidedly a claim on a portion of the peasant's land. It is somewhat difficult to understand what claim he can have superior to what would be enjoyed by a tenant holding a farm on an ancient and always renewable lease; but, as all Russians, proprietors or not, seem now to admit his title in some degree, and at least recognize the utter impossibility of dispossessing him, the abstract question is really not worth discussing.

As for the serf himself, profoundly ignorant as he may be of the principles of political economy, he has, nevertheless, a theory as to his own right of possessing the land which he has been in the habit of cultivating: or rather he has a conviction. "I belong to you, but the land belongs to me," is a peasant's saying, which has been often quoted in connection with the emancipation question. Mr. Porochin quietly observes that the answer of the master to this saying of the serf has not been made known; but in connection with the abolition of serfdom it probably would be, "When you no longer belong to me, the land given to you to live upon will no longer belong to you." This is, or at least, was, the view of the matter taken by the great majority of Russian proprietors when the question of emancipation was first started; but it is a view which has never been held by the Russian Government, and which is in opposition to the earliest and most cherished belief of the Russian peasant. Whenever proprietors applied, during the last two reigns, for permission to liberate their serfs, the reply made to them invariably was, "Liberate them, but give them enough land to maintain them." There have been instances of individual nobles, at the commencement of the present reign, emulating the generosity of the Toula nobility in 1838, and proposing in the fulness of their hearts and the emptiness of their pockets to "let the foolish rustic go," that they might retain his land for their own purposes; but such propositions were left without action in the office of the Minister of the Interior, and the emancipating landowner, on *these* terms, did well if he escaped without a reprimand.

The serf, too, unlettered and unversed in the mysteries of economical science as he is, has a traditional belief on the subject of his emancipation, which curiously enough, is in perfect harmony with the history of serf-emancipation in Prussia, in three parts of Poland, in Hungary, and probably in Austria generally. He finds his *corvée,* or task-work, gradually diminishing, while there is no diminution in the land set apart for his use. The end of this constant progression will, as he thinks, be a total abolition of the *corvée,* the peasant-land still remaining in the possession of the peasants. All he knows about the matter is that the land belongs to him, and that he belongs (but in his private opinion ought not to belong) to his master; that his master formerly required six or seven* days' work in the week from him, that he was then satisfied with five, then with four, and latterly with three, and that during the last year women's weekly task-days have been reduced to two. Some day, he believes, and before long, now that an Emperor has really taken pity on him, the task-work will be done away with altogether, and his time, equally with his land, be left at his own disposal.

This gradual diminution of the *corvée*, without injury to the peasant's claim to his land, certainly took place in ancient Poland—for the Constitution of 1791 legalized and rendered permanent (unless both the contracting parties consented to a change)

* Both the Emperor Paul, and, after him, the Emperor Alexander I., found it necessary to issue edicts forbidding noblemen to make their serfs work on Sundays. The Emperor Paul had even endeavoured to limit the task-work to three days in the week, but without general success; and, until the publication of the celebrated manifesto of March 3, 1861, there were still proprietors who were not ashamed to exact six days' *corvée* from their unhappy peasants. It is not astonishing, then, that on some estates, under the new system, the land has not been sown, and that on others the crops have been left to rot on the ground.

all kinds of agreements between peasants and proprietors, showing plainly that agreements between them of different kinds existed. Moreover, Kosciuszko, in the Act of Independence, published in the name of the Polish nation in 1794,* recognizes serf-obligations of numerous degrees, and modifies them as they had evidently been modified before. The serf who owes the work of six days *per* week to the proprietor has to give four days; the serf who owes four days has to give two; the serf who owes two, one; the serf who owes one *per* week, one *per* fortnight.

In Hungary, when the peasants were emancipated with their land by the Austrian Government, after the insurrection of 1848–9, the *corvée* had already been reduced by the proprietors to two days a-week on some estates, and one day a-week on others, while the general position of the serf had been alleviated in a variety of ways; so that every year he approached more closely the state of a free labourer, without for that reason being called upon to give up his ancestral fields.

In Galicia, after rejecting several petitions from the Polish nobility in favour of emancipation, the Austrian Government itself emancipated the peasants. As the object of this measure, which was put in force two years after the Galician

* *Bibliothèque des Archives Diplomatiques—Pologne*, p. 377.

massacres, was to strengthen and encourage the peasant and to weaken the proprietor, the former received all his land, and the latter (like the proprietors of Hungary) received no indemnity. Ultimately, however, the Galician proprietor was nominally recompensed up to about a third of his losses by Government in bills of doubtful value, for the payment of which a good solid tax was laid on the province generally. But though the proprietors did not wish to be ruined in either country, the necessity of liberating the peasant *with* the land was generally recognized, both in Austrian Poland and in Hungary.

In the Grand Duchy of Posen the serf and his land were emancipated together. The peasants had about a third of their masters' estates made over to them, for which they were to pay a third of the estimated money-value of the *corvées* up to that time executed by them. After the revolution of 1848, the perpetual annual rent of five thalers, which the peasant on the average paid for the land ceded to him, was capitalized, and State bills, bearing interest and redeemable at certain periods, for the capital represented by the rent were given by way of indemnity to the proprietor. These bills, unlike the Austrian ones, possessed at once a marketable value, and were quoted at par on the Exchange. The peasants under the new arrangement had and have to pay to the Government, instead of to the proprietor, five and a quarter thalers, instead of five, and for twenty-three years (up to the year 1871) instead of for an unlimited period.

However, without looking out of Russia, at the fate of other serfs, or even beyond his own village, the Russian peasant had—and, it is to be feared has still—the belief that liberty means, for him, the right of cultivating his field and garden (if his they really be), without paying anything, either in money or work, for the privilege of doing so.

The proprietor has, for the most part, regarded the emancipation of the peasant as a measure for rendering the latter free to employ himself as an agricultural labourer or farmer, at a wage or rent, but giving him no title to any portion of land as absolute property.

The Government has taken a middle view between these extremes, and has failed to give satisfaction to either party. Unable, without indemnifying the proprietors, to assign to the peasants the land to which hitherto they themselves had been assigned; and equally unable, not to say afraid, to deprive the peasants of their hereditary cottages, gardens, and fields, to give them merely the freedom of the birds, it hit upon this expedient,—to declare the serf, while pretending to liberate him and leaving him his land, "temporarily obliged" to continue his task-work, or his money-payments in lieu thereof; and to force the proprietor, while assuring him of the inviolability of his rights to the whole of his estate, to give up (on the average) two-thirds of it. Under the emancipative decree of the 19th of February, 1860, neither is the proprietor at liberty to dispose freely of his land nor the peasant of his labour.

The manner in which the details of this decree (already modified, and which must of necessity be modified still further) were decided upon, is probably well known. The nobility of the various provinces, upon the invitation of the Emperor, formed committees for the preparation of projects of emancipation. These projects were forwarded to a central committee sitting at St. Petersburg, and composed, for the most part, of Government functionaries, whose duty it was to compare them and to elaborate a final scheme, which was submitted for approval, and in due course approved by the Council of State. It was then confirmed by the Emperor, and a ukase based upon it was published by the Imperial command in all the newspapers, proclaimed in all the churches, exhibited on all the walls of the capitals and principal towns, and made known in every possible way in all the villages of the Empire. Imperfect as the scheme was, it nevertheless conferred immense benefits on the largest and the most unfortunate class in Russia; for, if it left the peasants subjected to a system of forced contracts, these contracts were, by comparison, highly advantageous to them, and it abolished once and for ever all that was demoralizing and degrading in serfdom. It did not solve the problem that had to be solved; but it at least raised the peasant in the scale of humanity, and effectually emancipated him from the arbitrary rule of the proprietor. The moment that the ukase appeared, all the odious vile part of the old system ceased. The serf became a peasant, with appointed duties, and accountable for his manner of performing them to the law alone. He has not yet reached the promised land, but he has crossed the Red Sea, and this is the cruel bondage from which he has been delivered:—

1. From the power of the master to make him work without paying him wages.

2. From the power of the master to punish him without proving or even advancing any specific charge against him, and to maltreat him generally.

3. From the power of the master to marry him against his consent, and to give his betrothed in marriage to another.

4. From the power of the master to send him at any time to the army, or, on paying his very

moderate travelling expenses, and without accusing him of any offence, to Siberia.

Whatever Alexander II., occupying, perhaps, the most difficult position in which any man living could be placed, may have left undone, in the way of ameliorating the condition of the peasant, he has certainly saved the Russian peasant from much possible cruelty, and the Russian nobility from the opportunity of committing many barbarous crimes.

CHAPTER XVI.

THE LAST MOVEMENT.—UNION AND DISUNION BETWEEN RUSSIANS AND POLES.

In spite of what Panslavonian theorists tell us about Russians and Poles belonging to the same race, and being therefore bound to love one another (as if all men were not bound to love one another by a far higher law than any that is likely to be laid before us by political ethnologists), we have now fresh proofs, if any fresh proofs were wanted, that they can hate one another as though they belonged to entirely different branches of the human family, and as though it were a natural thing that different branches of the human family should make it their chief object to destroy one another. Although Poles and Russians doubtless share some national characteristics, although by temperament and habits of life they both differ very much from the Germans, and although Poles and Russians often associate in St. Petersburg and Moscow on terms of friendship, yet, on the whole, they have hitherto been brought together far more by common antipathies than by common sympathies.

In cases of real friendship between Poles and Russians I have always noticed that this friendship might be, and almost certainly was, based on similarity of pursuits, literary, scientific, or artistic.

Thus, in St. Petersburg and Moscow you may meet writers and professors who associate freely, and do not ask one another whether they are Russians or Poles.

Also, a Polish violinist and a Russian pianist can play a duet together without fighting.

But this only proves that the liberal arts have softened their manners, and do not permit them to be ferocious. Ask a Polish historian and a Russian historian separately what each thinks of the claim of the Russians to the provinces seized at the first three partitions; ask a Polish and a Russian philologer whether the dialects spoken in those provinces ought to be called Russian or Ruthenian, and whether, simply as a question of science, they ought to be classed with the Russian or with the Polish language; ask a Polish and a Russian ethnologist whether the Russians are a Slavonian race, or a Finnish race which has merely adopted a Slavonian tongue; ask a Polish and a Russian politician whether the principle of election which is found in so many spheres of Russian life owes its existence to a national love of liberty, or to a national and Mongol-like instinct to appoint chiefs and delegate all authority to them; finally, ask Poles and Russians at random whether Tsar (in Polish, Czar) is derived from the Tartar word *khan,* or is true Slavonian for king or emperor; whether the modern Russians ought to be called Russians or Muscovites;* whether Russian despotism is an Asiatic or a European product; whether Peter destroyed the germs of a free government already existing under the Tsarate of Muscovy, and took the worst features of the modern Russian system from the despotic Courts of France and Imperial Germany, or whether he

* The Russian Grand-dukes could not knowingly have borrowed their sovereign title from their greatest enemies. "Tsar" is, moreover, really a Slavonian and not a Tartar word, a fact which Miękievicz not only admits, but builds more than one theory upon; as, for instance, that "Nebuchodonosar" means "nie-bogh-odno-Tsar" ("There is no God but the King"); that "Belshazzar," "Belisarius," mean "biele Tsar" ("the white king"), and so on. On the other hand, during the period of the Tsars of Muscovy the territory generally known to the West of Europe as "Russia" was the Polish province of that name. In the list of proper names at the end of Ainsworth's *Latin Dictionary*, "Russia" is described as "a province of Poland," also as another name for Eastern Sarmatia ("Eastern Sarmatia" is now Western Russia). At the same time, no one imagined that Muscovite was not Russian ground, or that the Muscovites did not speak the Russian language. The simple truth is, that (without making use of the word "Ruthenia," which meant "Russia" just as much as "Prutenia" meant "Prussia,") there were two Russias—Muscovite Russia and Polish Russia. So there is an English Britain and a French Brittany. (See, on this subject, No. 2 in Appendix.)

simply maintained an Oriental despotism of natural growth, and perfectly suited to the Russian character: on all these questions and on many more, the Poles and the Russians will give entirely contradictory replies. Even the Panslavonian Pole will sometimes forget bimself, and in his natural hatred of his country's oppressors—so far deeper and stronger than his love for any ethnological theory—declare that the Russians are only half Slavonian by race, and entirely Tartar by their political life; while the Panslavonian Russian will, in his turn, maintain that the Polish nobility is not of Slavonian origin at all, that the Poles in the days of their greatest glory abandoned Slavonian for Latin civilization, and the Slavo-Polish for the Latin language.

I need say nothing about the sort of concord which exists between Polish and Russian democrats, for the democrats of all nations are agreed up to a certain point. If, however, the Polish and Russian democrats should ever succeed in overthrowing the Russian autocracy, they would soon disagree about the future Poland.

Nevertheless, an attempt has been made to bring about an understanding between the revolutionary parties in both countries, and letters and explanations on the subject have been exchanged constantly during the last few months between the Central Committee of Warsaw and the editors of the *Kolokol*, in whose journal the communications have been published.

The general plan agreed upon was, that the members of the Polish Revolutionary Society should rise in Warsaw simultaneously with the peasantry and the Democratic party throughout Russia. The troops, when ordered to fire, were to refuse. Under these circumstances, the Russian Empire in its present form would naturally come to an end. The peasants were then to be endowed everywhere with the land for which they at present pay rent or perform task-work; and being also endowed with the right of voting, could not fail to re-elect the Emperor, after which the Russian Empire would go on much as before, only with autocracy established on a firmer basis than ever.

In the almost inconceivable case of success, however, the "Kingdom" was to be liberated and given over to the Poles; while the inhabitants of the provinces seized by Russia at the first, second, and third partitions were to be invited to make known their patriotic sympathies through the ballet-box of democratic despotism. If universal suffrage declared the birth-place of Kosciuszko to be Russian, as it has already declared the birth-place of Garibaldi to be French, then it was to remain

Russian; in the contrary case, it was to be given back to the Poles.

Of course, no people can be justified in fighting in the name of national independence if they require a ballot-box to tell them where their nation really is. Probably, however, the unhappy Polish revolutionists were willing to make any theoretic concession in order to come to terms with the revolutionists of Russia, and although the democrats have commenced the war it will not be for them to settle it, for the Poles of all parties are always ready to fight for their country, and persons of all classes and from all parts of Poland are now hurrying to the camp of General Langiewicz.

In speaking of parties in Poland, I must not omit to say a few words about the Marquis Wielopolski, the great political quack, who would rather Poland should die than that she should be restored otherwise than by the Panslavonian remedies prescribed by him.

The Marquis Wielopolski is celebrated as a man of determination; but it is not every one who will envy him that barbarous sort of firmness which enables him to keep his place in the Government while the Poles are being driven to despair by the course that Government pursues towards them. Two mistakes, however, are often made as to the Marquis Wielopolski's position. On the one hand, he is looked upon as a Pole animated by the sentiments common to the great body of his countrymen; and it is assumed that, in appointing him to the responsible office he occupies, the Russian Government wished to give some proof of an intention to carry out a policy agreeable to the Polish nation. This is a view entertained by many foreigners, who are not aware that the Grand-duke Constantine's *adlatus* is the most unpopular man in Poland, and that he is the only Pole who has ever openly proclaimed his belief that the cause of Polish independence is hopeless.

On the other hand, most of the Marquis's countrymen regard him as a man who, from ambition and love of power (to say nothing of meaner and quite impossible motives), will connive at any amount of cruelty and injustice that may be practised in Poland rather than resign his post. The fact that he did resign when his plan for recognizing the educational system and re-opening the universities was rejected, and only took office again in order to carry it out, does not seem to be taken into consideration; nor ought it to be, as in this instance he may have resigned from injured vanity alone. All that is remembered—and remembered with indignation—is that he was implicated in the recent barbarous measure of conscription, or proscription; and that after the massacre of April, 1861, when all the chief Polish officials were asking to be relieved of their functions, and the whole country was testifying, in every possible manner, its abhorrence of the conduct of the Government, the Marquis Wielopolski could see no reason why he should not continue to serve it as before, and gave it the full weight of his support after everyone else had abandoned it.

If, then, the Marquis is a patriot, his patriotism is certainly of a very peculiar kind. In fact, he has hitherto shown far less love for his countrymen than for a theory of his own, according to which his country is, some day or other, to regain, if not its independence, at least its integrity and its national life, under the protection and dominion of Russia.

In 1846, immediately after the failure of the impracticable Galician insurrection, and the organized massacre of upwards of one thousand proprietors, the Marquis Wielopolski addressed a very remarkable letter to Prince Metternich; writing it from the neighbourhood of Cracow, while the country houses all round were still burning, and the serfs (whose emancipation Austria had always opposed) were still wandering about, half mad with drink, spending in full liberty the money they had received from the Austrian officials as the wages of assassination.

The Galician proprietor told the Austrian statesman what effect this policy of his Government would have on the future policy of the Poles, and that, in the first place, it had re-awakened all that "inextinguishable hatred" which the Poles, as Slavonians, must always feel for the Germans. The author of the *Letter from a Polish Gentleman to Prince Metternich* had come to the conclusion that Poland had played the part of victim long enough, and that she ought to engage in no more hopeless enterprises, above all, as there was now no weapon which her enemies were not cowardly enough to use against her. Whatever speeches might be made on her behalf in Parliamentary Assemblies, whatever tokens of sympathy she might receive from public meetings, whatever articles might be published in newspapers and reviews, to prove that Russia, Austria, and Prussia had no right to set all the stipulations of the Treaty of 1815 at defiance, he was evidently convinced that these stipulations would be violated all the same; and that his unhappy country would never be more than an object of purely theatrical interest in the eyes of Western Europe.

He therefore proposed that the Poles should look for assistance and support to the only one of their three oppressors which had much to gain by a Polish alliance; that they should throw themselves frankly into the arms of Russia, and, forgetting the injuries they had received from the Russian

Government, think only of its power to rescue them from the tyranny of Prussia and Austria. Once united under the Russian Crown, Poland, he maintained, would have an important influence on the destinies of the Russian Empire, and would no longer be persecuted, if, instead of thwarting Russian policy for the benefit of Western Europe, she endeavoured to forward it for her own advantage and the gratification of her own legitimate revenge. The ultimate goal of the Marquis Wielopolski's designs was (and no doubt is) the formation of a great Slavonian Confederation, in which Poland would once more enjoy her national existence, and, thanks to the support of Russia, become an object, not of pity, but of terror to the Western nations.

It is now sixteen years since the Marquis Wielopolski first made known his conviction that Poland, having nothing to hope from her so-called friends, had better make the best possible terms with the most powerful and enterprising of her declared enemies. Like everyone else in Poland, he had taken part in the insurrection of 1830, but he proved that he had become reconciled to Russia by sending his sons into the Russian army; and he has given good evidence of his faith in his Panslavonian policy by sticking to it firmly through good and ill repute, or rather through ill repute alone, for hitherto it has never found the least favour among the Poles.

The worst of this policy is, that it looks so very like suicide. The Marquis has a plan for taming a bear which seems to consist in letting the bear devour him—or rather, not him, but his unfortunate countrymen. They may derive what consolation they can from the reflection that their brethren in Galicia and Posen will be devoured afterwards.

Nevertheless, when M. Wielopolski, after formally retiring from public life, was afterwards suddenly installed in office, and arrived in Warsaw with the Grand-duke to give authority to the system he was about to inaugurate, there did appear to be some little chance of its being attended with success. Eight additional gymnasiums (as the reader is already aware) were opened, the Warsaw University was re-established, and steps were even taken for restoring the University of Wilna in Lithuania. Unfortunately the authors of the new Panslavonian scheme had thought more of attracting Slavonians in general to Russia than of doing simple justice to the Poles, who were actually living and suffering under the Russian yoke. Professors of the four great branches of the Slavonian tongue—Russian, Polish, Bohemian, and Servian—were engaged at enormous salaries, and the provincial idiom of "Little Russia" and "Ruthenia" was elevated to the dignity of a language that another professor of Slavonianism at six thousand roubles a-year might be appointed. You might be thrown into prison or carried off to the army on the report of a spy, but it was at least gratifying to know that there were more literary dialects of Slavonian than of ancient Greek, and that a lecturer from Little Russia would demonstrate this so many times a-week at the Warsaw University, while you were serving as a common soldier in the Caucasus.

I have spoken of the democratic Panslavonian party, and of the one aristocratic, oligarchic, almost autocratic Panslavonian. I can think of no other party, properly so called, in Poland, though there are, naturally, several different opinions as to what policy ought to be pursued. Thus, there are some who would do everything to secure the assistance of the Western Powers, and especially of France. Others have but little faith in the Western Powers, and remember that in the days of the Duchy of Warsaw, Napoleon was always ready to throw over the Poles for the sake of a good alliance with Austria, or, above all, with Russia. A successful campaign against Russia might give the Poles the Kingdom, but Russia would still hold the Lithuanian provinces, and Poland would be as far from unity as ever.

I still think that Poland's best chance of gaining this unity is by means of Russia; and Alexander II., on his side, need not give up an inch of Polish ground if he would only resolve to carry out in a fair spirit the "favourite project" of Alexander I.

The worst of the position of the Poles is this: that whereas their country is in pieces, and they wish it to be made whole, yet the Western Powers will neither attempt to liberate it altogether, nor would they ever allow it to be united under the Russian sceptre.

Russia, however, cannot now solve the Polish difficulty by simply restoring the Constitution to the Kingdom; nor can she grant the Constitution at all without extending it not only to the Russo-Polish provinces, but to the Russian Empire generally.

I have no faith, however, in any particular solution. All I am convinced of is, that if the Poles remain true to themselves, their enemies will certainly fall out before long, and they may then come by their own again.

Nor would I trust to any definite line of policy. Hitherto, the Poles have, unconsciously, no doubt, followed the policy recommended by Rousseau to the Polish deputation who visited him immediately after the first partition. "They have swallowed you," he said; "don't let them digest you."

But the noblest and best policy (in the sense in which honesty is the best policy) is undoubtedly that which the venerable Prince Czartoryski adjured his countrymen to persevere in, almost with his last breath:—

"God, by the long life He has granted me, has," said the Prince, "permitted me to witness the entire history of the misfortunes of our country. I have been a witness of all those faults, deceptions, griefs and humiliations, which you, gentlemen, only know by tradition. In the midst of these various trials, the spirit of the nation has become modified and re-tempered, each trial purifying and rendering her more apt for a free and independent existence. During the most important period accorded to our forefathers for this work of national regeneration—a period which may be said to be summed up in the anniversary which we celebrate to-day—I have myself been participator, as far as my youth permitted me, in all the glorious efforts which have occasioned redoubled perfidy and violence on the part of neighbours resolved on the ruin of Poland.

"Nevertheless, I can say, with a heart full of gratitude towards God, that the nation has never before attained this dignified and calm attitude; never before have all Poles been so perfectly of one mind; and never, independent of any foreign interest and influence, has the term of our long adversities appeared so certain.

"I know not, gentlemen, if I shall be permitted again to speak to you in this place. Permit me, then, to recur once more to my hopes and to my fears, and to address myself for a moment to that country which, for more than seventy years has been the centre to which all my thoughts, all my sentiments, all my anxieties, and all the labours of my life, have turned.

"Descend not, O my nation! from this height on which peoples and Powers are forced to respect thee! Remaining there, thou wilt never lose sight of the object of thy hopes, and wilt approach it with more assured confidence. In the midst of thy cruel griefs, and of the despair to which cruelty and violence impel thee, reject the temptations of anger; do not abase thyself to combats unworthy of thee, which can only increase thy sufferings, if they do not entirely consummate thy ruin. Recollect that it requires more heroism to meet death with a bare bosom, than to defend life sword in hand. The greatest courage on this earth consists in not holding to life. To have this courage, being, at the same time, gentle and generous, free from every thought of vengeance or desire to injure even one's enemy—this is virtue indeed, and true political prudence. Shut thy heart especially against pride, for it degrades and vilifies the noblest impulses; but know, O people of Poland! that thy actual power and thy hopes for the future consist in the elevation of thy sentiments and the grandeur of thy virtues! The martyr for his faith and his country is always the precursor of victory, for he holds up the victim at the same time before God and before man, and covers his murderers with shame. It is not given to man to foresee events, especially when they are of so elevated an order as the facts which we are now witnessing. It is Providence itself which at present enlightens and inspires the nation: to it we should look for succour, and this succour will not fail us."

APPENDIX.

No. I.

EXTRACT FROM THE MARQUIS WIELOPOLSKI'S *LETTER FROM A POLISH GENTLEMAN TO PRINCE METTERNICH.*

We cannot help asking what advantage have we in fact derived from German sympathies? What are the manifestations of Germany from which the future independence of Poland may be expected? These questions are answered by the terrible position in which Poland is now placed. Death on the gallows, or by flogging, Siberia and the torments of the dungeon, exile and misery, have for a long time been the only consequences brought upon us by the policy of the great German Powers, who have hitherto only made use of the Polish national feeling as a tool for crippling the political advances of Russia. Applause was given to the Polish insurrection of 1831; Austria permitted a free passage through her territory to Poland for arms, money, and foreign officers; the inhabitants of Galicia, landowners who returned home after the fall of the same insurrection, received favours from the Government, by the remission of many arrears with which their estates were burdened. All this was done because Slavonians were fighting against Slavonians, whose bloody struggle was an enjoyable sight to the Germans. The severe measures of Russification adopted in the Russian part of Poland were ostensibly lamented, whilst every development of the Polish nationality was counteracted in Austria by that keeping down of intellect which is the political system of that Government, and in Prussia by the so-called civilization, which means (as it has been confessed by Mr. Flotwell, Wuttke, and others) a noiseless Germanization, tolerating only as much of Polonism as might be required to keep Russia in check by the Polish bugbear. The violent blows given by Russia to Polish nationality in order to murder it, were loudly complained of, but it was found very just to prepare the death of the same nationality by a lingering consumption and absorption, brought about by the withdrawal of the means of its vitality. Austria's hitherto veiled hatred of Polonism sufficiently betrayed itself when a foolish, puerile conspiracy of the Poles disconcerted, for a moment, the old political wisdom of that State, and seduced it into measures which may be compared with the celebrated Neapolitan counter-revolutionary alliance of the King and the clergy with the Lazzaroni, the Mammoni, and Fra Diavolo. The same occasion caused the press of Germany to resound with words of contempt and with the most worthless abuse against Polonism, pronounced with the greatest arrogance, it being declared that the destiny which Providence has assigned to the Poles was to *obey the Germans*, since everything remarkable that has ever taken place, not only in Poland, but also in Russia, is exclusively ascribed to German agency. Those very men, who so loudly utter, on the Rhine, the words *Fatherland* and *National rights*, curse the Pole who pronounces the same words. If we have hitherto laboured under the delusion that all our woes come exclusively from Russia, may the present state of our country teach us to know better! The persecutions in consequence of the Polish efforts, which had hitherto been considered as being solely inflicted by Russia, come now from the quarter where, a short time before, our hopes were placed, and with the addition of two new deadly weapons suspended over our heads, namely, the flail of the instigated peasants and the daggers of the new Polish demagogues, generated by the rank suppuration of the cruelly-irritated wound of the national body.

Thus, the Poles have been declared unworthy, not only of political rights, but even of the rights of humanity. It is not for them that the sunshine of national liberty was given, and now they are even precluded from the harmless enjoyment of domestic happiness in the quiet asylum of their rural retreats. It is true that they have remained Poles, but their Polonism consists in a Polish helotism; they nourish in their breasts the sacred flame of the love of their country, but the only arena opened to their patriotism is the dark cell of the fortress or the graveyard of their fallen fathers and brethren. They do not give up their rights and hopes, but the only right which has certainly been conceded to them, is the right of martyrdom. These are the final results which they have hitherto derived from their reliance upon Germany. Shall we, then, persevere in the same career, which we have hitherto followed, serving by our delusions the interests of German arrogance and selfishness? No! this idea is too absurd to be ascribed even to the most fantastical amongst us, and it cannot be entertained any more than that of an unassisted insurrection in a country the Government of which does not consider the instigation of bands of assassins and robbers as too wicked a means for suppressing the outbreaks of our despair. If we must, therefore, resign, on the one side, what is impossible and visionary, but on the other persevere in our indestructible national ideas, without which we should be nothing better than a contemptible, mulish, national monster, unprofitable to mankind, it seems that the most complete closing of the ways which we have hitherto either tried or meditated, may be regarded as a providential indication, which points out to us henceforward the only possible way of salvation. It is through the paths of misfortune and of apparent destruction that Providence often leads nations into more salutary ways; and as our need is now the greatest, we may therefore hope that God is the nearest. We cannot help having a greater confidence in the only way which still remains to us, namely, in the way which Russia offers to us.

The axiom *Vox populi vox Dei*, has been often, though not always, justified by facts. Now, as it has been really confirmed that the hitherto so-detested Russians were recently, on their entrance into Cracow, loudly greeted by the inhabitants of that city,* that they have frequently protected the same inhabitants from the oppression of the Austrian soldiery, and that they enjoy, in that city, such a popularity that the funeral of a Russian officer was attended by an immense concourse of people, who tore to pieces the velvet of his coffin,

* This alludes to the manifestation which the inhabitants of Cracow had really made in favour of the Russian troops, who saved that city from the pillage with which it was menaced by the Austrian general. See the despatch on the subject from General Mansfield, British Consul at Warsaw, to the Foreign Office, quoted by D'Angeberg (*Recueil des Traités*).

and kept it as a relic, in order to manifest, in the presence of Germans, the sympathy which the Slavonians felt for a Slavonian; now, as such a universal popular manifestation could not be produced except by a spontaneous impulse, it must be considered particularly as a *vox Dei*, because the undefined instinct of the common people exactly coincides, in this case, with the logical inductions of the reflecting Polish politician.

Now, if all of us who remain under the Russian, as well as the German Governments, shall abjure the Russian antipathies which have hitherto animated us, and joining, in a cordial and conscientious manner, the elevated political tendencies of Russia, supporting this new destiny of ours with all that zeal and perseverance with which we have hitherto opposed Russia, then it must follow, as a matter of course, that the national spirit, which has hitherto been weakened on account of its being exclusively Russian, will grow into a powerful Slavonic spirit, and be able to meet, with all the fulness of its strength, the wiles and intrigues of a foreign opposite policy. The best sap of Russia will become profitable to her gigantic body only when her great and painful wound shall be healed. She will cease to barbarize herself by the severities which she is employing against us; she will rapidly advance in her interior, in the career of national civilization and the progress of a truly Slavonic civilization will never be hostile to the cognate Polonism, and will be still less able to absorb it. The Polish nationality, for which it is now necessary to struggle, will be secured and animated in its further development. The action of the Russo-Slavonic spirit will penetrate, without impediment, into the borders of envious Germany; and it may easily embrace the other cognate Slavonic nations. Thus, perhaps, a not very remote futurity may show the possible existence of several confederated Slavonic States, amongst which the Polish would, in conjunction with others, attain, under the hegemony of Russia, that national *self-standing* position which is due to it much sooner and surer than by the hitherto-followed way of German sympathies.

In order to obtain this result, we need not, as has hitherto been done, have recourse to insurrections and sacrifices of blood and property; we need no longer, for the advantage of the Germans, expose ourselves to the torments of an heroic martyrdom. The only thing which is required is a sincere, unfeigned, cordial alliance of spirit and feeling with Russia, who is now more and more advancing in civilization. This merely moral alliance will, through the position of our country, as well as through the eminence of the Russian policy, soon become a real confederation. The present frontiers of the German portions of Poland will soon be perceptible on the maps only, and in the difference of the colours of the frontier-posts; in every other political respect this partition wall will soon disappear before the power of the Russian influence, friendly to the Poles, and which will prevail throughout the whole of ancient Poland, even before the Prussian and Austrian eagles will have retired from the German absorption to which already millions of Slavonians have succumbed; and the mighty flow of the Russian national-political stream will bring us of itself to the long-wished-for goal.

Let us, therefore, no longer hesitate in seizing the only possible resolution. The time for a useless and tormenting expectation is now past. It could formerly be called a patriotic resignation; or, perhaps, served to indulge the personal idleness and comfort of some. These narrow prospects are no longer allowed to us. Surrounded as we are by the spies of the police, by revolted peasants, who thirst for our blood and property, by the murderers of our fathers and brethren, and, finally, by the Communists who have penetrated into our very ante-rooms, can we any longer think about comfort and quiet, even in the interior of our homes? And hesitation is death to us. We are, therefore, compelled to enter our only road of salvation; we must sincerely offer the Russians the hand of future friendship, and make the first step towards it, in order that those Slavonic brethren of ours should see that our intention is real, and that we are acting on our own accord.

No. II.

THE SOVEREIGN OF RUSSIA'S TITLE.

THE United Provinces and the King of Prussia had already, in 1711, acknowledged Peter's right to the title of Emperor: but the Courts of London and Paris withheld their consent. During the negotiation pending between those Courts and Peter, several despatches passed between Lord Carteret, Secretary of State, the Cardinal Dubois, and Sir Luke Schaube, English Ministers at Paris.

"Le cardinal," writes Lord Carteret in one of his despatches to Sir Luke, dated Jan., 1721–2, "croit qu'on pourroit accorder le titre de *l'Emperour* au Czar, de manière que les couronnes n'en sussent point prejudiciés."

"Le Roy [George I.] a trouvé la réponse très sage, que le cardinal a faite aux ministres du Czar touchant la demande du titre *d'Emperour*. Nous agirons de concert, avec son Eminence dans cette affaire. Et pour luy donner les éclaircissements; qu'elle souhaitte, toûchant ce qui s'est passé entre la Grande Bretagne et le Czar à l'egard du titre, je vous envoye un extrait, qui a été tiré des regîstres de nos archives, pour luy être communique. Les ministres *Moscovites* ne font nullement fondez en ce qu'ils alléguent que ce titre a été accordé au Czar comme une partie de la satisfaction dans l'affaire de Matueof. Il est constant que l'on ne fit alors aucun changement à cette occasion là.

"En examinant le stile, dont les roys de la Grande Bretagne se sont servis, en écrivant aux Czars de *Moscovie,* on est remonté jusqu'au tems de la Reine Elizabeth. On trouve qu'on leur a toûjours écrit en Anglois, et que cette princesse.

"An 1559. Se servoit du stile *d'Emperour* et de *Highness.*

"1616. Le Roy Jaques I. de celuy *d'Emperour* et de *Majesty.*

"1633. Le Roy Charles I.

"1666. Le Roy Charles II.

"1687. Jaques II. et Guillaume III. de celuy *d'Emperour.*

"1689–90. De *d'Imperial Majesty.*

"1707. La Reine Anne s'est servie du stile *d'Emperour* et *d'Imperial Majesty,* jusqu'à l'an 1707, et alors on commença à écrire *Commander,* &c., et *Czaric Majesty.*

"1708. En 1708 le 19 Juillet et le 19 Septembre, *commander* et *Imperial Majesty;* et le 9 Novembre de la même année, *Emperour* et *Imperial Majesty.* En 1709, 1710, 1711, *Emperour* et *Imperial Majesty.* En 1712, 1713, 1714, *Emperour* et *Czarean, Czarish*, et *Imperial Majesty*, tantôt l'un, tantôt l'autre, et souvent *Czarish* et *Imperial Majesty* dans une même lettre. En 1714 le 27 Septembre, le stile de la lettre de notification de l'avénement du Roy à la Couronne, est, *Emperour* et *Your Majesty*, et dans plusieurs autres lettres depuis ce temps, la *Czarish* ou *Imperial Majesty*, et quelquefois *Your Majesty* simplement. Voicy le titre entier :—'To the most high, most potent, and most illustrious, our most dear brother, the great Lord, Czar, and Great Duke, Peter Alexejewitz, of all the Greater, Lesser, and White Russia, Self-Upholder of Muscovia, Kiovia, Ulodomiria, Novogardia, Czar of Cazan, Czar of Astrachan, Czar of Siberia, Lord of Plexoe, and Great-Duke of Smolensko, Tueria, Ugoria, Permia, Viatkya, Bolgaria, and others, Lord and Great-Duke of Novogardia, and of the Lower Countries of Czernegorsky, Resansky, Rostovesky, Yeroslave, Beloorzersky, Udorsky, Obdorsky, Condinsky, and *Emperour* of all the Northern Coasts, Lord of the Lands of Iversky, Cartilinski, and Gruzensky, Czar of the Lands of Caberdinsky, Czereasky, and Duke of the Mountains, and of many other Dominions and Countries, East, West, and North, from

Father and from Grandfather, Heir, Lord, and Conqueror.'"

Lord Carteret, in a letter to the Cardinal Dubois, writes: "Le Roi concoura sans difficulté avec sa Majesté très Chretienne, à faire ce que V. Eminence jugera convenable, par rapport au *nouveau titre* que le Czar demande, et un parfait concert à faire espérer à ce prince une telle complaisance pour servir à le gagner, et à nous faire tirer fruits de son ambition." Jan. 30, 1721–2.

And in a despatch to Sir Luke Schaube, he thus expresses himself: "Le coûteme icy a toûjours été d'écrire aux Czars de Moscovie sur du velin enluminè peint et doré, comme on fait aux Empereurs de Maroc et Fez, et à plusieurs autres princes non-Europeens, lesquels selon cette coûtume seroient également fondez d'insister sur le titre d'Empereur. On n'a jamais voulu changer l'usage étably, quoique les Moscovites l'ayent fort solicité durant l'ambassade de my lord Whitworth a Moscow. Ce ministre s'excusa toûjours d'en faire la proposition. Il leur dit, qu'il le leur donneroit le titre, sans difficulté, tel qu'il le trouvoit établi; mais qu'il ne leur conseilloit pas de remuër cette matière, ni de s'éclaircir trop soigneusement sur quel pied on leur donnoit ce titre. Des Moscovites crûrent son avis bon pour lors. Quand my lord Whitworth, et Mr. l'Amiral Norris fûrent chargez d'une commission auprez du Czar à Amsterdam, ils n'eûrent que des lettres de cachet, dont le stile étoit *Votre Majesté;* les ministres *Russiens* en firent d'abord quelque scrupule, mais n'y insisterent pas." *

* From Sir Luke Schaube's State Papers, in the collection of the Earl of Hardwicke, quoted by Coxe (*Travels into Russia, &c.*, vol. i. p. 400).

No. III.

THE BARON AND HIS WIFE; OR, THE FORCED MARRIAGE.

By the Countess Rostopchin.

Circulated in MS. in Moscow and St. Petersburg.

A Knightly Ballad.

THE BARON.

Attend, ye servants and vassals,
To your gentle master's call;
Judge, without fear of my anger,
For I am ready to hear the truth,
Judge of the quarrel known to you all.
Though I am powerful and renowned,
Though I am omnipotent here,
I am powerless at home;
For ever disobedient
Is my troublesome wife.

II.

I saw her an orphan,
And took her all ruined,
And with my mighty hand
Gave her my protection.

I dressed her in brocade and gold,
I surrounded her with an innumerable guard,
And, lest the enemy should lure her,
I stand over her myself with a dagger.
Yet dissatisfied and melancholy
Is my ungrateful wife!

III.

I know that with her complaints
She brands me everywhere.
I know that before all the world
She curses my shelter and my sword.
She looks askance from beneath her brows,
And repeats a false clatter:
Prepares vengeance, sharpens the knife,
Kindles the fire of domestic war.
She whispers with the monks,
My deceitful wife!

IV.

Contented and rejoiced,
My enemies look on,
And foster the factious anger,
And flatter her busy, restless pride.
Give me just counsel,
And judge which of us is right.
My tongue is severe but not deceitful.
Now, listen to the disobedient one:
Let her defend herself,
My guilty wife!

THE WIFE.

Am I his slave or his companion?
That God knows! Was it I that chose
A cruel husband for myself?
Did I take the vow?
I lived free and happy,
And I loved my freedom;
But I was conquered and made captive
By my wicked neighbour's bloody invasion.
I am betrayed, I am sold:
I am a prisoner and not a wife!

II.

In vain the cruel yoke
The Seigneur thinks to gild;
In vain my holy revenge
He seeks to change into love.
I need not his generosity,
Nor do I want his protection;
And I myself can teach the meddlesome
To pay me peaceably the tribute of respect.
By him alone am I humbled:
I am his enemy and not his wife!

III.

He forbids me to speak
In my own native tongue;
He will not allow me to sign
With my inherited coat of arms.
Before him I may take no pride

In my ancient name,
Nor pray in my ancestors' eternal Church;
A religion not her own
His unhappy wife is forced to adopt!

IV.

He has sent into exile, into imprisonment,
All the truest and best of my servants,
And has given me over to persecution
To his slaves and spies.
Shame, persecution, and slavery,
Are the wedding-gifts he brought to me;
And is it I he forbids to murmur?
And am I suffering such a fate,
To hide it from everyone—
I, a wife against my will?

THE VASSALS' REPLY TO THE BARON.

Printed in the "Northern Bee."

We are chosen, Baron, by you,
To judge conscientiously
Between yourself and your deceitful wife:
If it please you, we will speak.
Her family we are all acquainted with,
And we all know of her doings.
She never was virtuous,
And was unable to live at home;

And it does not astonish us now
That the woman should talk insolently.

II.

They were three sisters * when they lived
Together in their own family. Then how many
times
They were sold under the hammer
To empty lovers for an hour!
With such a life, is it astonishing
That lawful marriage is not for them?
What is a husband to them but a constant enemy?
To be free from the marriage-tie is their ideal of
liberty;
Therefore it does not astonish us now
That the empty woman should scream.

III.

To the wild screams of the silly coquette
You should not listen, Baron.
You have other dutiful ones;
And, without her, many wives.
Put on your gauntlet of power,
And pat her while she is quiet;
But when she makes the least noise,
Then chastise the young person well.
And it will not astonish anyone
If the woman is instantly silent.

* Poland, Lithuania, and Ruthenia.

IV.

Whether you are a slave or a companion,
The question is not difficult to decide.
You are a wife, if your husband
You will obey and love ;
A slave, if again, injudiciously
You throw yourself into the midst of tumult,
Forgetting the lesson you have already received :
Then chains are ready for you.
And it will not astonish anyone
If the Baron should crush you.

V.

Unjustly and hypocritically,
You say that you were sold.
But into the hands of the Baron, not once alone,
You were given up by victory;
War decided your fate.
Remember, now, how many times
You showed mercy to us :
But, apparently, your strength did not last ;
Therefore it does not astonish anyone
That you should have lost credit.

VI.

Now, who forbids you to chatter
In your own native tongue?

And who forbids you to pray
In the temples of your ancestors?
No one! you chatter nonsense
At the dictation of foreign writers,
Your faithless friends.
Chatter; pray; but keep quiet,
And then it will not astonish anyone
If the Baron should pardon you.

VII.

But it was not the wife who wrote those verses,
It was a poet in a cap who wrote them.
She has no small talent,
But, unfortunately, she is without sense.
It is not worth while to be angry with her,
Nor even to talk to her;
But simply to threaten her with the finger,
And order her to return;
And it will not astonish anyone
If the Baron should pardon her.

No. IV.

ADDRESS FROM THE INHABITANTS OF WARSAW, 1861.

THE following is an abridgement of the "Address from the Inhabitants of Warsaw," which, during the last two years, has been circulated, reprinted, and re-circulated by tens of thousands in all parts of Russian, Austrian, and Prussian Poland. I have omitted sentences, but those which I have retained are translated word by word. The Address has the merit of setting forth in a comparatively short space all the grievances of the Poles. It presents, moreover, their only general programme, though the Poles of Galicia and Posen (who possess certain slight, but undoubtedly useful, political privileges) cannot be expected, and ought not, to adopt it equally with those of the Kingdom. The Address states that the three Powers, with different modes of government, have all the same intentions towards Poland; and, in the same way, the inhabitants of the various parts of Poland, with different forms of protestation, have all the same intentions towards the three Powers:—

"To all our Countrymen on Polish Soil, 1861.

"The criminal union and superior force of Russia, Prussia, and Austria have violated the holiest laws of God and humanity, and have deprived Poland of her political existence. Over the torn fragments of our native land rule foreigners, our foes, who, though governing after different modes, are, nevertheless, all aiming at one object—to complete the criminal destruction of our country.

"Their rule is falsehood, injustice, illegality, and slavery. They are robbing us of the language of our ancestors; they are sowing between us suspicion and distrust—quarrels between peasantry and landlords, between Christians and Jews, between Ruthenians and Poles.

"They will not permit us to extend civilization. In our schools they employ the Russian and German languages, and give such instruction as tends only to falseness and confusion of sense. They have abolished the high schools and Universities, and will not allow us to establish schools for the poor.

"Our religion and priests are despised by the Muscovites, and they deprive us of the liberty of worship and prayer. Taking from us our just laws and our liberal institutions, they would also remove us from God, not permitting us to pray for the happiness of our native land. Destroying morality, virtue, and courage, they would produce dissoluteness, enervation, and luxuriousness. Limiting commerce, fettering the professions, and checking free intercourse, they burden us with enormous taxes and strive to sink us in misery and ignorance; because the miserable and ignorant do not know their rights.

"They thrust outlandish officials upon us, and carry off thousands of our youth in their Muscovite and German legions to destruction in distant countries, commanding them to shed their blood for foreign and not for Polish causes. The rule of Russia, Austria, and Prussia in Poland is a constant crime, which prevents the progress and liberty even of other nations. Their common interest in stifling us brings them together, and joins them in an indispensable alliance, in the presence of which the freedom and prosperity of other countries also suffer. Though the liberty of Poland interests the whole of Europe, nevertheless, we must only count on ourselves. On ourselves alone depend our happiness and liberty.

"Demonstrations are only useful at certain times and opportunities, but as for risking an armed rising without reckoning our forces and elaborating a material power—of that we must not think. The time for an armed rising will come, and then—having no more differences to torment us, and being strong of one accord and certain of victory—we shall advance to the attack. For the present we must fight our cruel foes with other arms.

"They have dominions, unjust laws, cannons, and bayonets; we have God, our national spirit, our just necessities acknowledged by everyone, and the moral force with which Heaven endows the injured and persecuted, a great and powerful force, which already, last February, vanquished for a short time our cruel foe. The Governments are not able to deprive us of this force, but, as for arms, they are still strong enough to take them from us.

"The nobles, animated with good intentions, must forthwith, though at the sacrifice of some material advantages, introduce the farm-rent law where it is not yet established, that through it the peasantry may become proprietors. They must establish schools for them and instruct them; for as long as the peasantry are not citizens so long will the yoke last upon us.

"And you, peasants, have confidence in your landlords, for on your agreement with them depends your happiness and that of the whole country. A landlord who strikes a peasant or a peasant who listens to agitators and is led to rise against his landlord, are equally criminals towards the nation.

"Do not believe the Government which has never kept one promise, but has always betrayed us. Seek no help from it, for it will give it with poisoned hands. Decide your quarrels and lawsuits among yourselves, and do not seek satisfaction in the tribunals and public offices.

"Our brothers in Lithuania and in Ruthenia who, ages ago, united of their own free will with Poland, should repel the advances of the Muscovites and Germans, who are only endeavouring to disunite them from their countrymen of Mazovia* and of Great and Little Poland. All these countries, as far as Dantzic, form one Poland, and all their inhabitants, in spite of different social degrees, conditions, languages, and religions, are nevertheless fellow-countrymen and Poles.

"Putting our faith in God, to whom we offer prayers in all the churches for the deliverance of our native land, let us reject luxurious and dissolute living and all useless gaiety. Let us dress in black as a sign of the affliction in which we are plunged; let us dress in Polish costumes, but without persecuting those who wear other costumes. Let those who understand foreign languages, especially German and Muscovite, speak them to no German or Muscovite on Polish soil.

"Avoid bad men, and all such as pollute themselves by taking service under the Government.

* The Province of which Warsaw is the capital.

Drive them away from your circle. Nobody must abase himself and injure his country *unpunished*.

"Instead of seeking for bread in the army or in any vile service, seek it in industry, agriculture, commerce, and other honest occupations.

"We must not spend our money uselessly; but let us give it willingly for patriotic purposes, for supporting the poor, for arms, and for Polish books and pictures. Let us help and support one another through all need, and we shall soon rise to a power through which we shall be able to expel our enemies.

"There is no hope whatever from the Government, so expect nothing. Provide for the wants of the country through association and union, and when the time arrives we shall all know how to stand on the field of battle and vanquish with arms. In this way, and not by resorting to useless provocation, we shall in time obtain general happiness and a free and independent Poland.

"Poland for ever!

"And let no one spare his labour, his money, or his life.

"THE INHABITANTS OF WARSAW."

AUTHORITIES AND BOOKS REFERRED TO.

A CALL to Repentance. Skarga.
Actes de Congrès de Vienne. Klüber.
Address to the Young Generation. Mikhailoff.
Analysis and Parallel of the Three Polish Constitutions. Lelewel.
Annual Register, 1772 and 1777.
Appeal from the Old Whigs to the New. Burke.
Appel à la Presse Libérale.
Archives of Poland. D'Angeberg.
Archives of Russia. D'Angeberg.
A Voice to the Inhabitants of Cracow.

Book of the Polish Pilgrims. Miçkievicz.

Correspondence with the Government of Russia, &c.
Coup d'Œil sur la Pologne de 1815. Hoffman.
Cours de la Littérature Slave. Miçkievicz.

Dieu c'est le Mal. Proudhon.
Du Développement des Idées Révolutionaires en Russie. Herzen.

Encyclopédie du Gens du Monde.
Epistolæ. Bishop Zaluski.

Faux Démétrius. Mérimée.
Fréderic II., Catherine, et le Partage de la Pologne. Frédéric de Smitt.

Geography of the Middle Ages. Lelewel.
Guerre aux Infants, &c., à Wilna. Lelewel.

Histoire de la Lithuanie et de la Ruthénie. Lelewel.
History of Friedrich II. Carlyle.
History of Poland told by a Grandfather to his Grandchildren. Lelewel.
History of Russia. Oustrialoff.
History of the Consulate and the Empire. Thiers.
History of the French Revolution. Louis Blanc.
History of the Polish Kings. Lelewel.
History of the Polish Legions. Dombrowski.
History of the Reign of Stanislaus Augustus. Lelewel.
History of the Thirty Years' War. Schiller.

La Décade Historique. Count de Ségur.
La Pologne. Forster.
La Pologne, Pittoresque et Illustrée. Chodzko.
La Proprieté c'est le Vol. Proudhon.
La Prusse et le Traités de Vienne.

La Régénération Sociale de la Russie. V. Parochin.
Latin Dictionary. Ainsworth.
La Verité sur la Russie. Prince Dolgoroukoff.
L'Église Catholique sous la Russie. Abbé Lescœur.
Le Prince Adam Czartoryski. Le R. P. Felix.
Les Mémoires d'Oginski.
Les Slaves. Miçkievicz.
Letter from a Polish Gentleman to Prince Metternich. Marquis Wielopolski.
Letter to Lord John Russell. Mitchell.
Life of Dr. Johnson. Boswell.
L'Odyssée Polonaise. E. Regnault.

Mémoires. Guizot.
Memoirs of Kubalski.
Memoirs of the Courts of Berlin, Warsaw, &c. Wraxall.
Memoirs. Sievers.

Opisanie Varshavi. Istomin.
Opocha. Count Leon Skorupka.

Parliamentary History, 1791.
Panslavism and Germanism. Count Valerian Krasinski.
Patriotic Letters. Wiebitski.

Recueil des Traités, &c., concernant la Pologne. D'Angeberg.
Richard Cobden, Roi des Belges.
Russia, by a Manchester Manufacturer. Cobden.

Statement of Facts and Arguments on the Subject of Poland.
State Papers. Sir Luke Schaube.

The Autonomy of Galicia. Count Leon Skorupka.
The Rambler. Dr. Johnson.
Travels into Poland, 1784. Coxe.
Treaties on Studies serviceable, &c., to the Writer of History. Lelewel

Untergang des Polen. Professor Raumer.

Year-book of the Israelites (1861).

INDEX.

CPSIA information can be obtained
at www.ICGtesting.com
Printed in the USA
LVHW100431110522
718424LV00003B/111

9 783375 004316